BODY POLITIC

BODY POLITIC

J. M. Gregson

9011225498

Chivers
Bath, England

•

Thorndike Press
Waterville, Maine USA

This Large Print edition is published by BBC Audiobooks Ltd, England, and by Thorndike Press, USA.

Published in 2003 in the U.K. by arrangement with Constable & Robinson.

Published in 2003 in the U.S. by arrangement with Juliet Burton Literary Agency.

U.K. Hardcover   ISBN 0–7540–7261–4 (Chivers Large Print)
U.K. Softcover   ISBN 0–7540–7262–2 (Camden Large Print)
U.S. Softcover   ISBN 0–7862–5414–9 (Nightingale Series)

The text of this Large Print edition is unabridged.
Other aspects of the book may vary from the original edition.

Set in 16 pt. New Times Roman.

Printed in Great Britain on acid-free paper.

British Library Cataloguing in Publication Data available

Library of Congress Cataloging-in-Publication Data

Gregson, J. M.
     Body Politic / J. M. Gregson.
        p. cm.
     ISBN 0–7862–5414–9 (lg. print : sc : alk. paper)
     1. Legislators—Crimes against—Fiction. 2. Police—England—
Fiction. 3. England—Fiction. 4. Large type books. I. Title.
PR6057.R3876B63 2003
823'.914—dc21   2003047359

CHAPTER ONE

'Of course there are things wrong with the country,' said Raymond Keane. A winning frankness was one of his strongest cards in friendly company, and he reckoned they didn't come much friendlier than the lady with the elaborate blue hat and the little smear of cream on her upper lip.

'You mean people sleeping in cardboard boxes and so on?' she said, anxious not to miss her cue, determined to keep her MP with her for a little longer before he moved on, as she knew he must, to the next smiling listener, to the next vol-au-vent and warm white wine.

Raymond watched the patch of cream bobbing as she spoke, like a white horse on a choppy sea. 'That, of course,' he said. 'Though I think we could agree that most of the people who clutter our city streets have chosen their own fate. I was thinking more of the way we have to look under our cars in the Commons park for bombs before we drive away.' Middle-aged ladies in Gloucestershire liked a little frisson of vicarious fear, he knew that from experience. It was years now since he had checked for bombs, but the danger card was still one to play to build up a little sympathy.

The gathering was going well. The conservatory of the big house, Victorian in its

1

proportions as well as its design, made the crisp winter day outside seem warmer than it actually was: only the leafless trees and the bright red stems of the dogwoods beyond the wide green lawns revealed that the bright blue sky beyond the double glazing was in fact a winter one.

Raymond Keane had his professional equipment in good working order. The smile was practised but the brown eyes remained earnest, never setting into the enamelled mask he had seen in less able Westminster men. No one knew better than he the benefits of a safe Conservative seat, especially now that what had once seemed comfortable majorities were under threat in many parts of the country. In this part of Gloucestershire, where the Beaufort rode regularly and royal estates were discreetly hidden behind ancient trees, his support might be diminished but the seat was rock-solid safe.

He managed a substantial gulp of his Muscadet as he moved on to converse with a local squire. He was well used to these functions after five years in the seat; he thought he managed better than anyone else in the room the manipulation of a plate of food and a glass of wine, a process which clearly needed three hands but had to be managed with two. Thirty feet away, over the head of a lumpy girl and two more of the hats, he caught Zoe Renwick's eye.

It held his only fleetingly: he was happy to see again how discreet she was, what a good politician's wife she would make, in due course. Her look said, 'How soon can we get away?' but there was no urgency, no impatience in the question. More important, the man who was reaching for another brown-bread square of smoked salmon was not even aware of her swift glance over his shoulder. He resumed the tidal flow of his views on immigration without even a suspicion that he had lost the attention of his bright young listener for a vital instant.

Raymond began to move unhurriedly towards the door, chatting to a succession of supporters as he made his circuitous way towards escape. The chairman of the local association, as practised as he was in reading the hidden agendas of gatherings like this, edged equally imperceptibly towards the wide double oak doors from the other side of the room, until this slow-motion pavane culminated in a meeting of the two on the polished parquet near the exit.

The grey-haired chairman said softly, 'Time you were on your way, Raymond?' He was tactful enough to suggest a crowded schedule rather than a simple wish to be finished with a necessary evil of constituency politics. His MP had earned his corn, if that wasn't too crude a phrase for such a decorous gathering. Keane had done all that was required, with a graceful little speech to set this fundraising exercise in motion, a couple of gentle jokes about the contrast between this get-together and that being attended at this moment by his Labour 'pair' in a northern working-men's club. He had turned a nice compliment to the ladies who had worked so hard to set up today's function, keeping it light but thoughtful; all these things made it easier to raise enthusiasm and volunteers for the next function at Easter.

The chairman surveyed the animated heads in the now cheerfully noisy conservatory. A few people had already left. The MP must not be first away, but neither should he stay too long, for that might suggest that he was desperate for support, or not as busy as his publicity always suggested. The chairman said in a low voice, 'I shouldn't bother to say any goodbyes, or it'll take you half an hour to get out. Just melt away discreetly. I shall do the same myself in another ten minutes.'

Raymond needed no further encouragement to do what he had always intended to do at this point. In twenty minutes, he was back in the cottage with Zoe. In another five, they were in bed together, making relaxed, unhurried love, their clothes dropped by the bed like snakes' discarded skins, the public personas they had assumed for the lunchtime assembly of the party faithful abandoned just as eagerly.

Presently Zoe lay back, fixing her brilliant blue eyes on the moulding in the centre of the

4

old ceiling, stretching her arms above her head and clasping her hands beneath the masses of dark blonde hair. 'Well, do you think they approved of me?' she said.

Raymond caught the intoxicating mixture of fresh sweat and expensive perfume from the armpit near his face, then nuzzled recklessly into it, making her giggle as she clasped an arm lightly across his head. 'You were great,' he said in a muffled voice. Then, lifting his head and shifting a little to look down into her face, he said, 'I thought you were quite good at the wine and cheese, too!'

'I wasn't looking forward to it, you know,' she said. But she was relaxed now, staring contentedly from her lover's face to the ceiling, knowing within herself that she had carried it off well, this inspection by the pearls-and-cashmere set and the local landowners.

'You were fine, darling,' Raymond said contentedly. 'But I always knew you would be.' Secretly, he was relieved. A new fiancée was always a risky step for a divorced politician, even though the constituency likcd to see you with a wife at election time. He had pretended to her in advance that today was more trivial than he had felt it to be.

But he needn't have worried. Zoe had handled it as if she had been bred for it, treating the elderly women with just enough deference, showing just enough spirit to win over susceptible husbands without raising their wives' hackles. He would take her to all the Party functions from now on. A month from now, they would announce the date of their wedding. By the time of the next election, Zoe would be snugly established as one of the most photogenic of parliamentary wives. Perhaps, in due course, of ministerial wives . . . But he was in no hurry about that. At forty-one, time was still on his side in these things.

'It was all a bit too smooth for me.' Zoe's voice, suddenly serious, pulled him abruptly back to reality. 'I thought politics was about getting things done. We seemed a long way from the problems of the country when we were exchanging pleasantries at Darnley Court today.'

It was true. He had forgotten how divorced from reality these things could seem to an outsider. Which Zoe still was, essentially. 'We *were* a long way from any problem-solving today. Those gatherings are a necessary evil, if you like—keeping faith with the people who form the hard core of Party membership, reassuring them that they still matter in a world that's changing too fast for some of them to understand. And raising useful funds, of course. But I agree: nothing to do with politics, in the sense of getting things done. That happens at Westminster. And even there, more in the committees than in the public debates in the House, most of the time.'

'I just feel that twenty-eight thousand voted

6

for you, and the vast majority of them have lives which have no connection with those of most of the people I spoke to this afternoon.'

'That's true enough. Perhaps you should come along to the constituency clinics sometimes, once we're officially a team. That's where you'll feel in touch with real life. Where you can even help people, sometimes.'

'I'd like that. Only when we're officially united, though. I wouldn't want people to feel I was just there as a voyeur.'

She was right, as usual. People in distress wanted to see only their MP, and even then they lost faith pretty quickly if you weren't able to offer real help. He told her about the woman whose husband was in real pain, but had been told he had to wait another three months for a gallstones operation, of the woman whose daughter had disappeared who could get no sympathy from the police, of the couple trying to bring up children in a street where prostitutes patrolled for four hours each night. And of the questions he planned to ask in the right bureaucratic places to get something done for these people.

The recital of these glimpses of an MP's working life cheered him. Beneath his enjoyment of the trappings of power and his love of the good things in life, Raymond Keane genuinely wanted to use politics to improve the state of his country and the fortunes of the people he represented, and it was good to remind himself of it. But he was still enough in love with Zoe to be afraid of appearing pompous when he spoke of serious things. 'That's enough about work,' he said firmly. 'The rest of the weekend is ours. And I know how I intend to spend the first part of it!'

He threw his arm around the slim shoulders beside him and drew her body against his. 'Does Muscadet always make old men so ambitious?' she said as he slid beneath her. 'I must remember to order a couple of cases!'

It was much later, when the early winter twilight had dropped upon the room and they lay in pleasant exhaustion on their own sides of the big bed, that Raymond said, 'I trust that chap who threatened to kill me at the constituency clinic won't come back again.'

At first, she thought he was joking, and in a way he was. 'Oh, it's nothing to get upset about,' he reassured her when she pressed him. 'Every MP will tell you that he has his quota of nutters who threaten violence. It's a way of letting off steam for them to threaten the nearest person they feel has any real power. Nothing ever comes of it.'

It was a phrase that was to nag at her for many of the strange days which followed that weekend.

CHAPTER TWO

Police wives do not mix with each other as much as outsiders might expect. This is not so much because of considerations of rank; the police hierarchy is not as rigid as that which operates in army married quarters, where officers' wives find it difficult to meet on equal terms with the wives of lower ranks, and even the sergeants' mess sets up its own social barricades.

Nonetheless, the sorority of police wives is not as intense as might be imagined. Policemen themselves do not encourage it, for one thing. There is almost a freemasonry within the force about the unwritten rules and taboos of conduct, and most policemen are still chauvinist enough not to wish to share the code with their spouses. Every policeman, from the humblest beat copper to the CID superintendent, has things in his career he would rather not discuss, things he has often not confided even to his wife.

But men—and the ethos of the force is still overwhelmingly male—gossip, at least as much as women. The gossiping female and her tight-lipped husband are a pair set up by male propagandists over the years. The same copper who remains tight-lipped about his own conduct when speaking to his wife gossips to

9

her about the weaknesses of his colleagues. And he knows that those same colleagues will certainly have prattled about his own weaknesses to their partners. Hence he is not anxious that wives should be able to compare notes too often.

The job has enough stresses to bring a divorce rate which keeps comfortably ahead of the rising national average, without personal secrets passing among a circle of wives. Policemen have affairs like other people, with members of the public as well as with the steadily increasing number of female police personnel. Secrecy, in the guise of discretion, is bred into them from the moment they begin their training, and they are happy to extend this into a caution about their personal affairs.

There are exceptions, of course, especially when officers have worked with each other for a number of years and trust each other absolutely within a professional relationship. The wives of Superintendent John Lambert and Detective Sergeant Bert Hook had got to know each other quite well over eight unhurried years of gradually increasing contact. They did not see each other more than once a month, even now, but when they did, they were immediately at ease with each other.

Eleanor Hook rang Christine Lambert when she knew both their husbands were still at work. The phone rang as Christine was

10

putting her car in the garage, so that she arrived rather breathless at the instrument. She was curiously glad to hear her friend's voice on the other end of the line; it was company of a sort, and she realized suddenly that she needed that.

'You sound puffed, Christine. Did I catch you at the other end of the house?'

Christine could hear the sound of the Hook boys in the background, two boisterous but likeable lads of ten and eleven. 'No, I was just coming in from the car.'

'Kept late at school again? You're too conscientious, you know.' It was a routine admonition to a friend. But Eleanor knew how much she would like the lively and diligent woman on the other end of the phone to educate her own boys.

'No, I've been to the breast-cancer screening unit for a test, that's all.' Why, Christine wondered, did one always feel the need to hide anxieties about health, even from friends? 'Nothing important: I was just due for the routine scan. I can scarcely believe it's five years since I was last done, but they tell me it is.'

'I must go myself when I get the chance. I'm forty-three now, you know.' It was characteristically open. The Hooks had married late, and happily. Perhaps because Eleanor knew she was taking on the police force with the man, they had not had the traumas which Christine's marriage had endured in its early days, a full generation ago now. 'I'm ringing to ask a favour, I'm afraid.'

'Ask away.' Christine found herself curiously glad to be wanted, to assert the ordinary rhythms of life after the efficient sterility of the breast screening unit, where human concerns seemed part of a mass production line.

'Could you baby-sit the boys for us on Saturday night? We've booked for the D'Oyley Carte at Malvern, and my mother can't do it.'

'Of course I can. What are you going to see?'

'*La Vie Parisienne.* It's so difficult to get Bert to go out these days. I don't want to miss it.'

'How's his Open University course going?'

'Quite well, I think. He's always reluctant to admit it, but I think it is, despite the fact that he never has enough time. I know he enjoys it.'

'Nobody doing a full-time job ever has enough time to study. I think he's performing miracles to have got as far as he has.' She resisted the temptation to talk more about Bert, to keep talking for talking's sake. It was a very unfamiliar urge for Christine Lambert, who was normally so brisk and self-sufficient.

She was about to ring off when she remembered something. 'There was one condition John imposed on any baby-sitting, if you remember.'

'What was that?' Eleanor could tell from the tone of voice that this was only half

12

serious.

'If John baby-sits for Bert, your worthy husband has to agree to try out golf.'

Eleanor laughed, her genuine amusement edged with just a trace of nervousness; these men were just big boys really, and they could be just as stubborn. 'You won't get Bert to go near a golf course, you know. Game for upper-class twits, he always says.'

'I know he does. John used to think so too, at one time. But he won't make Bert go into a golf clubhouse. The arrangement as far as I remember was just that Bert would agree to try hitting a basket of golf balls at a golf range. Quite painless, really. Unless he gets the golf bug, of course.'

'Not much danger of that, I'm afraid. I'd really quite like him to take up some outdoor activity. He doesn't get enough exercise, since he packed up his cricket.'

'You're willing to risk being a golf widow?'

'I can't see much chance of that. Sometimes I'd like to kick him out of the house, anyway.'

They exchanged a few more views about the childishness of men and their phobias about chasing small balls around the countryside. It is sobering to consider how mighty decisions can spring from such tenuous conversations.

*   *   *

On the Sunday morning, Raymond Keane's

13

business partner came to see him at the cottage. Raymond found the meeting more difficult than any political exchange he had had in the past year.

He had been fiercely heckled by students in Manchester, but that was only par for the course, the kind of robust evening anyone making his way in the Conservative ranks must take on with enthusiasm. A hostile reception in such places even gave some kind of kudos within the Party; it indicated that the opposition in the country saw a man as a figure to be reckoned with.

This was something altogether different. He had never seen Chris Hampson so annoyed. The fact that he had good reason did not make things easier. He wished now that he had not chosen to meet Chris with Zoe in attendance. He had thought to show her his easy mastery of a new situation, but he was now not at all sure that he was going to be seen in a good light in this.

Like many MPs, Raymond Keane found it useful to have a source of income outside the House. It made one less dependent on the often unpredictable whims of the electorate and the Party moguls. It was also an insurance, a life that was there to be resumed if politics lost its attraction as a career or a source of interest. Many of his colleagues were lawyers, who went into city practices in the mornings when parliament was sitting. Raymond had

Gloucester Electronics; until now, he had seen that as a more lucrative and worry-free income source.

Now suddenly it was not worry-free. Chris was beginning to hector him. The fact that he had right on his side did not make the experience any easier for Raymond to bear. 'Computer software doesn't sell itself, you know,' said his partner.

Chris Hampson was five years older than Raymond, who realized guiltily that he had not seen him for over three months. His hair was greying as well as thinning; the lines round his deep-set grey eyes seemed to Raymond more numerous than he remembered them. Raymond leaned forward. 'I know it doesn't, Chris. I'm sorry I've been too busy in the House to give you the help I intended. I suppose it's because you always seem so much on top of things that I rely on you to—'

'Don't fob me off as though I was one of your voters!' Chris shouted angrily, hearing the words bounce off the walls of the small, low-ceilinged room in the cottage. 'You know damn well that things are difficult. The competition your bloody Party is so keen on fostering is cutthroat.' Hampson could hear his wife's voice urging him on, telling him not to let his smooth partner get away with excuses.

'I'm not fobbing you off, Chris.' Raymond spoke quietly, recognizing the advantage which calmness would give him as his partner's temper rose. Chris had always been the technical one, clever in developing products, but less at home with words. He could handle him, as he always had. 'Oh, I admit I've not been able to give the business the attention I would have liked to, over these last months. But if you were in difficulties, you should have let me know. I'm sure—'

'I did let you know. I've left messages on your blasted answerphone four times. I've faxed you at Westminster, I've faxed you here at the cottage. Once you faxed back that you'd be in touch. The rest of the messages you just ignored.'

'Oh, come on, Chris! You knew I was going to be busy in the House. I've agreed to front that video for the States, and I'll do it in the spring. Just give me a bit more notice if you need help, that's all.'

It sounded reasonable: Raymond was good at that. It looked to the future, to the promises of jam to come, and not to his omissions in the immediate past. Hampson was no fool, but he was a straightforward man; although he was aware that he was being outflanked and was determined to resist, he was not sure of the tactics he should adopt, whereas the man sitting relaxed on the other side of the shining oval coffee table seemed not to have to think but merely to act instinctively.

Chris said sullenly, 'You can't just shrug things off. You never turned up for the meeting with that fellow who wanted to represent us in America.' He saw his opponent raising his eyebrows in that enquiring manner, that gesture which suggested without words that his accuser was a liar, and said, 'You must remember promising that. I was especially anxious that you should be there. You wrote it in your diary, a good six months ago. Moira was there at the time—she said she'd make sure you were in Bristol for the meeting.'

Hampson remembered with his mention of the name that Moira's successor as Raymond's partner was in the room. He glanced abruptly at Zoe Renwick, that cool, intelligent presence who had sat without a word on the sofa at the side of the room, forgotten as the argument intensified and the two men became preoccupied with each other. Her pale, assured face answered his guilty glance with a small, reassuring smile, but she remained silent, as if her composure could reassure him that he had not after all made a faux pas.

Where Hampson had been all excited, uncoordinated movement as his temper rose, Keane had hitherto remained resolutely still. Now he waved a hand in a small, dismissive gesture, as if to signify that he was above the petty concerns which dominated his business partner. 'You needn't be afraid to mention Moira. Zoe and I have no secrets from each other,' he smiled, with an affectionate glance at the elegant blonde woman on the sofa. He did not wait to see if she answered his smile. His concentration was on Hampson.

He spoke now like a statesman, explaining to a minion why lesser affairs must always be subordinate to the affairs of the nation. 'I remember the occasion well. I was on a trade mission in Italy at the time. You should have been informed that I wasn't available. If my secretary didn't get in touch with you, I can only apologize.'

His expression was artless and reasonable, his hands opened almost imperceptibly towards Hampson as they lay on the arms of his chair. Chris wanted suddenly to punch that handsome face, to shatter the careful dentistry of that slightly open mouth which seemed to be taunting him. He found himself gripping the arms of his chair to keep control. 'This is my life, Ray. It's all I've got. It may be a tinpot little business as far as you're concerned. But it's been a lucrative one. So far.'

Keane ignored the implied threat. 'Of course it has. And it isn't tinpot, it's very important. And I'm grateful to you for carrying the brunt of the development over the last few months, but—'

'Last few years, you mean!' Hampson almost exploded in the face of the other man's insouciance. This time he found he was no longer concerned about the effects he made. Shouting was an outlet, and an outlet he needed if there was not to be physical violence.

18

'I'm just about sick of your damned excuses. Either you pull your weight or you get out!'

His threat rang round the room. It was followed by a silence which seemed more profound for the passion which had preceded it. Hampson's heavy, irregular breathing was the only sound to be distinguished. He was trying unsuccessfully to control it, but succeeding only in making it even less rhythmical.

Raymond Keane took his time, letting the interval stretch almost unbearably for the other two people in the room. Then he said, 'Perhaps you haven't read the details of our agreement recently, Chris. It's a partnership, on equal terms. We split the profits as we have always done.'

'Not if there isn't equal work, we don't.' Hampson gasped the words out. He was so astounded at the other man's effrontery that he could scarcely articulate them.

Keane was at his most urbane now, riding on his opponent's discomfiture. 'I'm afraid you'll find that isn't so, Chris, if you look at the terms we agreed when we set up the firm. Nothing is said about the degree of input of the partners. It's difficult to evaluate these things, in any case. Since you seem to have documented Moira's presence so clearly, you will no doubt recall that she was there on another, earlier occasion, when we discussed my election to the Commons. It was agreed

19

that my higher political profile, with its position in the public eye, would be valuable to a small firm like ours.'

'It's what you talked about at the time, not what we agreed. I didn't get the chance—'

'The public image is what I'm contributing to the firm, what I'm working hard to build up. And that is what we agreed at that time. I'm sure Moira would confirm it, if you think it's worth disturbing her.'

He glanced at Zoe for confirmation, though he knew that she could not give it: she had never met his former mistress. He managed to imply both that he lived a free and open life, so that there was no embarrassment in discussing a former lover with the woman he now planned to marry, and that Hampson might be unfeeling enough to disturb Moira, who was now an invalid, in pursuit of his selfish ends.

Chris said harshly, 'I'm not talking about the small print of agreements. I'm talking about what's just and equitable.' He was pleased he had managed to get that phrase out. He sat on the edge of his chair, glaring challengingly at his partner. He hated the smoothness which he had so admired in Ray Keane in their early days. He had never expected it to be turned upon himself.

Keane shrugged his shoulders, smiled a smile which expressed his surprise at how little the other man understood of the world.

'What's just and equitable is a very vague concept. It's capable of different interpretations by different people, Chris. As I'm sure you will appreciate, upon reflection.'

He looked again at Zoe, smiled at her over Hampson's downcast head, trying to assess what effect this was having on her. Power was supposed to be the ultimate aphrodisiac for women, and he was asserting his power now in this quiet, almost claustrophobic setting. He had no doubt whose will would prevail in this conflict, however much right Chris might have on his side. Zoe stared back at him steadily for a moment, then switched her gaze to the man sitting frustrated on the edge of his chair.

Keane had won now, and all three people in the room knew that. Hampson said dully, 'We can't go on being successful if you don't pull your weight. We'll need to talk about it.'

'Of course we shall. Let's just give it a few days, for both of us to cool down.' His smile said that only one of them really needed time to cool down, but that he, Raymond Keane, successful businessman and rising MP, was used to being magnanimous about these things.

He stood up, signifying that their business was concluded. Successfully, as far as he was concerned. He ushered Hampson to the door, preventing himself with difficulty from throwing an arm across the other man's shoulders. The rigidity of the taller man's torso and arms warned him that Hampson was still seething, so that any form of physical contact might be a mistake.

Keane said, 'I'll be in touch, Chris. At the end of the coming week. I'll definitely phone you this time, I promise.' It was his first acknowledgement that there had been substance in the older man's complaint.

He stood in the doorway of the old cottage to watch his partner drive away, beaming a false fondness as he waved him into the distance.

Zoe Renwick watched Hampson's departure from behind the low leaded-light window. She had seen a ruthless display of power by Raymond Keane which bordered on cruelty. And what was worse, he had revelled in it. It was a facet of her husband-to-be that she had not even suspected. She found it quite disturbing.

CHAPTER THREE

The man in the trees watched Chris Hampson drive away from the cottage. He was curious about this visitor for a little while, as he had been curious when he watched him arrive forty minutes earlier. But his interest in this stranger did not last for very long. It could not contend in his mind with the hatred, steady and intense, which he felt for the man who remained within the house.

There were still a few leaves on the beeches and oaks, and the rich orange needles of the larches had not yet dropped to the dry ground beneath them, as they would do by the year end as the frosts grew sharper. They gave him concealment enough, but whenever he felt the need of it, the tall firs on the edge of the wood provided him with deeper cover.

It was dark as he moved beneath these, dark as in those northern forests of Europe, where the trolls controlled a darker world and the nights scarcely conceded daylight at all at this time of the year. On some days now, the man felt that he would be happier if it were dark all the time.

He flapped his arms occasionally behind his screen. His sparse frame should have shivered, but he wore so many layers against the cold of the December day that he scarcely felt it. He was warmed by the fire of hatred which burned within him against Raymond Keane, MP and hypocrite, who had proved a false friend and a smiling, polished enemy.

Well, he could play that game too. A man could smile and smile, and be a villain. The man who had first said that had also been a little uncertain about how he should proceed with his revenge, at first. But he had killed his man in the end. The people who gave him such curious looks as he went in and out of his

23

house nowadays would be surprised to know that he knew about things like that.

The man in the woods went on another of his small, slow perambulations, his hands deep in his pockets, his lips lifting slightly at their edges.

*   *   *

Sunday morning was not a fair time to spring unwelcome surprises upon a man.

Detective Sergeant Hook was struggling hard, but he was a fish that was already hooked and only had to be landed. He knew the rules of the game, and as a sportsman he knew that when the wriggling was over he would have to accept them.

'Eleanor had no right to say that I'd do any such thing!' he said gruffly.

'But she did. And now you must,' said John Lambert gleefully. 'As your superintendent, I have to insist upon your completing the bargain, however reluctantly.'

'But golf. Bloody golf,' said Bert gloomily. 'Bloody, bloody, bloody GOLF!'

'There you are. You're beginning to get the vocabulary already. You could be a natural for this game.'

'Who wants to be a natural in such a damned stupid game? It's the worst thing that could happen to a man. You'll have me drinking gins and tonics and voting

Conservative within a year, if you have your way.'

'A man's politics are his own business,' said Lambert sententiously. 'There's no reason why golf should affect your brain, if you keep it under proper control.'

'A man's soul lost, for the sake of a night's baby-sitting,' said Hook glumly.

'All this talk about souls is an overreaction. I blame this Open University degree of yours. Is Ibsen on your course, by any chance?'

'Ibsen wouldn't have gone anywhere near golf,' mused the downtrodden Hook.

'That explains a lot. Most of his characters talk like people short of a physical challenge,' said Lambert breezily. He decided to turn the knife. 'You were bought very cheaply, actually. The boys were quite charming. We chatted about football for a while, and then they went to bed like lambs when we told them it was time.'

'Damned little traitors,' Hook moaned. 'They never do that for us.'

'I expect they'd been threatened with all kinds of retribution if they didn't behave,' smiled Lambert, thinking back ten years and more, to the days when he needed baby-sitters for two lively daughters. 'Anyway, I want you to know that they were as good as gold. But that doesn't mean you don't have to pay the forfeit. A basket of fifty balls at the driving range.'

'Not today. I need time to adjust to the

idea,' Hook said firmly.

'Right, you shall have it. We'll leave it until after Christmas and the New Year. That'll let you dwell on the challenge to come. Monday, January the second. We'll lunch at the Miller's Arms afterwards. If you've any appetite left after you've compromised your soul and your afterlife.'

Lambert pushed himself back against the seat of the old Vauxhall Senator and eased the car away from the kerb. That date would give him a full two weeks of teasing, in a period which seemed likely to be thin on serious crime.

'All right. Monday the second of January it is, if that will shut you up,' said Hook dolefully. It would never do to let Lambert know that he was beginning to look forward to the activity. Hitting a dead ball when you decided you were ready to hit it must be quite easy and exhilarating.

And it would be a one-off, of course. He would never ever join a golf club.

*   *   *

Inside the warm thatched cottage with its cheerful fire, Raymond Keane found after Chris Hampson had gone that his display of power was not quite the aphrodisiac the sexual pundits said it should be.

Zoe Renwick was cool, even apparently

26

abstracted. He followed her into the small, neat kitchen and clasped his arms round her waist from behind her. 'Penny for them?' he murmured into her ear. He was excited already by a scent which might have been no more than expensive soap, by the soft touch of her hair and her neck. She tossed her fair hair in a gesture of dismissal, and he had more sense than to pursue any sexual plans in the face of her coolness.

Zoe made them sandwiches and a pot of tea for lunch. She came and sat carefully opposite him rather than beside him, holding her hands out briefly for a moment towards the fire, though the room was already warm from the central heating.

The lounge had two windows, but they were quite small, designed in the days when the primary concern in these thick-walled dwellings was to keep in all the available heat. In the soft half-light, with the reflection of the fire flickering against her pale face, Zoe's strong features had a Scandinavian beauty.

He could imagine her wrapped in thick woollens in a ski-hut, her long legs curled beneath her after an exhilarating day on the piste. Or even off it, on runs they had found for themselves: they were both strong, experienced skiers, and that would allow them a more private place to spend the long, contented nights. Raymond stretched his legs towards the fire, revelling in the thought.

Later, when her mood softened, he would take her to bed.

When she did not speak to him, he picked up the Sunday paper, turning automatically to the business section and its thoughts upon the Chancellor's latest strategy. Zoe looked for a moment at his square face, studying the nose which had been broken and reset a fraction off centre. She thought for a while about how little you could sometimes deduce of what went on behind features which were so familiar to you. Then she said, 'I think we should go to see Moira together.'

It was such a complete surprise to Raymond Keane that he almost showed his bewilderment. Then his politician's practised skills took over. He paused for a moment, digesting the idea whilst he appeared to be weighing it. Zoe must have been more upset than he thought she had been when Hampson had mentioned Moira Yates this morning. Damn Chris! Couldn't he have had a little more sense than to bring an ex-mistress into their argument?

Raymond said as calmly as he could, 'Do you think that's really such a good idea, old girl? I'm—'

'I'm not your "old girl"!' She was outraged by the expression, as she had never been before. But had he ever used it to her before? It seemed to ring in her ears with the note of an earlier era. Perhaps he had used it with other women, and that was why she was suddenly so furious with him. 'And yes, I do think it would be a good idea. Unless you still think that there are things about your relationship with her that need to be hidden from me, of course.' It was cheap, but it was out before she could stop herself. She was horrified by the sudden desire to hurt him she felt within herself.

'Don't be silly, darling. I've been perfectly open with you about her, and about all of my past life, if it comes to that.' That was true, he thought. He certainly loved Zoe now, and wanted to marry her. He had been more honest with her than with anyone else in his life; he was sure of that.

'And Moira knows it's all over between the two of you? And she knows about me?'

'Yes, yes. I told her about four months ago. Told her I was going to marry you. Even before I told you, as a matter of fact.' For a moment, as her bright blue eyes flashed suddenly up into his face, he wondered if this had been too blunt, though he had only been trying to reassure her. And it was true enough: he had been glad to offer his marriage plans to the intense Moira as a signal that their affair was now conclusively finished, that there was absolutely no possibility of its renewal.

'I still think I should come with you to see her.' Zoe stared into the fire, her face set like a small girl's, deaf to the arguments of those around her.

'It's just—well, just that I'm thinking of her, you see. She's not a well woman, by all accounts.'

'Agoraphobia. Nothing physically wrong, you said.' Zoe quoted him exactly, as if implying that she would reserve her own diagnosis until she saw the patient. She was a ward sister in a private hospital, though she claimed no expertise in psychiatric illnesses.

'No. But her brother said when I rang that she still can't leave the house. I haven't seen her for over two months, you know.'

He brandished his lack of concern for the discarded woman like a virtue, Zoe thought. 'I know you haven't been to see her. And you don't propose to see her again. You've told me all that. I think I should come with you.' She offered no reasons, because she was not sure herself why she was so determined to go.

All she knew was that the resolution had formed at the moment when Chris Hampson had brought the woman's name into this morning's argument. Before she saw Raymond with Chris, she had had no intention of going with him to see this other woman whom he had loved. Perhaps she would see other new aspects of Raymond Keane, this man she had thought she knew so well.

Raymond looked at the still, set face, considering arguments, rejecting each of them in turn as he saw the resolution there. He still

30

didn't know anything about this woman, he thought, even though he was determined now to marry her, to have her at his side for the rest of his political career. This stubbornness, this small undiscovered part of her, was a new excitement, even if it was a little disturbing.

'All right,' he said. 'We'll go this afternoon.'

She nodded, relaxing imperceptibly, still not looking him in the face. Perhaps she should warm to him for conceding the point without further argument. Instead, she felt a surge of enjoyment in her victory. It was the first real contest they had ever had.

*   *   *

It was a little over an hour before Raymond and Zoe left the cottage. The bright winter sun was already low. It shone brilliantly into their faces over the wood, almost touching the tops of the dark firs; in another half-hour it would be gone, and the cold and the silence would have this unpeopled world to themselves.

Peering into this brilliant light, there was no chance that the pair would see the man who watched, but he moved automatically behind his cypress nevertheless. The woman wore a thick fun fur, its hood raised like a halo round the pale oval of her face. But her court shoes showed him that she had no intention of walking far. Just visiting someone, then; they would probably be back quite soon, the man

31

who watched decided.

The blonde woman hurried behind Keane to the haven of the XJ12 Jaguar, folding herself gracefully into the passenger seat by the time her companion had opened the big door on the driver's side. No word had passed between the two from the moment when they had appeared in the wide low doorway beneath the thatched eaves of the cottage.

The observer watched the Jaguar roar into life, then pour soft clouds of white smoke from its exhaust into the still air. The car reversed from its position alongside the old building, then purred slowly away down the lane. He did not emerge until the last notes of the engine had died away and the car had long disappeared.

Then he walked swiftly in the opposite direction, his movement a welcome release from the long vigil opposite the cottage. Two hundred yards down the lane, he retrieved his van from its position beneath the trees, where the forest workers' wide track entered the woods. He made no attempt to follow the Jaguar, was not even curious to know where it had gone.

What he had to do would be done here. He was sure of that now, though he had not worked out the details yet. It would need to be when Keane came here without the woman, of course; he had no quarrel with her. But there were occasions when the man arrived here alone: he knew that from his observations.

That was the benefit of careful, unhurried planning. He was almost ready to make his move now.

CHAPTER FOUR

When Raymond Keane rang to ask if he might come to see her, Moira Yates answered the phone herself.

Her former lover's voice was uncharacteristically uncertain on the other end of the line; she thought she had never heard him so diffident. Perhaps that helped her confidence; although she had not heard Raymond's voice for many weeks now, she found herself perfectly assured in dealing with it.

'There's no need to treat me as an invalid,' she said. 'I'm perfectly all right within my own home, you know.' She listened as he went on haltingly, her mouth forming a curious smile. Then she put her hand over the mouthpiece and said to the two men who were watching her, 'He's bringing his new woman along to see us.'

Dermot Yates sprang to his feet, alarm starting into his wide brown eyes. 'I don't think that's a very good idea,' he said. 'If you'll just let me speak to him—'

But his sister turned gently away from him, cradling the phone against her neck like a pet kitten. 'That will be perfectly all right, Raymond. We shall look forward to seeing her.' It was the first time in months that she had spoken his name, she reflected, and it had not been difficult. She felt thoroughly in control of the situation, despite the concern of the two people behind her. She put the phone down quickly, pretending she had not noticed her brother's protective hand stretching to take it.

The second man in the room felt the sick apprehension one only feels when one fears for a loved one. He had known Moira for twenty years, since he had first met her as a raw young Irish girl of sixteen. For most of those years, Gerald Sangster had been in love with the girl who had blossomed so quickly into a poised, dark-haired beauty. It was a hopeless love, as she had told him gently on several occasions over the years, but that did not diminish the pain.

But the heart accepts no logic, and when Raymond Keane had suddenly deserted Moira, Gerald Sangster had quickly reappeared in her life. Each of them knew that he cherished the hope that even at this stage she might take him as a permanent partner, though neither of them voiced the thought. She could name her own terms, and she knew it. Yet life is cruel enough to dictate that she

34

was less likely to accept him because of that very thought.

But the spirited, independent girl had shrunk beneath the shadow of illness in the months since Keane had finished with her. She was a brilliant horsewoman and a county tennis player, but now the strong arms which had controlled the liveliest hunter had wasted a little through lack of use, the shoulders which had launched so many blistering backhands were hunched. Gerald had thought many times as he looked at her in these last weeks that you would never have taken her for an athlete, and the thought had seared his aching heart. She had confined herself first to house and garden and then to the house itself, until she shrank nowadays even from an open door to the world outside.

Gerald went across to her now and took her hands in his, kneeling before her chair on the thick Persian carpet. It might have been a self-conscious gesture, but it came perfectly naturally to him in his concern, and Moira was too sunk into her own thoughts to find the move theatrical. 'Do you really think you should take this on, love?' He had taken to adding that little word of affection to the end of his exchanges with her, as his northern mother had once done. She had used the term indiscriminately, but for him it was a small assertion of his closeness and concern. 'There's still time for us to ring him back for you. He'll understand, I'm sure. He won't know how ill you've been, you see, and—'

'Oh, but he will, when he sees me.' She had that abstracted, brittle air they had noticed in her so much as her illness had taken its hold and she had refused to leave the house. But today she was animated, not lethargic. She got up now and went to look at herself in the wide gilt-framed mirror over the marble fireplace. She lifted the tresses of dark hair, holding them back above her ears for a moment, noting the odd strand of silver that had threaded lately among the sable, nodding what appeared to be satisfaction.

She could see the two concerned male faces behind her reflected in the mirror, and for a moment she studied them, until she apparently decided that they too were as they should be. She had the air of a woman checking the tidiness of a room in preparation for visitors, but in her case she checked the human pieces rather than any inanimate furniture. 'Cheer up, me boys!' she said. 'He won't bite you, and sure it'll soon be over.'

The Irish accent which had almost disappeared over the years had edged its way back into her speech since the agoraphobia had taken a stronger grip on her. Dermot saw in her a woman guying her younger, more innocent self.

The two men looked at each other, recognizing this sudden resolution in her,

36

bizarre because she had shown so little interest in anything for weeks. Dermot said, 'I'll go and get a tray ready. I think we have a fruit cake in the tin.' He went into the small, neat kitchen, where he had cooked only for one in the seven years since his divorce. He had been happy to take in his beloved younger sister when the tragedy of her break-up with Keane had beset her. But he had not bargained for the illness which followed hard upon it.

Moira was twelve years younger than him; she had always been a girl to him, applauding his successes on the rugby field in the old days, sharing her own tennis triumphs with him when he had ceased to play seriously. She had seemed to him a golden girl, as she gathered adulation as a young adult. He found it difficult to come to terms now with her illness, so unexpected in this laughing, extrovert sister. He busied himself rattling cups and saucers on to a tray in the small kitchen, wondering miserably how he was to help her to cope with this latest crisis.

Through the open door to the lounge, he heard Gerald's low, concerned tones as he talked to the woman he had loved so hopelessly for so long. 'It's bound to be a bit of an ordeal for you, love. I'm sure you can handle it, but do remember that we're here to help if you need us. Just give us a look—there's no need to say anything, we'll understand. We'll soon get the two of them to go, if you want us to.'

Gerald Sangster went on in the same vein, his anxiety making him speak too much, causing him to repeat himself in the face of the abstracted silence of the woman who sat with her hands in her lap, as upright and still as a sculpture.

Dermot Yates was irritated as he listened. He washed his hands at the neat modern sink, scrubbing the nails which had collected dirt as he worked in the garden. He had been glad to take advantage of Gerald's presence to get outside in the crisp winter air for a little while. It allowed the emotionally distressed pair in the house a little privacy, he had told himself; he did not like to admit that he was apprehensive about leaving Moira on her own in the house these days.

Through the efficient double glazing of the windows, all sound was diminished; Dermot saw rather than heard the big Jaguar turn carefully into the drive of his neat modern house. He went back into the lounge, with the vague idea that they must present a solid front to what he now regarded as the enemy. He had never liked Raymond Keane, even when Moira had been so attached to him. Now he was sure the MP was responsible for her illness, which had started almost from the moment of his desertion.

Yet when the knock came at the door it was Moira who was swiftest to react, moving easily into the hall, welcoming the uncertain pair on the doorstep as if she were a practised hostess and this was a perfectly normal social occasion. 'Good to see that the coming political figure still has time for his old friends!' she said to Keane. He had half expected her to be stiffly distant, half expected her to come forward and kiss him without passion. Instead, Moira took the hand he had never proffered determinedly between hers, looked past him, and said, 'And this must be . . .'

'Zoe. Zoe Renwick.' The tall woman pushed past Raymond and shook hands briefly but firmly. Moira felt too close to her to take her in in detail. She had a vague impression of good teeth in a swift, unaffected smile, of fair, straight hair, of jewel-bright blue eyes. But her own eyes must have been filled with moisture, for she saw the other woman as through a window with rain upon it, swimming in and out of clear vision. She was glad to sit down.

All the things which Raymond had prepared to say seemed now false to him, in this house where he had never been before, with this woman whose body he had known so intimately and whom he now had to address in front of strangers. Everything he had thought up to say over the last weeks was designed for an exchange between the two of them.

Now she was ill, a laughing extrovert suddenly pinned within a narrow private world, and he spoke as if he were a hospital visitor at a bedside: there seemed no other way. 'How are you feeling?'

Dermot and Gerald looked at each other. It was a question which seemed designed for them, but neither wanted to answer it in front of the patient. Instead, it was Moira who said, 'Bright as a button, really!' At that moment she looked it, sitting on the edge of her armchair like a precocious child who knows she is the centre of attention. 'So long as I don't leave the house, of course.'

For the first time since they had sat down, she took her eyes off Keane and looked at the other two men, sitting together anxious on the sofa. 'I'm doing my best, aren't I, me boys?'

Gerald Sangster was irritated by the way she dropped the Irish accent on to the last phrase. It seemed as if she was applying a deliberate taunt to those who cherished her in front of this man who had caused her illness. He said, 'We thought we'd get her into the garden today with the sun out, perhaps get her at least as far as the gate, but . . .' He stopped helplessly, realizing too late that he had fallen into the old trap of speaking about her as if she were not there with them .

'. . . But I'm not a very good patient, I'm afraid.' Her brilliant black eyes were back on Raymond Keane. 'I mean to be good, of course, but then I let people down. But then you'd know all about that sort of thing.' It was the first barb she had offered him, delivered

40

with a dazzling smile which removed every line from her face. For that moment, she dropped at least ten of her thirty-six years, seeming again an ingenuous, vulnerable girl.

Keane did not know how to manage this. He wished only that he had never come here; he had never envisaged anything like this. He would not have minded her having a go at him, flinging her hurt and resentment in a final exchange, which would have closed this particular chapter in his book. But that would have been in private. He had not thought of her like this, an invalid with an audience who watched over her, listening and weighing his every reaction, exploiting her position as he had never seen her do in the days of their intimacy.

Raymond looked at Zoe, sitting silent and apparently composed beside him. He said desperately, 'We just thought we'd call in whilst we were in the area for the weekend, you see.' He was speaking apologetically to the two men in the room, not to Moira. And Dermot, taking his cue, bustled away to bring in the tea and the slices of cake.

It was like a more sinister mad hatter's tea party, Zoe thought later, with herself in the role of Alice and only Moira seeming to know the rules. The four sane people in the room exchanged whatever small talk they could manage, about the splendour of the winter day outside, about Dermot's domestic expertise, about the convenience of this neat modern house on the edge of the village.

And all the time the four of them were listening for the interventions of the fifth voice in the room. Moira's contributions had a strange awareness, an insight into the anxieties which lay beneath the polite exchanges. She behaved like an intelligent but vulnerable child, who understood none of the rules of safe adult conversation. When Dermot spoke of the convenience of a modern house, she said abruptly, 'I prefer old cottages. Like Raymond's. We had some good times there, you know.'

The last phrase was darted without warning at Zoe. The new woman in Raymond Keane's life studied the pattern on her china cup resolutely and refused to be drawn into a reply. She remembered her early medical experience of young people hooked on drugs, who often had this brittle, uninhibited confidence after a fix. She would like to have known what if any medication Moira Yates was receiving for her agoraphobia. Despite herself, Zoe found she was fighting images of Raymond in bed with this startling woman. And she knew in that moment that this had been Moira's intention.

Raymond Keane found himself applying the rules he had adopted for his public exchanges to his private life. 'If you're on a loser, cut your losses quickly,' was one of the rules he applied

42

to political exchanges. On this occasion, he could not call briskly for another question. He looked at his watch and said, 'Well, we mustn't trade on your hospitality for too long.' He pushed his cup and saucer on to the small table beside his chair and pulled himself clumsily to his feet. 'Busy weekend, I'm afraid!'

'I'm sure it is.' Moira had not taken her dark eyes from Zoe's face. She now allowed her gaze to travel down the curves of the blonde woman's slim figure. Her small, knowing smile degenerated momentarily into something very near a leer. Then she rose in turn and stood facing Raymond Keane. 'I shall watch your career with interest. From afar, of course.'

'Thank you. Thank you. And when you are better, which I'm sure will be soon now, you must come and have lunch in the House one day.'

He was more nervous than he could remember being in years, and his sentiments dropped into the abruptly silent room like the most hollow of political platitudes. Everyone was standing now, but no one helped him out, no one offered a crutch for his feeble stumblings. The two men saw no reason to rescue a man they disliked, and Zoe was aware that any intervention from her could only make matters worse.

She knew now that Raymond and this woman had been very close, that he had treated her shabbily when Zoe came into his life. He had pretended to her that his affair with Moira was finished when he met her. He had come here today to dismiss her finally from his life—and found that she had turned the tables completely upon him. This was Moira Yates's dismissal of Raymond Keane.

And for the second time that day, Zoe found she had no wish to rescue Raymond from a situation he had brought upon himself.

It was obvious that the other woman in the room was enjoying being the central, unpredictable figure in the scene of Keane's discomfiture. As she ushered them into the hall, Moira addressed her words of dismissal to Keane alone. 'It's been good to see you again. And to find you so little changed. I wish I could say the same for myself.'

It was a blatant invitation to frame a denial, and Keane was unwise enough to fall for it. 'You look as beautiful as ever. I'm sure you'll be back to normal by the time we meet again.'

She neither nodded nor denied it, but threw him the last and most dazzling of her smiles, underlining with it the falseness of his compliment. None of the people there believed that he would ever visit her again.

Zoe did not look back, but Raymond Keane could not resist the temptation to turn towards the house as he reached the gate. Moira, the woman who nowadays shied away from even an open window, was standing in the doorway of the house, an actress playing out the final effect of a scene she had dominated, that brilliant farewell smile still fixed firmly upon her features.

Only the two men who stood behind her in the darkness of the hall saw the tears upon her cheeks as she shut the door and turned back towards them. 'I did well, didn't I?' she said.

CHAPTER FIVE

It was Sunday afternoon when Raymond Keane took Zoe Renwick to see Moira Yates, the woman she had displaced in his affections. By the evening of the following Wednesday, the embarrassment of that meeting seemed already more than three days behind him.

It is easy for an MP to keep busy, to remind himself that private concerns should be submerged beneath the swirling waters of national events. And these last three days of the parliamentary session had not been without their satisfactions. He had voted in a two-line whip motion on defence cuts. He had managed to ask a 'planted' question of his leader at Prime Minister's Question Time on the Tuesday—in effect it had merely offered congratulations to the PM on his prompt actions to quell the latest urban riot.

His question had meant that the nation—or

at least that fraction of it that chose to listen to *Yesterday in Parliament*—had heard his clear articulation and confident tones amidst the bear garden of Question Time and the Speaker's ritual calls for order. More important, the fact that he had been suggested by the Party hierarchy to be this conduit of admiration for the PM confirmed that he was a coming man, in other people's minds as well as his own.

That Wednesday, he even concluded some action on behalf of a troublesome constituent of his, Joseph Walsh. He had been taken aback by the man's vehemence at his clinic in the constituency, but not for long. Politicians were perforce accustomed to dealing with the occasional harmless loony, who thought an MP could achieve far more for them than the system actually permitted. And the man had lost his daughter, after all. He deserved a certain amount of consideration, even if nothing could be achieved for him.

Raymond had asked the appropriate written questions of the appropriate minister, and received the appropriate answers in writing from the civil servants in her department. Now he wrote to Joseph Walsh and told him nothing could be done, enclosing a copy of the minister's reply to demonstrate how diligently he had pursued the matter.

A busy week so far, then, but not without its modest achievements. Raymond allowed himself a bottle of the excellent parliamentary claret with his dinner. With parliament now suspended for the Christmas recess, there was time for a little relaxation. He began to plan out his movements for the next three weeks.

*   *   *

On the following morning, in the neat modern house in Gloucestershire, Dermot Yates watched his sister anxiously, assessing the effects of the visit of Moira's former lover and his new mistress upon the invalid in his care.

Moira had seemed exhausted after her brilliant performance—Dermot could only see it as that—in discomforting Raymond Keane. She had been all intensity, full of a sustained, almost unnatural concentration upon the part she had chosen for herself, whilst Keane and that strangely dignified blonde woman had been in the house. But the effort had told: she had been very quiet since Sunday, moving about the house like a convalescent who had pushed herself beyond what her resources will support.

Thursday was one of those quiet December days when the sun shines softly through the leafless trees and the day is unnaturally mild. Dermot tried unsuccessfully to get his sister out into the garden, to breathe the air which had once been such a delight to her, so necessary a part of her life.

47

She made the coffee for them in mid-morning, and he was pleased by this departure from the lethargy which had dropped its hand upon her like a malign presence over the last months. She opened the window to call in her elder brother from the garden and he was emboldened by this small concession the agoraphobic was making to the outside world to keep her there while he spoke. He said, 'We could have our coffee on the terrace, I think, if you put your sheepskin coat on. It's sheltered there, and the sun is right on it at present.'

Moira regarded him for a moment with a simple, uncomplicated love, even looked with seeming longing at the spot he had indicated, where the honey-coloured sun poured softly into an alcove, around which the brown clematis stems intertwined with a climbing rose which still carried its last three obstinate blooms, as if refusing to believe the calendar. Then she shook her head firmly, and he saw her shutting him as well as the suggestion out with the movement. 'I can't, Dermot. Not yet.' She shut the window carefully in his face, as if the security of her self-imposed prison was supremely important to her again.

He had to go through the kitchen to the dining room to make contact with her again. He found her putting ginger biscuits upon a plate. She pushed them towards him, then grabbed one and dunked it suddenly into her own mug of coffee, dismissing further argument with that abrupt gesture. It was uncharacteristic of her, too, he thought. He could not remember seeing her dunk biscuits in tea or coffee since she was a child. She looked for a moment at her brother's troubled face and said, 'I'll be all right soon, I think. I'm feeling better each day now.'

He was not convinced; but how could he tell her tactfully that her actions did not support that view? She turned away from him and went over to the shelves of books that ran from floor to ceiling on the other side of the dining room. She stood motionless whilst he studied the upright back, which had remained erect over many a mettlesome horse, marvelling at this stillness in a woman who had always been so active. He wondered what was going on in her mind, for he did not think she was looking at the books at all. He had left his rubber boots at the door when he came in from the garden. Now he set down his beaker and moved across the carpeted room on silent, stockinged feet to study the profile he knew so well.

He had half expected the eyes to be filled with tears. Instead, he found that an odd half-smile sat upon her lips. And the dark eyes, though as unseeing as he had expected, were dry and brilliant.

In the next hour, the doctor would be making his weekly call. Dermot was suddenly glad of that support. But this did not seem the moment to remind Moira of the visit.

*   *   *

Twenty miles away from Moira Yates, in a bungalow with a large, well-kept garden on the edge of Oldford, another woman was drinking coffee. But Christine Lambert sat alone, and she was scarcely conscious of whether she drank her coffee or not.

Indeed, when she remembered it, after staring for a long time at the movements of a robin in the winter garden, she found it was almost cold. She leant towards the table beside her and picked up the letter again, with its official heading, its bland, impersonal wording, its unconvincing assurance that this second summons was not necessarily anything to be anxious about. 'Not necessarily,' she repeated aloud to herself, fastening with her teacher's practised expertise on the key phrase in this welter of bureaucratic reassurance.

She did what she had not done in years, not done since the bad old days of twenty years ago, when she had been left in the house for days on end with only toddlers, and had almost left her husband and his whole damned police force. She rang John at work.

'Superintendent Lambert?' said the efficient voice. 'Yes, I think he's in his office. I'll put you through.'

She realized then that she had been half

hoping he wouldn't be there. It was unusual for him to be available at the station. Unlike most people of his rank, John Lambert did not conduct cases from his office, where the head of the team usually stayed, but went out to the scene of the action. It made him an eccentric in the modern police force. For years, his colleagues had doubted how long such behaviour would be tolerated. But Lambert's methods had survived the arrival of a new Chief Constable, as many had not expected they would. In the big cases, the murders and the other crimes of violence, Lambert got results. The hierarchy was wise enough to allow him a little licence, as long as he pulled the rabbits from the hat so regularly for them.

He picked up the phone at the first ring. Christine was scarcely ready for it, wondering if he was going to bite her head off for this unexpected intrusion into that other, working world she had long since resigned to him. She said foolishly, 'John?' as if she had not recognized the voice she heard so often on the phone when he rang her.

'Christine? What is it? Is it one of the children?'

He was concerned, not abrupt. For that small kindness, she was absurdly grateful to him. 'No, it's nothing like that. Nothing serious really. There's no need—'

'I'll be home in an hour. Or is it more urgent than that?'

'No. There's no reason for you to come home at all, really. I'm being—'

'I'll be there in an hour.'

'I'll make you some lunch, then. And please don't—'

But the phone was down and he was gone. She was immensely relieved that he should have known immediately how anxious she was, that she had not needed to spell out her exaggerated fear to him on the phone.

Endurance in marriage brought its rewards, in the end.

* * *

In a smaller house, with a garden much more neglected, on the outskirts of the city of Gloucester, another solitary figure turned another official letter within his hands.

But Joe Walsh had no one to ring with his news, no figure to bring the reassurance of common sense and proportion into the dark world in which he increasingly lived. It seemed, indeed, so dark this morning that he could detect no chink of light within it. Until he determined upon the one fierce, explosive action he would himself achieve, which would dispel the darkness with a sudden, blinding flash, bringing a blaze of light so brilliant that it would make it impossible to see what lay beyond it.

He looked again at the House of Commons

crest upon the notepaper, at the three short paragraphs which were meant to dismiss his daughter for ever, at the confident, illegible scrawl of a signature which said, 'I am a busy man and this is all that your daughter is worth to me.'

Already he could have recited the letter by heart, but he looked again at those phrases which stung his eyeballs like acid: '. . . matter has now been thoroughly investigated . . .'; '. . . facts of the incident have been established as clearly as they ever will be . . .'; and last and worst of all, ' . . . can only advise you to reconcile yourself to the fact that this was an unfortunate accident . . .'

The pain on his unblinking eyes was almost unbearable. Then, abruptly, it eased, and the phrases which had been so painful swam before him, as the salt tears sprang from nowhere, brimmed on the lower rims of his eye-sockets, and ran unchecked down his cheeks.

Well, Mr High-and-Mighty, uncaring, sodding, bloody Keane, there was more than one type of 'unfortunate accident'. You've had your chance and failed, Keane. Just as I knew you would, like all the rest. Now it's time for your punishment, you smooth bastard, you false, uncaring, fucking friend. I've watched you for long enough: now it's time to act.

He did not normally use obscenities, and they brought a kind of relief. He went on shouting them for some time at the impassive walls of the silent house, which had ceased to be a home when his daughter had been carried from it in the narrow oak coffin.

He would get Keane. And without being caught himself. He did not care for his own safety, now that Debbie was gone, but his revenge would only be complete if it went unpunished. The man who had killed Debbie had got away scot-free; when he killed the man who had so miserably failed to avenge her, he would get away scot-free too. The justice of it pleased him. Somewhere in the recesses of his memory, that phrase rang a Shakespearean bell.

Unfortunately, it was not a warning bell.

CHAPTER SIX

John Lambert looked at the letter, his face made longer by the deepening lines of the last few years. To Christine's great relief, he did not make light of it.

He made the ritual comfortings, as they both knew he must. 'Quite a high percentage of people have to go back for a second scan after these mass screenings, you know.'

'Yes. Well, not all that high, actually. About four per cent, I believe.' She had checked that already.

And how many false alarms were there among those? And how many genuine cases of breast cancer? The questions started up in both their minds, but neither of them wanted them voiced aloud. Christine said, 'I don't know why I should feel so cast down by it. I've been expecting it somehow, ever since I went to the unit last week for the first screening.'

She expected him to say, in his knowing, commonsense way, that she was probably imagining that, now that this had happened, that it was a kind of phoney, retrospective knowledge that she had had. Instead, he nodded and said, 'You were very quiet, the night after you'd been.'

'Was I? You'd never have noticed that, you know, at one time. It was the night I agreed to baby-sit for Eleanor, if you remember. I thought you were more excited by the thought of getting Bert Hook hitting a golf ball!'

Suddenly, she was in his arms. Neither of them knew who had made the first move towards the other. They subsided clumsily on to the big settee, laughing their relief in the contact, seeking out each other's lips, allowing their mouths to dwell long and tenderly upon each other.

'This is a turn-up, cuddling at lunchtime,' he said eventually, holding her so that they could look into each other's eyes, smiling his wish that this might be nothing more than a trivial diversion from the steady tenor of their middle age.

'Special occasion,' she said. 'You don't have a neurotic wife demanding your attention every day of the week.' It was true that they were not much given to casual physical contact. They never kissed each other ritual goodbyes in the morning, like some other couples they knew. But now she took his hands from behind her shoulders, and ran them softly over the breasts which were now suddenly so suspect.

He smiled, an intimate, tender smile, wanting to offer assurance, helpless in the knowledge that he could not. 'They feel all right to me, lass,' he said, in a clumsy parody of her northern roots.

'Maybe they are. Probably they are. We'll know soon enough.' It was she who comforted him now; she felt happier in that role, bred into her over the years, of soothing away childish ills and anxieties.

'You haven't felt any lumps or anything?' he said, feeling awkward and heavy in his maleness, wanting to tell her he understood this female complaint. Yet how could he ever do that? He wished that one of his daughters could be here, cursed the nature of modern society which split families and took daughters away from their roots to be with their husbands. His concern was all for Christine; and yet he felt helpless, as he never felt in his work.

She smiled at him. 'No lumps. It'll be a false alarm, you see. Just the silly apprehension of a menopausal idiot.'

He scrambled to his feet, his head bouncing away one of the big tinselled spheres she had hung up for Christmas decorations as she tried to distract herself. 'Just so long as you don't stop me getting a golf club into Bert Hook's big hands,' he grinned.

'Don't tell anyone else,' she said as he was at the door. 'I don't want your colleagues to know what a panicky old bat you've got at home. Sorry I interrupted your day.'

'No great matter,' he said. 'It's a quiet time anyway, coming up to Christmas.'

When he looked back a fortnight later, that seemed the most ironic statement of all.

*   *   *

Gerald Sangster went to see the love of his life on that Thursday before Christmas. The hopeless love. He told himself he realized that now, as everyone else had realized it years ago. But his heart would not allow him to let go of Moira Yates, however clearly his brain spelt out the situation to him.

Dermot Yates tactfully left the pair on their own. He said that he would be glad to get out of the house for a break, to do some belated Christmas shopping. Probably there was some truth in this. The doctor assured him that

57

Moira could be left on her own in the house, but he had not chosen to leave her without company on many occasions as her own reluctance to set foot beyond two or three rooms in the house had become more marked with the passing weeks.

Moira and Gerald Sangster chatted in desultory fashion through the afternoon. They knew each other well enough not to be embarrassed by the long pauses in their talk. But it was the talk of old friends, rather than the intimate exchanges that Gerald always envisaged and never seemed able to engineer. They were easiest when they talked of the old days, when they had been part of a crowd of young people, when they had been the most gifted of a group who played serious tennis, when he had towed the horsebox around the south of England to the scenes of her various equine triumphs.

Nostalgia is a powerful pleasure among old friends, uniting them in happy remembrance of times past, reminding them of common interests, mutual friends, and the joyous successes of years gone by. Carefree times, they always seem, in the retrospective glow of that selective memory which is one of the human defences against darker thoughts.

Sangster brought the conversation back as gently as he could to the present. He tried to explore the depth of Moira's present depression, for he had researched agoraphobia since she had become its victim, and his reading suggested that depression of some kind lay always behind its fears. Whilst he hinted gently that the only solution lay within herself, she retreated gently behind the fences she had built around her as she had receded into her illness.

When Gerald was eventually irritated into a more definite suggestion, she turned her eyes for the first time to meet his. He expected anger, and for a moment irritation did flare in those large, near-black pupils which had given him so many sleepless nights over the years. Then she relaxed, grinning at him, teasing in a way he remembered from happier days. 'You mean I should snap out of it!' she said.

'No, I wasn't thinking of anything so—'

'You're right, though. It's what the doctors say, too. They don't put it as directly as that, of course. They say that, "the solutions to psychological disorders of this kind will most usually be found within the patient herself." I prefer your version, Gerald, "Snap out of it!" '

It gave him a ridiculous pleasure to hear her use his name. She had not done it much during the months of her illness. Not knowing what to say, he found himself bumbling on about his lack of medical knowledge, going nowhere.

This time it was the invalid who had to rescue him. She came across and sat beside him on the sofa in the darkening December room and took both his hands in hers. It was the first time in months that she had volunteered any physical contact with him, and for an instant his blood pulsed in his temples with an absurd hope that it was he who was to be her salvation, he who was to lead her as a lover from the barless prison within which she had caged herself.

It was the opposite. She looked him again full in the face and said, 'I will come out of this, Gerald. I can feel that, now. But the rest of my life won't be spent with you, you know. I'm sorry.'

She didn't say any more. Neither of them needed more. He held on to her hands for a full minute, in what he felt now would be the last intimate contact he would ever have with the woman he loved. He did not want explanations. Yet he was driven into words, as much to break the spell of this exquisitely painful silence as in search of explanation. 'It's him, isn't it? Keane!' He spat the name harshly, as if it were an obscenity.

She snatched her hands away at that, as he felt he had known she would. Her eyes stared out at the twilight, her profile turned to marble. He felt her seeping away from him as she said, 'It may be. I don't know. I think I'm almost rid of him, now. But I can't live with you, Gerry. I'm sorry.'

The words hit him like a bludgeoning with a sand-filled sock. He stood up unsteadily, surprised that he had enough control of his limbs to move in a normal fashion. 'I'm sorry, too, Moira. Perhaps . . . Well, perhaps when . . .'

He could not go on. He wanted to say that perhaps when she was better things might be different, but he could not face the certainty of the renewed denial that would bring. He said clumsily, 'I think I'd better be off now,' unable to frame a decent excuse for an abrupt departure. He knew that Dermot would be away for an hour at least yet, but he needed to be out of this claustrophobic house, away from the woman he loved before she could retreat even further from him. She did not come to the door with him, and he did not look back for the face he knew would not be there.

That night, fury welled within Gerald Sangster, surging over and drowning the pain of his rejection by Moira. It was not her face which was framed by his anger, but the confident, urbane countenance of the man who had rejected her, who had cast her into this illness which Gerald now felt was the source of all his pain and frustration.

Raymond Keane had suffered nothing for what he had done to his lovely Moira. He had installed that new blonde woman already in her place. And his political career was going from strength to strength. Well, he couldn't be allowed to get away with it. He wasn't the only enterprising and determined man in Moira's life. Gerry had built his own prosperous business, and he had the resources and determination to bring Keane down, if he put his mind to it.

It was the only service he could render now to Moira. The only one she would allow him to make. He would not fail her. He had no idea yet what he would do.

But he would make sure her revenge upon Keane was swift and effective.

*   *   *

Gerald Sangster would have been surprised at what was happening to the blonde woman he had last seen on Keane's arm.

Even as Sangster began to formulate his action against Keane, Zoe Renwick was reviewing her relationship with the MP. She had had a trying day as ward sister. There was sickness among the staff as flu began to make its winter rounds. There had been a little spat between two normally quiet nurses about the duty rotas for Christmas and New Year. For the first time in her experience, the notion that parents of small children were given priority in Christmas leave had been challenged, and she had been called upon to adjudicate.

In the afternoon, there had been a death— an expected one, but one which tore at the emotions none the less for that. Death in the smaller, more intimate world of a private hospital shattered those close to it more than that inevitable event did in the large and busy wards of the National Health Service. The grieving relatives, even with their breathy, well-meant thanks to those who had nursed the departed through these last days, made an unavoidable impact on the other patients in this quiet, contained world.

By the time she got back to her flat in the evening, Zoe was quite exhausted. Her mind came back again, as it did in every spare moment, to that curious gathering on Sunday, when Moira Yates, flanked by her brother and her faithful champion of many years, had confronted her former lover and his new mistress. Try as she might, Zoe could only think of the meeting in terms of a confrontation.

And what of her own part in it? Why had she chosen to be present at this embarrassing encounter? Had it been mere curiosity to see the woman she knew Raymond had lately loved so deeply, however much he might make light of it now? Had she been anxious to oversee and confirm Raymond's exchange from his former lover to her? It was understandable she would need reassurance, after all: Raymond Keane was expecting her to become his wife.

And she had expected, even been anxious, to become that wife. Before Sunday. She did not like what she had seen in herself that day, but she liked still less what she thought she had seen in Raymond. There had been a streak of cruelty in her wish to be so inappropriately present at this farewell to Moira Yates; she saw that clearly now. There had been a part of her which wanted to see herself triumphant and the former mistress put down. It was despicable in her. And it had not worked out that way.

That strange, febrile woman who had taken such unexpected charge of the proceedings had been the winner of the strange battle she had conducted in her brother's antiseptic modern house. Zoe had found herself suddenly jealous of her, of her easy intimacy with Raymond Keane, of her ability to discomfort him so easily. Zoe had been treated as if she did not exist, until Moira chose to acknowledge her presence. And for Raymond, when he had been in the orbit of that strangely powerful dark-haired witch, Zoe had indeed been unimportant, almost unnoticed.

She had known by Sunday night that she could never marry Raymond. She had been appalled by the casual, exuberant cruelty of his treatment of his business partner, Chris Hampson, on that Sunday morning. The fact that he had been showing off to her, asserting his power and inviting her to admire him, had made it much worse, for she had felt herself drawn into his behaviour. It showed what he thought of her, how little he knew of her, that he expected her to applaud him in this.

And then that encounter with Moira Yates in the afternoon. He had planned to be as cruel to that strange woman as he had been to Hampson, she was sure. And he would have expected Zoe to applaud him in that cruelty also. She was glad now that that flashing dark-haired woman had so discomforted Raymond, that she had been there to see it. It had been painful, but the scales had dropped from her eyes.

Everything Raymond had said since he had left Moira Yates had only confirmed her revulsion for him: his preoccupation with recovering his own composure; his repeated statements that Moira would never have made a parliamentary wife; above all, his total failure to take account of the way the meeting had affected Zoe and her relationship with him.

When the phone shrilled suddenly in the quiet room, she started so violently that she spilled most of her drink on her lap. It was evidence of how much on edge she was, she thought as she picked up the phone.

It was Raymond. He had been drinking; for the first time ever, she resented that, acutely and irrationally.

He was not drunk, but his voice slid a little carelessly over the syllables as he said, 'I've almost wound things up in the metropolis. One or two people to see tomorrow. Then I should be able to get away to the cottage. See you tomorrow night?'

65

'Not tomorrow. I—I'm working.'

The lie fell clumsily from her trembling lips, but he was too drunk, or too complacent, to recognize it. 'Saturday, then. Christmas Eve. Mistletoe and no nighties! I'll look forward to it, my love.'

The endearment was too casual, too presumptuous. She wondered how many other women it had been offered to in the past. Such things had never worried her when she loved him. 'All right. I don't know what time.'

'Be in touch, then. Goo' night, old thing.'

He put the phone down before she had to frame a reply. Zoe knew that she was one more small task achieved, one more item to be ticked off on his list of tasks for the day. This was the well-organized political man, making his way, putting his wife in place as part of his visible parliamentary baggage.

Staring down at her phone, Zoe Renwick realized how close she had come to ruining her life.

CHAPTER SEVEN

Zoe was right about the man who was still officially her fiancé. Raymond Keane was ticking off the jobs he still had to complete at the end of a busy parliamentary session.

He did not go as far as putting Zoe on his

66

list, of course; he did not need to be reminded to ring her. But the rest of his tasks and assignments formed a neat handwritten list in the back of his diary, and on Friday morning he checked it and did indeed tick off the ones which had already received his attention.

He had already delivered his professionally packaged gifts of perfume and chocolates to his secretary and his parliamentary research assistant. The latter was an earnest, bespectacled girl who was still young enough to be besotted with his charisma; she worked like a slave for the man she was willing on to ministerial office.

He took his bottle of whisky down to the caretaker of the Westminster block which contained his London flat, remembering like the good politician he was to ask about the progress of the man's student son, thereby securing for himself a disproportionate burst of affection and a reputation as a thinking and caring man.

He dictated four routine letters into his dictaphone machine and left the tape for his secretary. By midday, he was on the M4, the big Jaguar purring quietly at the 78 m.p.h. the Chief Constable had assured him was the safe limit as far as motorway police were concerned. He concentrated his mind on the meeting ahead, which was more than just another routine matter. There were fences to be repaired.

He parked the Jaguar next to Chris Hampson's Granada and walked into Gloucester Electronics to find that Christmas was still being kept at bay. There were a few coloured paperchains in the main office, a row of cards strung along the wall, but everyone was still busily employed in company work. A notice on the top of the filing cabinets sternly reminded staff that, 'We have guaranteed all our customers that all orders received by December 20th will be dealt with before Christmas', and the small factory hummed with the sounds of cheerful industry.

He found Chris Hampson characteristically busy in shirt sleeves. His partner had always led by example, long before 'hands-on management' had become a fashionable term. In answer to Raymond's routine enquiry, he said curtly, 'Business has picked up, as it always does in the last weeks before Christmas.'

'So you were being unnecessarily pessimistic when we spoke last week at the cottage.'

'No. What I said then had nothing to do with this. As a matter of fact, the order book for the new year is thinner than it's ever been. I shall have to lay some of the lads out there off by the end of January.'

Hampson, his grey hair tousled with effort, looked older with even the thought of that. He had never come to terms with the harsher aspects of industrial life. Raymond said, genuinely wishing to be helpful, 'Would you like me to come down and give them the bad news? Assuming it should be necessary, of course.'

'Tell people you've never seen that their services are no longer required, you mean? No, thanks. I expect you'd quite enjoy it, but I'll do it.'

Raymond kept control of himself, determined not to be offended. 'Sometimes it's better to keep these things as impersonal as possible. Wouldn't it be better if they blamed me than you?' Raymond could already see himself incorporating his bravery into political speeches about the hard facts of industrial life. When election time came round, it would remind his listeners that he was a working capitalist, still in touch with the pulse of British economic problems.

Chris Hampson's lined, experienced face was red with his sense of injustice. 'Be better if you got out into the world and used your contacts to get us some orders. Leave the routine stuff to me.'

'Look, Chris, I haven't the time. And politically I have to be careful of what I do. I can't be seen to be using my position to the advantage of the firm.'

It was no more than a routine excuse: there was no question of government orders being placed with a small firm like theirs. But it was the wrong thing to say to a man looking for help. 'You didn't say that when you went off to parliament,' said Hampson furiously. 'The whole basis of your downing tools here was that you'd make use of what you called your higher profile to bring in orders. And what's happened? As times have got harder for us, you've not wanted to know. The rougher things get, the less we see of you!'

It was a long speech for a man who lived by actions rather than words, who had to force himself into the harshness of disagreement. Chris Hampson stood toe to toe with his partner, panting like a boxer at the end of a vigorous exchange. Their eyes were not more than a yard apart.

For Raymond Keane, this was the worst possible scenario. He had called in at the works to make peace, hoping that his emollient skill with words would heal the breach between him and Chris, or at least paper over the cracks until things improved in the business. Not for the first time this week, he was finding that the generalities which got him by with a wider audience were not being accepted in a more personal situation.

He gave his partner a smile that was supposed to convey the understanding he brought from a wider perspective. 'If times are hard, we'll just have to cut back, Chris. It's a fact of industrial life. You know that as well as I do.'

'Good. I'm glad you feel like that. I'm glad

you accept the situation. Because neither you nor I will be taking anything out of the business this year.'

Hampson got his first spurt of satisfaction in this confrontation, as he saw alarm spread over Keane's handsome, well-fleshed features. 'Now wait a minute, Chris. That wasn't what I was implying at all. I need the money from the firm, I've planned my life around it for the next—'

'Well, you can just unplan it then. I'm not getting rid of good men from the shop floor whilst an absentee landlord takes a fat income out of the place. You'll be getting nothing this year, Ray. Just be glad you've got that parliamentary salary, including the rise you so thoughtfully voted for yourselves, to keep you going.'

All his resentment, not just of the complacent man in front of him but of the harsh industrial climate in which good men and a good business were cast upon the rocks, came pouring out in the phrases. Keane, with the moral ground shifting fast beneath his feet, retreated into the politics of power. 'Read the terms of our agreement. The partners have a right to a minimum of thirty thousand a year. I shall be taking mine. You can do what you damn well like. Sack another couple of men, if you need to.'

He turned upon his heel and walked without pause out of Hampson's room, through the curious upturned faces of the outer office, out into the coolness of the car park, to the wide driver's door of his Jaguar. This wasn't what he had intended. He had meant to look at the books with Chris, to discuss what action they might take to improve things, to work out what might be the best working role for himself in the coming year. Confronted with the personal opposition of one man, he had lost his cool and gone over the top, as he would never have done in a party matter.

As he drove out of the car park, he saw Chris Hampson's white, infuriated face at the window of his office.

*   *   *

Raymond Keane was glad to turn between the familiar high gateposts of the Gloucestershire house where he had grown up. As the car moved between the banks of rhododendrons, along the curving gravelled drive where coaches and horses had once driven, he felt for the first time protected from a world which had turned hostile with his partner's outburst.

His mother's face lit up when she saw him, as only a mother's will. 'You look tired. You've been working yourself too hard, as usual, I expect,' she said.

He was reminded of those years long gone, when he came home from Eton to parents

72

anxious for news of his boyish excitements in the term that had gone. After his row with Hampson, it was a real relief to relax in the totally uncritical ambience of his mother's house.

'This place is too big for me, you know,' she said, repeating the thought she raised now almost every time she saw him. 'I should move to somewhere smaller. But nowhere smaller seems to have the privacy I'm used to here.'

'Nor the elegance, Mum,' he grinned. He stuck to the form of address which had been fashionable years ago in his boyhood, and she loved it. We are always children to our parents, and they like anything which seems to arrest the advance of the years and confirm that notion. 'You've got this place just as you want it; it would take you years to lick anything else into shape.'

'I miss your father at this time of year. He always enjoyed playing the country squire at Christmas.' Raymond's father, a jovial landowner who had kept up an old tradition of London philandering, had died seven years earlier. His mother was now seventy-six, but still vigorous in mind and body. 'It's a pity you can't be home for Christmas yourself.'

For the first time, he regretted that it could not be so. He felt an unexpected desire to nestle for a while in this cosy, predictable world, where his status was assured and his privacy would be respected. He had told his mother months ago that he would be spending Christmas with Zoe: he had promised Zoe that they would spend Christmas in the cottage together. He said, 'It is a pity, yes, Mum. But I'm staying here tonight, so we'll have a full day just to ourselves. And we shall be here on New Year's Day, you know.'

'Yes. I shall look forward to seeing Zoe again,' said his mother briskly. She was far too proud of her independence to indulge in any outburst of self-pity or recrimination. 'I expect I shall enjoy my Christmas with Katherine and the children, anyway.'

Raymond grinned. His mother must be the only person left alive who did not call his elder sister Kate. 'Of course you will, Mum. We both know how much.' The unruliness of her four grandchildren was a secret between mother and son, the source of much rueful laughter and a string of awful stories.

It united them in easy, humorous reminiscence. By the time they had finished the roast beef she had prepared for him, they had agreed that with the help of the daily cleaner and the twice-weekly gardener, she could manage in the old house for the foreseeable future.

He rang Zoe that evening, but she was not at home. When he rang a second time at ten o'clock, there was still no reply. He left a message on the answerphone. 'I expect you've had to work late. I'll be at the cottage on

74

Christmas Eve as we arranged. I should be there by five at the latest—probably rather earlier than that. Looking forward to seeing you then. All my love.' He had grown used to these machines by now, but they were still impersonal. He wished he could have spoken to Zoe; he pictured her, cool, efficient and infinitely desirable in her ward sister's uniform.

Beside the phone in her flat, a grim-faced Zoe played his message back twice, then erased the tape. Then she left her half-empty cup of tea on the sink and went and poured herself a stiff whisky. It was dangerous, drinking alone, they said, and she had seen the results often enough. She did not drink much at any time, and never alone. But she had never had to plan anything like this before.

*   *   *

In the damp darkness beside Raymond Keane's empty cottage, Joe Walsh decided that the owner was not coming tonight, and stole softly away. It did not really matter; he had only come out here on the off chance. And the man would be down here for Christmas, whatever happened: he was sure of that. There was no need to hurry.

CHAPTER EIGHT

The weather was turning cold at last. It had been unseasonably mild for several days, but now the wind was from the east, light but chilling: straight from Siberia, the weathermen said. Children waiting impatiently for Christmas were put into scarves and balaclavas; the bookies had shortened their odds against snow on the twenty-fifth.

On Christmas Eve, Raymond Keane drove the forty miles from his mother's large house to his isolated cottage. It was a dry cold: there was no danger of ice on the roads yet. But he drove slowly, enjoying the freedom of having no formal schedule. For a man used to the straitjacket of a strict timetable, it was a holiday in itself to be able to leave when he fancied and arrive at whatever time was congenial. He was almost glad now that he had not arranged any definite time to meet Zoe at the cottage, though her failure to respond to his calls still puzzled him.

The last leaves had fallen from the forest trees as he drove through the southern Cotswolds. The green of the fields was a muted, winter green; tomorrow they would be white. Although the occasional beech hedge still lined the lanes with russet, the colour in this December landscape was mostly that introduced by man, and confined to the gardens around the villages.

The pyracanthas and cotoneasters were still well berried against the mellow buff stone of the older houses. But the brightest berries of all were on the holly; he had never seen such an abundant crop, reminding him of the festival at hand. A quiet Christmas in a Cotswold cottage: it was almost an English cliché, as one of his colleagues from an urban northern constituency had reminded him when he mentioned his plans for the recess.

He realized as he skirted Gloucester that his chosen route would take him past the end of the road where Moira Yates lived with her watchful brother. Almost before he knew he had done it, he took the alternative road, a slightly longer route which avoided the outlying suburb where Yates lived. He had concluded that particular chapter in his life: there was no way he was going to risk opening its pages again.

Keane smiled a little at his own superstition in avoiding the area. But there was a logic to it, after all. There was no chance that a woman with agoraphobia would be abroad, but it was just feasible that he might have seen that protective brother, or that faithful spaniel of a lover who sat so abjectly at Moira's feet. There was no sense in inviting the possibility of such embarrassment. That Sunday-afternoon visit to the house had been quite enough mortification for him.

The wind had dropped when he got out of the warm car beside the cottage. The long, low bulk of the thatched building loomed above him, a darker shape against the blue-black of the sky behind it. No light within it; Zoe was not here yet, then. He paused for a moment before he went inside, savouring the absolute silence of the country night after the incessant hum of life in London. The stars he could see above the treeline were brilliant as new-cut diamonds against the heavens; there was no moon as yet. It was already freezing; there would be ice on the puddles before the night was out.

He switched on the lights in the lounge and the kitchen, turned on the water at the stopcock under the sink, set the boiler throbbing, listened for a moment to the pump forcing the water round the radiators. The sounds of the house coming alive were curiously comforting to him. It would be warm by the time Zoe arrived. For a moment he indulged himself with images of the bedroom. The duvet would have its own attractions in this weather. And tomorrow, Christmas Day, he would light a fire, and sit with her in the comfort of the warm house, watching the flames which had been so necessary to the former owners of this quiet place, which were to modern man no more than an added luxury, a novelty in a world of domestic comfort.

He plugged in the television set in the corner of the long beamed lounge: checking the news was an occupational tic for a politician. There was little of it. Snow in the Scottish glens; colder weather moving rapidly south. The roads were already packed with people journeying home for the Christmas break. A girl had gone missing after hitching a lift on the M4 three days previously. The police thought there was 'serious cause for concern'. Raymond smiled grimly: that was public-speak for, 'We think she may well be dead.' Otherwise, there was no news; the pictures of the snow might have been taken from the Decembers of other years.

When he had had a drink, he'd bring in his holdall from the car, and put Zoe's present, which the shop had wrapped so carefully for him, in the corner where the tree was to go. He must get the tree out from the garage, and string the lights upon it; women liked the trimmings of Christmas.

It would take the thick old walls of the cottage some hours to warm up. Raymond, sitting on the sofa in his car coat, still felt the cold of the room around him. Somewhere in the house, there was a small but efficient fan heater. It had been put away when it was not required during the summer. At first he could not remember where: it was curious how it took you time to adjust to the geography of a second home, even when all the furnishings around you were familiar. He remembered, once he mustered his concentration. The heater was beside his desk in the small study along the hall.

As he rose to retrieve it, every light in the house went off.

A fuse. Perhaps something to do with the lights being put on all together and suddenly after a period of disuse, he surmised vaguely. Well, he knew where the fuse-box was. In the old walk-in pantry off the kitchen, where it had been sited when he had the house rewired. There were candles there, too, and a torch, if he remembered right. Power cuts were not the rarity in Gloucestershire that they were in London; they usually had two or three during the winter. So be prepared, as he had learned long ago in the boy scouts.

He fumbled his way to the door, his fingers clawing his way along the uneven plaster between the ancient oak framing. It was curious how monstrously bulbous it felt, when you were proceeding totally by feel. It took him quite a long time to find his way along the hall he had thought so familiar to the door of the kitchen. The pump seemed to have gone off too, for there was no sound now of circulating water. But the pilot light gave him a tiny illumination; with eyes beginning to adjust now to the darkness, he could pick out the white doors of fridge and oven as his landmarks. He found the dark wooden door of the pantry quite quickly, fumbled open the old wooden catch on its door, and pushed it inwards.

He was reaching up to the mains switch when the cord tightened around his neck. He had both hands clawing at it in less than a second, but he still had no chance to utter the cry which rose into his throat. The sound died there, as the thin cord cut into his flesh and the wood at its ends twisted and twisted behind his neck.

Raymond Keane died quickly, his hands flailing for a moment towards the invisible ceiling of the pantry, his assailant twisting the awful pressure about his neck ever tighter as he sank to his knees, feeling his own weight hastening him into oblivion. He was conscious of a brief wonderment that this should be happening to him, of a blinding, explosive light in his head.

Then he slumped dead upon the stone floor of the small room. His assailant breathed heavily for a moment, checked that there was no movement in the pulse in the neck. Then the hand which had lately dropped the cord upon the unsuspecting throat reached up unhurriedly to the mains switch it had switched off less than two minutes earlier.

CHAPTER NINE

Christmas night in the Cotswolds. Behind the closed doors of family celebrations, there is merrymaking of different sorts.

Detective Sergeant Bert Hook has put away his Open University books for the day. The boys have got bicycles for Christmas, but it is dark now, and Eleanor can rest, for the bikes are back in the garage and their riders safely back at the family hearth. The boys are watching an ancient Morecambe and Wise show replayed on television as their last treat of the day. Once they are gone, Bert will open the port he so thoughtfully purchased for his wife.

Ten miles away in his unusually boisterous bungalow, Superintendent John Lambert, who set out several hours ago to play the jolly grandfather, has long since forgotten that this is all an act. He is reading the same chapter of *Winnie the Pooh* for the third time to a six-year-old boy, who falls asleep before it is over. Lambert's daughter Jacky watches her father with affection whilst she chats with her mother, diverting her concern for a whole hour from the second breast-cancer scan which has shadowed Christine Lambert's Christmas.

By nine o'clock, small children throughout the country are either asleep or getting fractious. But in the childless house of Dermot Yates, it has been a strange day. Various relatives have visited, but most have stayed only for short periods, as if they were visiting someone in hospital. And that is not an inappropriate comparison, for Moira Yates has for most of the day had an abstracted air, carrying on surface conversations perfectly sensibly, yet giving the impression that her mind is elsewhere, in some secret world which only she can visit. It is behaviour common to many people with her ailment, says the doctor. By the middle of the afternoon, she is looking very tired, and retires to her room to rest for an hour.

*   *   *

They ate at six, as planned. Dermot cooked the turkey and set the table for Christmas dinner for three; for Gerald Sangster sat down to the meal with them, as Moira had requested he should. Wine was drunk and crackers pulled; the chef was complimented; the three made routine, harmless jokes; in short, they pretended hard that this was a normal Christmas.

Dermot found himself wishing that someone would drink too much, become noisy, even rude. Anything to break the mould of good behaviour. It was all so decorous that it was false. He felt that all of them knew that, but none of them knew how to fracture the spell. Or rather, the one person who could have changed things chose not to. Moira, the one of whom they were both so careful, from whom they took their cues, was the only one of the trio who might have changed this strange atmosphere. If she realized that she had that power, she must have chosen not to use it.

Chris Hampson, at home with his wife and grown-up children, hugged the troubles of Gloucester Electronics to himself and tried hard to be seasonably jolly. At ten o'clock, the children drove away to their own homes, and he found himself suddenly very tired. He plodded steadily through the day's mountain of washing up, the steady physical labour an escape from the things he did not want to discuss with his wife. She was tired but happy after the labours of the day; she did not seem to notice his preoccupation. Returning carefully correct replies to her talk about the small triumphs of her table, the small problems of their children, he felt like an expert, defensive, table-tennis player.

Only Joe Walsh had spent the day alone. Or almost alone. The retriever, who had crept in from the boisterous house next door to the quiet he knew he would find here, put a sleepy head obstinately on his knee as the hands of the clock crept towards the end of what for Joe was the longest day of all. The brown eyes looked up into the gaunt face, the tail wagged brief appreciation as the hand moved almost reluctantly to caress the soft fur of the tawny head. Joe stared unseeingly at the television set which had droned for hours at the other side of the room. 'Good lad, Chester!' he said softly to the dog.

It was a relief to him to find he could still give affection when it was asked for. But dogs made no demand for words or effort. Presently he opened the door and said reluctantly, 'Better go home now, Chester.' He watched from his back door as the animal loped away over the white frost of his neglected rear garden and slipped through the hole it had fashioned in his hedge.

Raymond Keane's mother enjoyed the evening, once her boisterous grandchildren were out of the way. It was half past eleven before she said to her daughter, 'That Raymond has forgotten to ring us, you know. And he promised!'

'Give him a ring yourself, Mum, if you like. And wish him a Happy Christmas from us.' Kate grinned secretly at her husband as the old lady went to the phone. If Kate knew her brother, he would be in bed with the delectable Zoe by now. But not asleep. Well, serve him right for not ringing his mum on Christmas Day if he was interrupted in flagrante delicto.

Old Mrs Keane let the phone ring in the cottage a dozen times before she gave up, her face filled with disappointment. 'I expect they're out with friends,' she said. 'He might not have been able to ring.'

*   *   *

By two a.m. on Boxing Day, the vast majority of Christmas revellers were sleeping heavily in their beds. The temperature outside their houses was now well below freezing, and still dropping steadily. The Cotswold ground was frozen hard, the frost thick as a dusting of snow at the sides of the deserted lanes.

The vehicle carrying the corpse of Raymond Keane moved cautiously through the deep woods around his cottage, its lights the only movement in that silent, frozen landscape. The body was covered with a blanket and an old coat. It was unlikely that there would be police on the route of this final journey, but there was no need for unnecessary risks. Besides, the driver preferred to have those wide, unblinking brown eyes covered on this final journey.

It seemed to take a long time to reach the place, though the distance could not have been more than four miles. The car hesitated for a moment at the side of the road, then turned carefully through the ragged gap in the hedge, where years ago there had been a gate. On the uneven track between the young birch trees, it was more than forty yards to the chosen place.

Once there, the driver switched off the car's lights. There was enough light from the low crescent moon and the stars for the task that was left.

No great strength was needed now. The pool was below the back of the vehicle, not more than four yards away. The driver dragged the corpse out, hearing but scarcely registering the thud as it landed heavily on the iron-hard ground. The material at the bottom of the trousers gave the easiest hold: the mortal remains of Keane were dragged unceremoniously feet first down the steep slope of frozen mud and flung vigorously on to the surface of the pond.

For the person conducting this awful dispatch, there was then a moment of black farce that might have come straight from Hitchcock. The surface of the pond was already frozen hard. The body slid spreadeagled on to it, the white face staring unseeingly at the night sky. And lay there, its eyes glinting white in the light of the moon. For a long fifteen seconds, it seemed to the watcher as though the ice was already too thick for the evidence to disappear from sight. Then, with a noise which sounded in the living ears beside the pond like that of an alpine glacier cracking into movement, the ice broke, and the body of Raymond Keane disappeared into the black depths of the hidden pool.

The pieces of broken ice disappeared for a

moment with their sinister burden, then returned to the surface and settled again into stillness. The watcher wasted no more time. Within thirty minutes, the driver was back in bed like other, more innocent survivors of the Christmas festivities.

Nature was the unwitting ally of evil. By morning, the ice on the surface of the hidden pool was already over an inch thick. When the body rose towards the surface two days later, the ice was a three-inch ceiling above the water, imprisoning the murdered body against discovery for as long as the arctic conditions should persist.

CHAPTER TEN

'The news is out. Such as it is. I knew we couldn't keep it quiet indefinitely.'

The Chief Constable stared dolefully at the newspapers on his desk. Like most of his colleagues, he found journalists more annoying at times than criminals. At least criminals kept you in a job, whereas it often seemed that if you made the wrong move journalists would be delighted to put you out of one. And you knew where you were with felons, whereas the fourth estate could switch sides overnight, without notice, and often with no good reason. 'It's only because he disappeared over Christmas that we were able to keep it quiet as long as we did.'

George Harding was quite new in his post still. Despite voicing the ritual police suspicions of the press, he was much more at home with the media than his grizzled predecessor had been. They could be helpful at times; and even when they became a nuisance, he accepted that they were a necessary evil. He pushed the papers at Lambert.

The story had made the front page of *The Times*, but only in the bottom-left corner: there were no glaring headlines as yet. 'Mystery of missing Tory MP' was the heading, and the text beneath began soberly, 'There is still no news of missing Tory MP Raymond Keane. The promising backbencher was expected to spend Christmas and New Year in his Gloucestershire constituency, but last night had still failed to appear. His sister said yesterday that the family was "a little upset" by his failure to contact them, but saw no real cause for alarm. "MPs are busy people, despite what some of the public think," she said. It appears that Mr Keane has not been seen since he visited his mother's house on Christmas Eve.'

For most of the tabloids, the Keane story wasn't yet worthy of the front page. The *Sun* headlined its piece 'Rottweiler Ray goes missing', pinning a scarcely earned reputation for parliamentary dogfighting on Keane in the interests of alliteration. The article began, 'Eligible bachelor and aggressive parliamentary debater Ray Keane has gone missing from his Gloucestershire constituency. The MP, known as Rottweiler Ray since he savaged Labour ministers in Commons exchanges, has not been seen since Christmas Eve. His mother and his business partner both refused to comment on his absence last night.

'Keane's parliamentary research assistant, vivacious twenty-three-year-old Despina Mottershead, agreed that her employer was an attractive man, and thought that he might well have disappeared to the Continent, though she was not sure what country he might have chosen. She said she had no doubt that he would be back for the beginning of the new parliamentary session. "Mr Keane is one of the most responsible and dedicated of our younger politicians. I certainly expect to see him or hear from him within the next week," she said last night . . .'

Superintendent Lambert knew why he was in the Chief Constable's office. The hunt, which had so far scarcely been worthy of such a dramatic name, was to be stepped up. When the press chose to stir things up, they got attention, however much the police and other public services might deny the connection. That was real life.

'They haven't raked up the unsavoury

history of other disappearing politicians yet,' he said. It was the only consolation he could think of to offer the smartly uniformed man on the other side of the big desk.

George Harding smiled, ruefully rather than grimly, Lambert hoped. 'It's just the beginning, John. You know the pattern. Tomorrow, if there's still no news, we'll get some of the tales of gay MPs and scandals which have led to resignations. Anyway, we shan't be responsible for that. Keane will have brought it upon himself. If he chooses to disappear without telling anyone where he's off to, he knows what the press will do with the story. I take it we haven't any further news?'

'No, sir. But I wouldn't expect any, unless the man turned up of his own accord. We've put him on the missing persons register, but otherwise kept it low key, as we agreed. The family didn't want us to stir up a hornet's nest. His sister was more annoyed with Keane for not contacting his aged mum than worried about him. She seems to think he'll turn up when he's ready.'

'Has he done this sort of thing before, then?'

'No. Not as far as we can tell, without more detailed enquiries into his past activities.'

Harding pursed his lips. He was a handsome man, his hair now a becoming silver but still plentiful, his body comfortably covered with flesh rather than plump beneath the well-tailored uniform. The chances were that nothing was seriously amiss, that he would only irritate Keane when he turned up if they were too persistent now with their enquiries into his absence. But once the press was on to these things, you had to be seen to be doing something. If anything proved to be seriously amiss with the police reaction to the disappearance, they would use the blissful benefits of hindsight to hold an inquest on it. An unfortunate word. Harding said, 'Give it another day: if there's still nothing then, step up the activity. Let them see we're taking the matter seriously.'

Even Chief Constables cannot expect to know the moment when events will take such decisions out of their hands.

*　　　*　　　*

It was good to be out in the fresh air. Detective Sergeant Bert Hook sniffed it appreciatively. The British climate was as perverse as ever; on this second day of January, when winter should have been at its hardest, there was a hazy blue sky and a most unseasonable mildness. Over the edge of the Forest of Dean, May Hill was clearly visible; you would have a good view of the seven counties from there today.

Hook rejoiced to be out on a day like this, especially after a morning in court where a key witness had failed to appear and the Crown Prosecution Service had decided not to pursue the case. It must be therapeutic to be out in the fresh air, even for this futile activity. 'Blow the cobwebs away nicely, this will,' Lambert had promised as they stepped out of the car, 'and we can always count it as your belated lunch hour.'

Hook smiled sourly, turning the bright steel five-iron speculatively in his large, strong hands. 'I suppose golf at least gets you out into the countryside. Didn't someone call it a good walk spoiled?'

'Mark Twain. Who seemed otherwise a nicely rounded human being. Mind you, on the driving range, you don't get the good walk that homespun humorist offered you as consolation. But it's a start.'

'And a finish, as far as I'm concerned!' said Hook firmly. 'Remember, I'm here under severe protest, and only because you made it one of your daft conditions.'

'Give us your money, lad. I'm not paying as well as instructing.' Lambert took the coins from Hook and slipped them into the machine, watched the forty golf balls tumble into the basket below, and then put coins of his own in for another basketful. Might as well have a little practice himself, if he had to be here to oversee the novice golfer beside him.

Hook, maintaining his gruff exterior, followed the superintendent along the row of covered stalls to the furthest and most private of them. He was pleased to see that there were only three other people striking balls, two of them women, and that the five feet high wooden divisions between the booths would give a decent degree of privacy to his initial efforts in this ridiculous game.

Though he had no intention of admitting as much to Lambert, he was secretly looking forward to this. He got too little exercise these days. Since he had given up serious cricket at thirty-eight, he had done nothing beyond the widely spaced long walks and sporadic visits to the gym in preparation for occasional police medical tests. Golf might be a silly game, but it was played in attractive places, and you could go on with it for as long as you could walk.

Moreover, it surely couldn't be very difficult for a good cricketer. You approached a dead ball in your own time: no one came and hurled an unplayable delivery at you, or edged your perfect outswinger through first slip's fingers for four. It was partly the lack of challenge which had kept him away from golf over the years. But you had to lower your sights a little as you got older.

Bert teed the ball on the rubber stub provided and swung Lambert's five-iron speculatively a couple of times, as he had seen the men who earned such ridiculous sums from this game do on television. It felt quite easy: it was difficult to see why people made such a fuss about the technique involved in such a simple thing as hitting a golf ball.

He stood with feet on either side of the ball and looked at it steadily, then swung the club in a wide, graceful arc, preparing a modest response for his chief's surprise at the excellence of his first shot. There was no sound, where he had expected the echoing impact that was coming from the stalls behind him where other people practised. He looked to see the ball soaring in a graceful parabola over the green expanse in front of him, towards the hundreds of other balls which waited to be collected from the end of the practice area.

Lambert's attempts to control his mirth were pitifully unsuccessful. He spluttered for a moment, then burst into a long, relieving peal of laughter. Hook looked down, saw the reason, refused for a moment to believe it, then joined reluctantly in his mentor's hilarity. The ball still lay where he had placed it in the tee. 'We call that an air shot,' said the recovering Lambert. 'You should expect a few of those in the early stages.'

'Stupid game!' muttered Hook. He glanced malevolently at the offending ball, then set the club behind it and froze his powerful frame into intense concentration. If it had been cricket and he had been hit for four, he would have bowled a lifter, pitching just short of a length and rearing at the offending batsman's ribs. But there was no one to attack in this silly game.

He eventually produced a savage slash at the ball. This time he made contact, but only minimally, with the top of the increasingly tiny target. The ball dribbled forward and fell from the elevated platform to the muddy grass beneath it, coming to rest some ten yards in front of him. 'Bastard!' said Bert.

Lambert felt cheered by this evidence of a golfing gene in his sergeant. He had feared that the taciturn, nonswearing Hook might not have the vocabulary necessary for the serious amateur golfer. He need not have feared. Hook's next three efforts got the ball into the air, but with drastic slices, which took the ball at an angle of almost forty-five degrees to the line he had intended. Bert's language passed through the sanguinary to the scatological.

Lambert called from his instructor's position in the next stall, 'Just swing the club, don't snatch at the ball,' and managed to send a couple of high, straight shots of his own down the inviting green expanse in front of them, demonstrating his own relative competence at this activity. A muffled outburst from the neighbouring stall indicated that Hook had now added blasphemy to his vocabulary of golfing reactions. Perhaps there was real hope for him in this game.

Hook's initiation to the game took less than half an hour, though in terms of suffering it seemed to him much longer. Lambert was quite gratified by his own efforts. He should practise more often, he realized. He felt quite invigorated, and the accuracy of his last few seven-iron shots in the still January air had been highly satisfactory.

Bert Hook, on the other hand, stumbled away from the practice booth dishevelled and disorientated. His hair was tousled; his features were crimson with effort and frustration; he had lost a button from his unsuitable shirt and broken a lace in his unsuitable shoes with his final, titanic effort to dismiss an infuriating white ball far into the distance.

'You'll get better, with practice, Bert,' said Lambert patronizingly.

'I won't, you know. I bloody won't. This was a one-off. A debt of honour. All it's done is confirmed to me what a damned stupid game this is.' Bert flung the five-iron roughly into the boot of Lambert's car. 'Good sodding riddance to bad sodding rubbish!' he said with feeling.

Yet as they drove away and he seethed in the front passenger seat, Hook knew that he would be back. He wouldn't dream of admitting it to John Lambert, of course. But this daft game couldn't possibly be as difficult as he had made it appear today. He would meet the challenge, show he could cope with it, and *then* give up the game.

97

Lambert drove silently, with a slight smile lifting the corners of his mouth. He had noted his pupil's reactions with an experienced golfing eye, and he knew the temperament of Bert Hook. The fish was hooked.

*   *   *

It is a mistake to take on a boxer puppy when you are sixty-nine. The man flapping the lead decided that this warning should be inscribed in capital letters in every canine handbook, in every RSPCA publication, in the directives of the hallowed kennel club itself. He had covered seven miles and more of winter Cotswolds, with the dog covering a good four times as much. Now, when she should have been exhausted, she had disappeared.

'Daisy!' he called hopelessly. 'DAISY!' The woods might have been empty of all life, for all the reaction his shouting extracted. He hadn't even felt like a pensioner, until he got this wretched animal; now he felt older than his years, as he toiled unavailingly in the wake of this muscular bundle of energy. He got out the dog whistle his wife had presented to him hopefully on the previous day, panted for a moment, then summoned all his breath to blow a single long, high-pitched blast.

He waited for a full thirty seconds with diminishing hope. There was no sound in the high, leafless trees around him. Then, somewhere in the invisible distance, a rook cawed faintly. He wondered bleakly if it had been disturbed by Daisy. If so, she was a long way off.

He went back to the road and moved slowly along it, bellowing the dog's name every two minutes, whistling in between times, cursing the day he ever let himself be talked into this purgatory. They had walked many miles before she went missing; surely he had a right to expect even a ten-month-old boxer bitch to be decently tired and obedient after such labour on her behalf?

They were into the early dusk by now, and he began to wonder what he would do if Daisy didn't reappear soon. At that moment, he heard a slight noise away to his left, near where a road ran away over the hills to Cirencester. A snuffling. Probably some wild creature, but it could be Daisy. He called her name, felt his heart lift in relief with her short answering bark. 'Come on then, girl!' he trilled encouragingly.

She didn't come. He turned off the lane, between ivyclad stumps which might once have been gateposts. He could hear the dog now, growling excitedly at something; she could not be more than thirty yards away, but he could see neither her nor the source of her interest.

Then suddenly he came upon both, fixed in a scene which would haunt him for months. A low, dark pond beneath the trees, and the dog up to her haunches in water, growling at something within a foot of her nose. The ice had gone from the pool with the thaw, save for a few half-melted grey slabs floating at the far end.

And between him and that ice, the grotesquely bloated body of what had but recently been a man, the arms and legs swollen within the clothing like those of a Michelin man, the eyes staring unblinkingly at the sky they would never see again.

CHAPTER ELEVEN

The Chief Constable's face was grave. Lambert looked a question as he took the proffered chair, and Harding nodded. 'It looks as though it's Keane,' he said. 'We shall know within a couple of hours; the formal identification can wait a little longer, if necessary.'

Already he was shaping the way the investigation would go, deploying his resources, considering the national spotlight this would bring to his force. 'Damned politicians! If he had to do away with himself, why couldn't he do it in London, and leave his own patch clear?'

'You think it's suicide?' said Lambert. Something told him it wasn't, but for a wild moment he hoped Harding had found something to support the idea. A message to someone, perhaps, or a previous threat to end it all in this way. He knew nothing of Keane other than the public pronouncements of the man, and from that suicide did not seem likely.

George Harding gave him a rueful smile. 'It's the most likely thing statistically, as you know. But no, I doubt it, as you obviously do, John. It's early days, but there doesn't appear to be any note, either at his flat in London or in his cottage down here.' He picked up a sheet from the folder in front of him. 'And his mother said he was, "cheerful and looking forward to his Christmas," when he left her. That was four days ago, of course, when our MP was merely a missing person.'

He sighed, wondering if the tall man opposite him was thinking as he was of the impact of today's news on that resolute old lady. Harding liked Lambert, even though most police wiseacres had forecast that there would be clashes between the new CC and his senior CID superintendent. Those who had thought that Lambert was a throwback to an earlier age and would be treated accordingly had forgotten that he was that most indispensable of police personnel, a thief-taker. Chief Constables were dependent for their reputations upon the successes of such men. Whatever their own skills in negotiating the minefields of public accountability, they needed the statistics of success to back them.

Harding looked at this shrewd, grizzled officer. 'You'll be in charge, of course, John.'

Lambert said, 'It will be high profile, sir. Assuming that it's going to be a murder investigation, that is.'

Harding nodded. He knew what Lambert was getting at. 'Don't worry about that aspect. I'll handle all the public statements, the press conferences, the television and the local radio. I may want you beside me on occasions, if this runs on for any length of time.' It was his way of saying that he was not shutting the superintendent out, not anxious to take all the credit for himself from a successful outcome.

He was assuming success, when that was anything but certain. But the men at the top had to do that: it was part of leadership. One of the things they taught you at management courses for senior police personnel. Harding would have done it anyway; optimism came naturally to him, and was one of the foundations of his success.

'Can I have my usual team?' said Lambert. He forgot the 'sir' as quickly as he always did, as his mind ran ahead to the first steps he must take. It meant no disrespect, was merely part of his impatience to get to grips with the realities of detection. He did not allow his subordinates to 'sir' him as they worked, except on suitably public occasions.

Harding smiled at him. 'And operate in your

usual manner, I suppose you mean?' They grinned at each other, the years falling away; for a moment they were both young coppers, eager to bring in a result. Lambert was unusual in his unwillingness to mount an investigation from CID headquarters, to run a team from his desk with only occasional sorties into the world outside.

As the phone shrilled on his desk, Harding ignored it long enough to say, 'Yes, you go out and get the smell of the case, John. As long as you bring home the bacon, I don't care how it's done.' He would have added the rider, 'Within the law, of course,' to most of his thrusting younger officers, but it was not necessary with this man. Lambert did not cut corners when it came to getting his evidence. That was taken for granted, and it was a major source of the building trust between the two men.

Then the Chief Constable picked up the phone and listened gravely to the voice which spoke animatedly on the other end of the line. He nodded twice, then said, 'Right. Superintendent Lambert will be in charge of the case. Pass all information to him—he'll keep me briefed. The murder room will be set up here in Oldford.'

It was the first time the word had been used. He stared hard at the instrument for a moment after he had put it down, then looked into the long, attentive face opposite him. 'You were right, John, of course. The pathologist made the usual noises about waiting for the PM, but he's pretty sure even out by that pool that the body was dumped there. That Keane didn't die by drowning.'

*   *   *

It took Lambert thirty minutes to drive the old Vauxhall Senator to the pond where all that remained of Raymond Keane had been discovered. He did not hurry, for he had Bert Hook beside him, and they discussed the little they already knew of the missing person that had suddenly become a murder case.

There was a pale winter sun behind a thin cover of white cloud, so that the landscape of the southern Cotswolds took on an impressionist look, with the bare tops of the forest trees shimmering in a haze against the winter sky. The streams in the bottoms of the gentle valleys appeared and reappeared like silvered ribbons, catching and losing the light as the car climbed and dropped over the slopes. The M5 was well behind them now, and they had left the main road to Stroud. There were few other vehicles visible in this area of agriculture and forestry. Most of the ploughing had been completed in autumn, so that they saw not a single tractor crawling over the arable areas. As always, this seemed a quiet place for evil to be abroad.

It would have been easy to miss the place

altogether, had it not been for the bright-yellow plastic ribbons and the single police vehicle. The plastic had been used to cordon off a rough rectangle extending from the lane to an area around the pond itself. The ambulance bearing the mortal remains of Raymond Keane was leaving as Lambert's old Vauxhall arrived. Although it had been obvious from its appearance that this had been a corpse for many days, the police had still had to wait for death to be formally confirmed by their doctor.

'There's no doubt that it was in fact Keane?' said Lambert to Sergeant Jack Johnson, the experienced Scene-of-Crime officer.

'Not to my mind. The clothes conform to the ones his mother described him as wearing when he left her house on Christmas Eve.'

Lambert nodded. 'We'd better get the formal identification completed as soon as possible. Is there anyone other than his mother we can use?'

'He was divorced. First wife hasn't seen him for four years, she says. Apparently there was a second wife in the offing. But there's a sister. She might be the best bet. He wasn't a very pretty sight when he came out of the water, though you and I have seen worse.'

Lambert turned to Hook. 'Can you contact the sister, please, Bert? And you'd better attend at the morgue with her when she does the identification.' Most murderers came from within the family, even when the victim was a public man. He had no great hopes in this case, but it would be standard procedure to study the bereaved woman's reactions.

Lambert looked back from the black surface of the pond down the forty yards to the road. Already what had been overgrown was now a track flattened by the feet of the investigators, even though the hefty police feet were clothed in the regulation plastic bags to avoid direct contact with the ground. Johnson anticipated his question. 'Presumably the body was dumped from a vehicle. But there were no wheel tracks when we got here. Probably indicates that he was brought here during that period of hard frost, when the ground was like iron.'

That could have been any time during the period from Christmas Eve to New Year's Day. So the killer already had fortune on his side. Or hers: Lambert made the detective's automatic reservation. But perhaps this murderer had not been lucky, and had calculated things to take account of the conditions; it never did to underestimate an opponent. 'We'll know more about how he was brought here when the autopsy has given us some idea of the method and time of death. But I expect you're right. No sole prints either, then?'

'Not so far. We've eliminated those of the man who found him. Elderly gent out walking his dog. Gave him quite a shock, I expect.'

*   *   *

Raymond Keane's sister Katherine agreed to identify the body. And to come at once. 'It will be better for Mother if all doubts are removed immediately,' she said.

Bert Hook was glad of her calmness on the phone. He was glad too that she agreed to come so quickly. It meant she would be able to see the body before they cut it up for the postmortem; they did a good job of sewing people up for the relatives these days, but he was not sure what the effects of decomposition would be on such restoration. Death was still a grim, unrelenting business, for those who had been close to the deceased. They were presented with less gore, fewer of the smells of human decay, than in the old days, but clinical advances sometimes only made human tragedy more poignant.

She met him at the mortuary. She wore a dark imitation fur coat; a small black hat sat precariously on an abundance of black hair which was not used to accommodating hats. She came dressed as for a winter funeral, thought Hook. She was composed, her black-gloved hands clutching a leather handbag without any feverish movement. Her face was very white, and the skin beneath her eyes was puffy, making the pupils seem smaller within their sockets. 'You should call me Kate,' she said.

Hook thought that would be irrelevant. He said, 'He's been in the water for some days: we don't know yet exactly how many.'

'A river?'

'No. A pond. And it's been frozen over for most of that time.'

She nodded. 'The flesh isn't much damaged, then?'

He realized that she had been preparing herself for the flesh being gnawed by rats or fish. Perhaps he should have said more on the phone. 'No, nothing like that. The face is a little—a little puffed up, that's all.' Like yours, but a lot worse, he wanted to say. He was shaken by a surge of sympathy for this woman he did not know, would probably never know.

He stood behind her as the assistant took her to the corpse in its steel box. She took a deep breath, breathed out with her eyes closed, then nodded briefly to the man, and he drew back the sheet to expose the head beneath it.

There was a sharp, rasping sound as she snatched in air. So her last image of the elder brother who had teased her, protected her, advised her, infuriated her, and just occasionally filled her with admiration would be of this smooth, inflated skin, stretched like a bloated white stocking over the features she knew so well. Raymond's brown eyes were closed, and she was grateful for that. Someone had combed back the hair while it was still sodden, so that it clung to the scalp, looking less thick than it had in life.

'That's my brother,' Kate said, and the attendant replaced the sheet quickly, as if anxious the vulnerability of that distended face should be protected as swiftly as possible.

The warm little waiting room outside was deserted. Hook completed the formalities of the official identification sheet, assessing with a practised eye how brittle the calmness of this seemingly self-possessed woman might be. 'If you could answer a few questions now, it would mean we did not have to disturb you at home,' he said quietly.

She looked up into his face for the first time, registering the rubicund, concerned features. Like the village bobby they used to have when she was a child, she thought inconsequentially. 'I should prefer that,' she said. 'I have young children at home, you see. I wouldn't want them to be affected by this.'

'It won't take long. First of all, I have to tell you that we suspect foul play in this matter. We shall know more certainly by the end of the day, but even at this stage—'

'Raymond was killed. You can be sure of that, Sergeant. He wasn't the type to commit suicide.'

This calm acceptance of murder was unusual; most people recoiled from the darkest of crimes. Perhaps she found the waste of suicide, with its disturbing implications for the rest of the family, less acceptable even than murder. Hook said, 'We need to establish who were the last people to see him. To build up a picture of—'

'Last persons apart from the one who killed him, you mean, of course.' She was disturbingly abrupt in her correction. 'I don't know of anyone who saw him after my mother. That was at around three thirty p.m. on Christmas Eve, apparently.'

She had been making her own enquiries, clearly. But Keane had been a missing person for a week before he became a murder victim and Hook became involved in this. He wrote the time in his notebook in his clear, round hand, giving himself a moment to think, deciding that there was no point in being oblique with this organized, almost impatient sister of the victim. 'Where was he going?'

'To his cottage. We already told that to the constable who came to see us when we reported him missing.'

He ignored her rebuke. 'Was he planning to meet someone there?'

'Yes. His fiancée. Or the woman who was to become his fiancée: I'm not sure it had been formally announced.'

So she wasn't quite as close to this brother as he had thought her to be up to now, thought Hook. Or at least, she wasn't quite up to date on the latest developments. 'What is this lady's name?' he said.

'Zoe. Zoe Renwick.'

'You've met her?'

'Just once. She's attractive. And well organized. Just the wife for a coming man in parliament, I'd have thought.' She ticked off the statements as though they were a list; Hook realized for the first time what her outward calmness was costing her. 'Have you and this Miss Renwick been in contact since Christmas Eve?'

'No. At least I haven't. My mother managed to contact her on Boxing Day, and found that she hadn't been down to the cottage after all.' She looked at him in surprise, as if giving him the credit for prompting an idea she should have thought of for herself. 'It seems odd we haven't heard from her since then, doesn't it? You'd have thought she would have been as anxious to know where Raymond had got to as we were.'

Bert Hook put away his notebook, thanking her for her help. He too thought that it was indeed very odd.

CHAPTER TWELVE

'It's years since I came to London,' said Lambert, as they followed the tide of grey-green winter coats towards the ticket barrier.

'The last time I drew into Paddington, it was behind a steam engine. A big green one,' said Bert Hook.

Lambert looked at him sharply. He was not always sure when his staid subordinate was pulling his leg, nowadays. It was just about possible, he supposed, if his sergeant had last come here as a small boy. Bert was a countryman, sure of his Gloucestershire roots; he had developed a consciousness of the ways of the larger world outside without needing to go much into it.

They took a taxi to Westminster. Even through the glass, the world between the streets of high buildings seemed to Lambert a noisy and alien place. That other self who had grown up here, who had been a city child on the bomb sites of postwar London, seemed a person he had known but almost forgotten, who had lived in a different land. 'The past is a foreign country: they do things differently there,' he murmured softly, almost to himself, and was irritated when Hook, looking out of his own window at the crawling traffic, said, 'L. P. Hartley.'

'You wouldn't have known that at one time,' Lambert said. 'You're supposed to indulge your superintendent, build up his sense of superiority.' He was tempted to mention golf, but decided to save such retaliation for another, more telling moment. He had a feeling they would need some light relief in the days to come.

Raymond Keane's parliamentary research assistant was waiting for them when they arrived. 'Despina Mottershead,' she said, holding out a thin hand with a nervous smile. She had dark straight hair and very large spectacles, which gave her the look of a startled owl.

It emerged quickly that she was genuinely upset by the news of Keane's death. She would lose her job with his going, Hook supposed, but he fancied her distress ran a little deeper than that. Clearly she was starry-eyed about the deceased man; he wondered how far Keane had reciprocated her feelings. He might have slept with her, or he might not even have noticed her. It was always one of the difficulties that you could never see a dead man from his own point of view, but only from those of a succession of other people.

Lambert eventually said, 'You told the press when he was missing that you thought he might be abroad. What was the basis of that thought?'

She looked both embarrassed and

apprehensive. 'I didn't really say that. The reporter said perhaps Mr Keane might be living it up on the Riviera. I said I didn't think he would be; and then he said had I any reason to think he might not have gone abroad. And of course I hadn't. I didn't really know where he might be if—'

'And the paper twisted it to suggest you thought he was abroad. I shouldn't worry too much about that.' Lambert spoke with the resignation of one who had been misquoted often enough himself. 'In any case, that's all irrelevant, now that Mr Keane's been found.'

'Yes. I can't understand who—' Her fist was suddenly at her mouth and she was fighting for control. Hook looked up at her from his notes, automatically estimating her emotions; policemen are professional cynics. But this time there was no doubt about it: the tears which now started into her eyes were genuine.

Lambert said gently, 'You've anticipated my most important question. Do you know of anyone who hated Mr Keane? Hated him enough to kill him?'

'No. No, I don't!' She fought for the control she felt she should possess: as a twenty-three-year-old; as a history graduate; as a new woman; as a person with a responsible job in the mother of parliaments.

To Lambert, who had daughters of his own, she looked behind her big, misting lenses more and more like a brave schoolgirl. 'You did research for him when he needed information, I believe.'

'Yes. Most of it isn't research as most people would understand the word. He gets letters and complaints from his constituents and the like. I follow them up for him, getting answers from various governmental departments and sometimes from other sources. I'm just a time-saver, really, in most of my work.'

She reeled off the modest explanation she had given many times before to her friends and relatives, the familiar phrases helping her to regain a measure of control. She spoke in the present tense, like many who find difficulty in coming to terms with a death.

Now Lambert spoke slowly, making sure she understood him through her distress. 'What we need to know, Despina, is whether you can think of anyone who has had a fierce dispute with Mr Keane in the last year or so. These things sometimes escalate, you see, especially if the person involved is not balanced enough to be objective about the answers he or she is given.'

'No!' The word was out almost before he had completed his explanation. Then, as if she realized it had been too impulsive for them, she said apologetically, 'I have thought about it, you see. I've been wondering ever since he was found and the papers said foul play was suspected. But there just isn't anyone.'

'Fair enough,' said Lambert, rising. 'Let us know if you have any second thoughts.'

'I'm sorry,' she said, like a student who felt she had failed some kind of oral exam. 'You might get something more useful from Miss Probert. That's Mr Keane's secretary. She has dealings with a much wider circle of people than I do, through his correspondence.'

Daphne Probert was a formidable, grey-haired woman, who oozed efficiency and had no doubt protected Keane from unwanted encounters when he had been alive. But she produced coffee for them, and drew from the top drawer of her desk the diary she had kept of her employer's parliamentary engagements.

She was around fifty, and far more detached from this death than the tremulous girl they had just seen. Because they were experienced in their questions and she was efficient and precise in her answers, they built up a picture of Keane's working life quickly. He had spent most weekends in his constituency, travelling down more often than not on Friday mornings, ignoring the Friday Commons business like two-thirds of his fellow MPs. Sometimes he had come back with the rest of the West Country weekenders in the jams of Sunday night, but he had preferred to motor up the M4 on Monday mornings whenever his engagements permitted it. She looked in her diary. After that last weekend before the parliamentary recess, he had come back to

London on the Sunday night.

She knew little of his life in Gloucestershire, and gave the impression that she had always thought it of minor importance. She was one of those people who, having lived in London all her life, considered that not much that mattered occurred outside the capital, and therefore saw no reason to leave it except for the occasional holiday.

Hook was kept busy writing, building up that profile of the dead man which was the core of all murder investigations. Lambert eventually said, 'This has been very helpful, Miss Probert. One of the difficulties of this case for us is obviously that a man of Mr Keane's background is dealing with a large number of people, by the very nature of his work. Are you aware of anyone who had a particular dislike for him?'

'Who disliked him enough to kill him, you mean?' For a moment, she rejoiced in the precision with which she dismissed what she perceived as a euphemism. 'No, definitely not. Most of the people who met him here were politicians or senior business people, of course.'

It was Lambert's turn to smile, at the notion that all such men and women should be above suspicion. 'What about your correspondence files? You must have dealt with some letters which were critical of Mr Keane, amongst the hundreds you receive, I suppose.'

She nodded. 'Every MP knows that he is bound to have a few nutters.' She produced the word daringly, as though this departure into slang showed how modern she could be when she unbent. 'There isn't anyone I remember as being particularly dangerous. I can check the files, if you like.'

Lambert smiled. 'I'm sure if there was a dangerous lunatic lurking among your correspondence, you'd be well aware of him, Miss Probert.'

She smiled, preening herself a little at the compliment. Then her brow furrowed and she said, 'There was one chap, now I come to think of it. But he didn't write to us, or I'd have remembered it. He rang, that was it. Came through to me on the telephone, very excited.'

'Do you recall his name?' said Lambert, studiously low key. People remembered things much less easily once you told them it was important.

'I don't. But I may have it somewhere in my notes. He left messages, you see.' She reached into the top drawer of her desk, pulled out a loose-leafed dictation pad, and began to turn its many sheets. 'Yes, here it is!' she said triumphantly. 'I remember it now, because Mr Keane said I was never to put this man through. I was to tell him to attend one of the constituency clinics, or put his complaint in writing. I gathered the exchanges had been going on for some time.'

'And what was the source of this man's displeasure?'

This time she liked the understatement. It seemed to her the proper parliamentary phrasing for that wild screaming she had had to deal with on the phone, when she had refused to put the man through and offered to take a message. 'Source of displeasure' was the sort of phrase she might have put in one of her letters, when someone had been really angry. 'I couldn't tell you exactly. The man wasn't very articulate, you see. But I gathered it was something to do with his daughter's death.'

'And his name?'

She looked down at her scribbled shorthand again, then smiled triumphantly. 'Joe Walsh. That's what he called himself.'

They were waiting for a taxi in the busy street outside when Hook raised his voice above the traffic noise to say, 'She's right, I suppose. The electorate is about a hundred thousand in our constituency, even though not all of them vote at elections. Our MP is bound to have been pestered by a few nutters.'

Lambert smiled. 'And a minority of all nutters are dangerously violent. At the moment, I'm hoping Joseph Walsh might be one of them.'

*   *   *

They went into the murder room in CID when

they got back to Oldford, to check with Detective Inspector Rushton that there were no dramatic developments in the case from the team of officers operating the routine enquiries a murder investigation always sets in train.

'The Scene-of-Crime team have finished at the pond where the corpse was found and moved to Keane's cottage,' Chris Rushton reported. 'No evidence of a burglary there, they say. Nor of a breaking and entering. Of course, we don't know yet where he was killed. If it was anywhere near that pond, he must have been lured there by someone, or driven out there in a car: it's quite a remote spot.'

And a good one for the disposal of a body, thought Lambert. Had it not been for an ebullient boxer bitch, the pool might have held its secret for a good deal longer. Hook handed over his notes from their meetings in London. Rushton would incorporate them in the appropriate file on his computer in due course. They left him working his way through a pile of notes at his elbow, his concentration upon the flickering green type on the monitor in front of him, as he fed in and cross-referenced the information that was coming in from the team of eighteen men and women now involved in varying degrees in this investigation.

When the work in a case like this one was at its most intense, Rushton had almost to be

120

prised away from his machine on some nights, his desire to incorporate each new scrap of information into his records bordering on the obsessive. Since his wife had taken his child and left him two years earlier, he had little social life and did not disguise the fact.

It was dark when a tired Lambert eased the big Vauxhall into the garage which had been opened for him at his home. 'I'm ready to eat as soon as you are,' he called through to the kitchen as he put away his coat in the big hall. 'God, this travelling exhausts me these days. Bert and I went up to London on the train. Perfectly comfortable, but—'

He stopped abruptly as he came into the kitchen and saw a white-faced Christine standing with her back to the sink. She said, 'I've been to the doctor, to get the results from that second mammogram. I told you it was today.' She had not meant it to sound like an accusation, but he had forgotten, and she knew it.

'Was everything all right?' he said lamely. Suddenly, he was hoping against hope that she was upset with him for forgetting, rather than because of what the doctor had said.

She smiled at him, seeing a strong man made suddenly weak by a thing he did not know how to deal with. 'You'd better sit down to hear. I had to.'

John Lambert lowered himself on to a kitchen chair, feeling for it behind him, his eyes not leaving her face. Christine switched off the radio which had been playing classical music at low volume on the windowsill behind the sink. 'Invasive carcinoma,' she said. The doctor had delivered the phrase to her as though announcing a bout of flu. She wondered what sort of message the words sounded now in her husband's ears.

Lambert raised his hands and set them carefully on the scrubbed deal of the kitchen table in front of him. It was as if the symmetry of their arrangement had become very important to him with the news. 'Will they operate?'

'Yes. No alternative. And as quickly as possible.'

'Yes. I suppose that's good. That they're going to get on with it, I mean.' He dropped his eyes to his hands, big, strong, and totally useless in front of him. After a moment he said, 'Will you lose the breast?'

'I expect so. I didn't enquire too thoroughly. I thought they'd better just get on with it.'

'Yes. So long as they clear it up, that's the main thing.' And with that banality, they were in each other's arms, without either being aware that they had moved. He held her tightly, wondering if even now as he crushed her against him he might be exacerbating the awful thing that gnawed at the body with which he was so familiar.

Christine broke away from him and went

into the bathroom and stood looking at herself in the mirror, looking at the crow's feet around her eyes, at the lines on the forehead of the oval face beneath the brown hair that was still without any grey. She felt the left breast that was going to be cut away, remembering when she had been a college student of nineteen, giggling with her friends at a dance when that same wilful breast had escaped from a cheap bra and she had fled in comic confusion to the ladies. That moment seemed at once a long time ago and very close to her. She wondered where her life had gone.

An hour later, after a meal with John that was punctuated by sporadic small talk, as if they had been polite strangers, she said, 'I've to go in tomorrow afternoon.'

'I'll take you.'

'Jacky will come over tomorrow night, I expect. I rang her. She said she'll bring something for a meal.'

'I can look after myself. But she'll want to see you.' It would be the first occasion when their daughter would be the strong one, looking to minister to her parents' needs instead of depending on them for support. He felt both old and weary; helpless, when he wanted to be a cheerful rock for Christine to rest on.

Later, he held her in the darkness, feeling her still wakefulness, moving his hands carefully over the cotton nightdress, too shy to let his touch stray to the breast which was the cause of all this trouble.

Long after his steady breathing had told her he was asleep, Christine Lambert lay quietly afraid in his arms.

*   *   *

Bert Hook was sometimes a source of amusement to his colleagues because they supposed him soft-hearted. So it was he who got the job of going to see old Mrs Keane about the death of her son. He could have been accompanied by a WPC, but preferred to go alone, knowing he operated these things best when he did not feel his own behaviour was being studied.

The big, ivy-clad Georgian house was very quiet as he drove between the high gateposts and up the curving drive between the banks of rhododendrons. There were a surprising number of houses like this still standing in Gloucestershire, many of them now occupied by successful postwar industrialists. Some of the larger ones which had kept their estates were occupied by the aristocracy; one or two of the grandest had even attracted royal residents.

This more modest but still gracious house might have been empty, for there was no vehicle, no sign of activity on the wide expanses of gravel in front of the impressive oak door. But Bert was admitted within a few seconds of his arrival by the middle-aged maid who seemed to be the only servant working in the big house.

Mrs Keane rose to meet him as he was shown into the spacious drawing room with its marble fireplace and three rectangular windows. She was clad from head to foot in black, as a mourner might have been in her grandmother's day. It was a custom which like many others had not long survived the 1914–18 war, but it seemed to a lonely old woman a fitting final gesture to the son she had never expected she would survive.

'I'm afraid there's no doubt now that it's your son,' said Hook. He had felt like an intruder as he stepped into the imposing hall. Now he spoke like a health visitor, watching the bereaved old woman for signs of collapse. Yet she had to be interviewed: she was the last person known to have seen Raymond Keane alive.

'I accept it's Raymond. Katherine rang me when she'd been to identify him. Was it you who was there with her when she did that?' Hook nodded. 'She said you were very kind.'

'I'm sorry to intrude at a time like this, Mrs Keane. We need to know whatever you can tell us about your son and the people he knew, you see.'

'Yes. But I'm afraid I knew very little about the life he led in recent years, Sergeant Hook.'

She looked infinitely sad at the thought, and he knew she was confronting a fact she found very unwelcome.

'We're pretty certain now that someone killed your son, you see, so we need to know what enemies were near to him in the last weeks of his life.'

'Yes. And obviously I want to help you. But I know very few of his new political acquaintances. Or any of the people he has met since he moved into politics, in fact. Parliament rather took him away from the family, but I suppose that was inevitable. He was doing rather well at Westminster, I believe.' Her pride surged suddenly through her reserve with the last sentence.

Hook said, 'Did he seem at all disturbed or nervous when he left here on Christmas Eve?'

'No. Rather the reverse. After a day and more with his aged mother, he was probably only too anxious to get away. But he was going to see that nice young woman Zoe Renwick, whom he was going to marry.'

'Yes. We shall be seeing Miss Renwick. I've already arranged an appointment with her.'

'I expect she'll be able to tell you more than me about his life in these last few months. He was expecting to meet her at the cottage. He'd tried to ring her from here, but he hadn't got hold of her.'

'And he was looking forward to seeing her?'

'Oh, yes. They were going to have

Christmas together, just the two of them. But he was bringing her here on New Year's Day.' She was suddenly anxious to defend her dead son against any charge of neglect. Bert had seen the reaction often enough in old women of humbler station; it was curiously touching in this straight-backed, patrician figure.

'We shall be seeing Miss Renwick very shortly. Is there anyone else who you think may be able to help us fill in our picture of your son? That's the way we work, you see. The fuller the picture we have of the way a person lived his life and the people he came into contact with, the better our chances of finding out how he died.'

She nodded, intelligence shining through her grief. 'There was another young woman, you know. A nice lady. Raymond decided that she wasn't for him a few months ago. Young people have to work these things out for themselves; it's more complicated than it was in my day. But I was sorry that they split up. I liked her very much.'

'And her name was?'

'Moira. Moira Yates. Lovely, lively girl. Excellent tennis player: I saw her win a tournament once. And a very good horsewoman too, I believe. She used to come here quite often, when she and Raymond were close. She and I got on very well together. I thought she'd have been good for him. Not that I've anything against the new girl, of course.'

She added the last sentence as a hasty qualification, still the anxious parent at seventy-six, anxious about her relationship with someone who might become a daughter-in-law, forgetting for a moment that there was no longer any need for such diplomacy.

Hook said, 'Thank you. We shall be seeing Miss Yates in due course, I'm sure. I believe your son had a business, in addition to his work as an MP?'

'Yes. Though he seemed to me to be neglecting it, leaving everything to his partner, since he became so interested in politics. But he said it was making good money, that they could get along perfectly well without him. It didn't seem very fair to Chris, but I couldn't interfere.'

'Chris?'

'Chris Hampson. Raymond's partner at Gloucester Electronics. Nice chap; I used to see a lot of him in the old days.' There was sadness again in the old, lined face, at the realization that she was now excluded from the developing projects in which she had once been so interested.

'Had he seen Mr Hampson in the days before his death?'

The old eyes glistened at him from their grey-black sockets; perhaps she was appreciating for the first time that the people she was mentioning would be involved in the investigation of her son's murder. 'Yes. Raymond went to see him on his way down here, as a matter of fact.'

'Was there any sort of dispute between them?'

'I don't know. Raymond wouldn't say any more about their meeting.' She looked down at the thick Persian carpet; plainly she thought as he did that there were implications in the dead man's reticence.

She did not call the maid, but saw him to the door herself. She stood still at the top of the wide stone steps as he drove away, dressed in black from head to foot, as static as a figure from Greek tragedy. The parent's loss of a child is the worst loss of all, thought Hook, who had never known a parent of his own.

CHAPTER THIRTEEN

The huge room took up half of the ground floor of the building. It was thickly carpeted and very quiet. Only about a quarter of the heavy armchairs and settees were occupied, and save for the occasional rustle of the turning pages of a newspaper, there was silence. It seemed another world from the busy streets of Cheltenham outside. You would never have known it was a hospital, thought Hook. Obviously you got the benefits from going private, even before you had paid.

Policemen are well used to hospitals. Long before they reach the exalted ranks of the CID, they get used to guarding injured witnesses; to watching people die; to sitting at the bedsides of injured criminals to protect them from their fellows; to wringing their stories from them as soon as the medicos allow it. The hushed and luxurious South Cotswolds Hospital had little in common with the spartan corridors where Hook had spent many long nights in his early police career.

There must be patients somewhere, he thought, but there was no sign of them in this plush reception area, which might have belonged to a prosperous industrial company anxious to impress its clients. Lambert was at the long desk, announcing who they were and the purpose of their visit. Hook could hear nothing of what he said from twelve metres behind him; even the superintendent seemed to have been overwhelmed by the prevailing atmosphere of quiet discretion.

They were directed to the second floor and another, smaller reception desk. There a smiling nurse in green told them that Sister Renwick was with a patient, but would be with them in a few minutes if they would take a seat. A man with a trolley served them real coffee, asked them if they wished to choose from the leather-fringed menu for the evening meal, and departed on silent feet, moving like the rest of this place on well-oiled ballbearings. There was still no sign of sick people, thought Hook: presumably there were some behind the soundproof double doors which had swished shut behind the porter and his trolley.

Sister Renwick arrived almost as quietly as everything else in this thick-carpeted place, smoothing down her blue uniform, holding out a slim, strong hand to Lambert as he struggled awkwardly to his feet. 'Zoe Renwick,' she said brightly, in the voice that must have calmed a thousand relatives. She swept off the curious white cap from her bright blonde hair with a single, practised movement of her hand. 'The management likes us to be conventionally uniformed—in the fashion of a previous generation of nurses,' she said, with a smile which showed them perfect teeth. 'It's supposed to reassure the customers that they're getting proper attention. Curiously, I think it actually succeeds in doing that, for many of the elderly patients.'

She was talking too much too quickly, about anything that came into her head. It was not an unusual reaction among people drawn into a murder enquiry. She shook hands with Hook when Lambert introduced him, then sat down to face them in this quiet little anteroom where she had talked gravely with so many anxious and grieving relatives. She directed her bright-blue eyes expectantly upon

Lambert, turning her black-nyloned knees a little to one side, sitting on the edge of her armchair with legs uncrossed.

Bert Hook doubted whether she was as calm as this pose suggested. She looked very attractive to him: it was easy to see why so many men found uniforms a turn-on in women. But Bert, reared in a Barnardo's home, had seen too many uniforms in his formative years. Nurses in uniform meant for him the nit-woman who came at regular intervals to examine the boys' close-cropped heads, moving along the rows of scalps, stamping them as safe for another few months, impassive as the woman who checked the dates on their library books. He wondered if those immaculately manicured fingers which now intertwined in that royal-blue lap had ever searched for nits in childish hair; it seemed unlikely.

Lambert said, 'I expect Sergeant Hook told you why we wanted to see you when he phoned.'

'Yes. About Raymond. I expected this. But I'm afraid I shan't be able to help you very much.' She was immediately tense and defensive, when she had determined not to be; she tried to breathe evenly, resolved to make herself take time to answer.

'Oh, you may be surprised how helpful you can be. We gather evidence from all sorts of people, you see. It's often only when we put it all together, when we get the complete picture, that the full significance of what people have told us emerges.'

'When you find discrepancies in people's statements, you mean?'

Lambert smiled at her, pleased that she had made the vague threat in his reassurance explicit. 'Sometimes the contradictions are interesting, yes. But people often make mistakes in good faith, and those are easy enough to sort out. If you simply do your best to answer honestly and fully, there should be no difficulty.'

Why, she wondered, did everything he said seem to be issued as a challenge to her? Perhaps she was merely hearing menace in his words, because she had things she was anxious to conceal. She felt a dryness in her throat, a scratching in her voice, as she said, 'What is it you want to know?'

Lambert looked at her calmly, assessing her state of mind, not troubling to disguise his scrutiny. A kindly man in most of his dealings, he could be quite ruthless in pursuit of the truth. This concentration was one of the first qualities he looked for in a detective, when he was considering personnel for transfer to CID. He said, 'You were engaged to marry Raymond Keane, I believe.'

'Then you believe wrong.' She allowed her anger to come out in the contradiction, then smiled nervously, attempting to conciliate. 'I was expected to marry him, yes. But we were never engaged.'

'I see.' He looked coolly into her eyes for a moment, until she dropped her gaze to the hands which twisted in her lap. 'And when did you last see Mr Keane?'

She took a deep breath, knowing this was going to be difficult, thinking of the questions which were bound to come. 'On the Sunday before he died.'

He raised his eyebrows at her, looking his surprise, trying to draw her into further words. When she offered him nothing, he said, 'You seem very confident about when he died. We haven't more than the vaguest idea of even the day of his death yet.'

'No. Neither have I. I don't know why I said that. I just—just sort of presumed that he must have been killed quite soon after he was last seen, I suppose. I spoke to his mother, you see, and we agreed that she should report him missing—this was a couple of days after Christmas. It seemed then that no one had seen him since Christmas Eve. I—I must have assumed that he'd died shortly after he was last seen, I suppose.'

She was talking too much, unable to stop as she stumbled towards an explanation, a retrieval of the blunder she had made through thinking too far ahead, beyond the apparently simple query he had put to her about her last meeting with Raymond. And this quiet, neatly

134

dressed snake of a man was allowing her to blunder on, listening to her fallibility, watching her every uncertain move. She looked from the lean intensity of the superintendent's features to the more reassuring roundness of the face at his side, but Hook was busy writing, recording the detail of her evasions.

She looked at the watch which dangled from the pin at her breast, wishing bitterly that she had not revealed at the outset that she was now off duty, wishing more profoundly than she could ever have thought possible for a conclusion to this. Lambert said, 'So you hadn't seen Mr Keane between December the eighteenth and the discovery of his body on January the third. And you left it to someone else to report him missing. That seems to indicate a notable lack of anxiety in one so close to the deceased. Or were you not expecting to see him in all that time?' He kept his tone neutral, just inside any note of insolence. Zoe Renwick was still helping them on a voluntary basis with their enquiries, though it would suit him if she did not realize that too clearly.

Her shoulders set squarely beneath the blue cotton of her uniform. She took a deep breath, making no attempt now to conceal her discomfort from them. 'I had decided not to marry Raymond. I wasn't looking forward to telling him that. It—it suited me that I did not have to argue it out with him, I suppose.' That at any rate was genuine, and it was a relief to her to deliver the truth.

'Why did you decide not to marry him, Miss Renwick?'

'That is my business, Superintendent. It has nothing to do with his death.'

'It would be better to let us decide that.'

'It was between Raymond and me. I never got the chance to tell him my reasons.' It was curious, she thought, that the exchange with Raymond which she had so dreaded should now give her an excuse for reticence with these strangers.

'And you think those reasons have nothing to do with his death.'

'I'm sure of it.' She was tight-lipped, determined. The strong-featured face which had looked so attractive when it had been broadened by her opening smile was now pinched and strained as the blue eyes stared not at her tormentor but past him.

'What arrangements had you made for the Christmas holiday period?'

'I was to spend it with Raymond. I should have gone to the cottage on Christmas Eve to meet him there. But I rang and left a message on his answerphone, asking him to ring me when he got there.'

'Did he ring you?'

'No.' She thrust her hands suddenly into the capacious pockets of her uniform, as if they were altogether too revealing to be exposed to their relentless gaze.

'Have you any idea why not?'

'No. Perhaps he didn't play back the tape when he got in. He was expecting me to arrive at any time, I suppose.'

'Did you go to the cottage? On that day or any of the following ones?'

'No. I had volunteered myself for Christmas duty here. I knew Raymond would want me to go and talk: it gave me a good reason not to.'

'Very well. So you did not see the man you had planned to marry, who apparently still thought he was going to marry you, after December the eighteenth. Can you give us some account of his last hours with you, please?'

'We spent the weekend together. At his cottage.'

Lambert wanted to ask her what had happened between them on this last weekend, but the questions which formed themselves in his mind seemed like prurient probings into the sexual exchanges between the pair. It was Hook, looking up from his notes, who said, 'Did you see anyone else over that weekend, Miss Renwick?'

She tumbled into an account of the Conservative wine and cheese at the chairman of the local association's mansion, piling on the detail breathlessly, feeling herself at least safe in this neutral area, which they could check so easily if they wanted to. She made it seem the centrepiece of the weekend, as if it had dominated all else, as if the weekend had been built around it. It was a relief not to be made to recall her last sexual exchanges with Raymond, those last tumblings in the familiar big bed in the low-ceilinged room beneath the thatch, which she was now reluctant to admit to herself had been so enjoyable to her.

But Hook established that the wine-and-cheese function was at the Saturday lunchtime, that they had spent no more than an hour and a half at the big house, that they had gone back to Raymond's cottage. She felt as he wrote the times down, as he recorded so meticulously the hour at which they had returned, that he was about to ask whether they had gone to bed then, to demand the details of the intensity of their physical passion on that last afternoon. Instead, he said quietly, 'Mr Keane left you on the Sunday evening?'

'Yes. He had to get back to London. He had appointments on the Monday in the Commons, I think.'

'Yes. We already have a full picture of his last week in London. It is his next weekend, his last hours, after he had come back to Gloucestershire, which we are now anxious to document. From Christmas Eve until whatever time he died.'

When this did not produce any comment from her, Lambert said, 'Let's complete the picture of your last weekend with Mr Keane,

138

then. Did you spend Sunday, December the eighteenth alone together?'

She had known this would come. And she wanted to tell them about it. The bare facts of the meeting, anyway. There was no point in trying to deceive them, when they were bound to find out about it from others. 'No, not all of it. We went to see Moira Yates.'

Zoe watched Hook write down the name carefully in his round longhand. Lambert said quietly, 'Who is that, please?' and she had no method of knowing whether the name was new to them or not, whether they already knew all and more of what she was going to tell them, from other viewpoints. 'She was Raymond's former mistress. The woman he was involved with before he met me. The woman who thought she was going to marry him, before I came along.'

She had got all of the worst of it out at once. Lambert raised his eyebrows a little, and she knew immediately the source of his surprise. 'You're wondering why I went with Raymond on that visit. Yes, I've wondered myself, since. Perhaps it was no more than curiosity, to see another woman he had once cared deeply for. Anyway, it was difficult for me, seeing her. I'd never met her before. And I shouldn't have gone. I realized that, as soon as we set foot in the house, but it was too late then.'

'Why did Mr Keane go to see her? It must have been embarrassing for him, surely?'

'Yes. But he felt he wanted to show her once and for all that everything was over between them. They hadn't seen each other for four months, you see. Not since he had met me, I think. And he was preparing to announce our engagement; he wanted to tie up loose ends before he did that.' The phrases Raymond had used when he had spoken to her about this seemed very banal now, as she brought them out to these strangers. And perhaps, after all, they had not been the full story. She saw now that his main object had been to make sure that his former lover did not become a political embarrassment to him in the months and the years to come.

She looked at the shrewd, still expectant face of Lambert and added, 'Miss Yates was ill, too. Had been almost since they split up, I believe. It was natural that he should want to reassure himself about her, I think.' She found herself wanting to give Raymond the full credit for his actions now that he was dead, to put the most favourable public gloss on his visit to that strange house.

He did not ask her as she expected him to do about the nature of Moira Yates's illness. She wondered again how much they knew about the other people who had been close to Raymond in his last days. Instead, Lambert said, 'Was anyone else present at this meeting?' and she felt he was testing her, inviting her to fall into some trap she could not see.

'Moira's brother was there. Dermot Yates. We were in his house, in fact. And a man whose name I cannot remember. An old flame of Moira's, Raymond said afterwards. He was certainly trying to be very protective of her. I can't remember his name.'

'Gerald Sangster, perhaps?'

'That's right.' They did know, then. Her blood ran suddenly cold at the range and effectiveness of the police machine. She could surely not hope to deceive these persistent, methodical men permanently.

'Did you see anything in this meeting to cause you concern?' When she did not immediately reply to the question, Lambert said, 'Did Mr Keane behave truculently, for instance? Did he do anything to arouse hatred in any or all of the three people you met on that afternoon?'

Relief flooded into her, with the thought that they were considering other people as candidates for this killing. Or was it all an elaborate ploy to put her off her guard? She had no idea of the way such men went about their business, and her ignorance was a breeding ground for the fear which rose to clutch so persistently at her heart. 'No. I didn't see anything like that. I don't know quite what Raymond intended. I never found out, because it was Moira Yates who controlled that meeting.' The memory of the woman's febrile dominance came back vividly to her, and for a moment its vividness thrust out even her own fear of what was going to happen.

'Controlled it?'

'She took over the whole visit. As if it were just a showcase for her. As if it were a scene designed for her to show how little she needed Raymond. How inferior his will was to hers.'

Lambert studied her carefully, then nodded. 'You have obviously thought about that meeting a lot in the last fortnight.'

Zoe nodded, forcing a little smile. 'It made a big impression on me. I realized that whatever else Moira Yates might be or might have been, she is a remarkable woman.' Powerful enough to use me as just part of the furniture, she thought; not many women have done that. And powerful enough to make me see things in Raymond Keane that I had not recognized in months of intimate contact.

Lambert wondered how far to pursue this. But, like most policemen, he shied away from the subjective. Establish the facts, all the facts, before you speculate, was his watchword with his subordinates. He could be a positive Gradgrind about gathering the facts in the first stages of an investigation. He said, 'What about the other two people who were present at this meeting?'

'As I said, it was at Dermot Yates's house. He's her elder brother, who's been looking after Moira during her illness. I gather there

142

are normally just the two of them in the house. He tried to control Moira—not very effectively. I think he was knocked off balance by the way she took over the proceedings. She was full of energy, and I got the impression that that was a surprise to him, that she had been listless for a long time.' She had forgotten that she had not specified the nature of Moira's illness, was speaking as if they knew as much as she did about it. 'Miss Yates has been suffering from agoraphobia. Hasn't been able to leave the house for months.'

'And what about Gerald Sangster? How did he react to her behaviour?'

She shrugged. 'I'm sure he was as surprised as Moira's brother by the way she behaved. By the energy she showed. By the effortless way she embarrassed Raymond and me.' She managed a little smile at her own expense at the memory, then looked Lambert full in the face, for the first time since much earlier in the interview. 'I'm sure that neither of the men had wanted the meeting. That was apparent to me when we arrived. They were prepared to be hostile to Raymond. To throw him out of the house, if he upset Moira. That was totally unnecessary. She was well able to take care of herself.'

Lambert nodded, encouraging her to enlarge on this. When she did not do so, he said gravely, 'You will be aware by now that we are in the early stages of a murder investigation. It is therefore important both that I ask you this, and that you consider the question seriously. Did you see anything in the attitude or the behaviour of the other three people at this meeting which would suggest a hostility, a hatred, if you like? Anything which would be strong enough to impel one, or perhaps more than one, of them to kill Mr Keane?'

Her pulse seemed to stop for a moment at the directness of the question, then resume with a rapid throbbing in her head, as if making up for its suspension. 'No. I didn't see anything like that. Not in any of them.' She wanted to offer him something, anything, to ease this intolerable burden of suspicion she felt descending upon herself, but there was nothing for her here, surely. She couldn't see that either of those subservient men or the overwrought, housebound Moira Yates would have had anything to do with Raymond's brutal dispatch from the world.

'What car do you drive, Miss Renwick?'

'A black Fiesta Sport 1600.'

'A hatchback?'

'Yes.'

She watched the burly sergeant make a careful note of the details. But the CID men seemed prepared to leave it at that. Perhaps, after all, they were not so anxious to trap her as she had thought. It was Hook who now said, 'Did you see anyone else in this last weekend

144

you spent with Mr Keane?'

It was a lifeline, of sorts. She didn't want to implicate anyone else, but she was realizing now if she was to protect herself in a murder investigation someone else might suffer. Somebody must have killed Raymond, and the police were eventually going to fasten on to one person, she supposed; a prime suspect, didn't they call it? She said slowly, her words sounding unnaturally clear in her own ears, 'We had one visitor. Raymond's business partner, Christopher Hampson.'

Her tone of voice rather than the words warned Lambert that this could be important. 'Was this a social visit, Miss Renwick?'

'No. No, I'm afraid Mr Hampson was rather upset.'

'He had an argument with Mr Keane?'

'Yes. Quite a violent one, as a matter of fact.' She felt the chill of her treachery, but she had to protect herself. And if Chris was innocent, it was up to him to look after himself, wasn't it?

'What did they argue about, Miss Renwick?' Lambert's voice was studiously quiet; he did not want her shying away from this now.

'About the business. I gathered it wasn't doing very well. Raymond had given me the impression it was forging ahead; perhaps he genuinely thought that things were better than they were. Anyway, Chris Hampson thought he should have been contributing more and took him to task about it. I wished I hadn't been there—I shouldn't have been. But I hadn't known it was going to blow up as it did.'

'Quite. And did they resolve things?'

Zoe took a deep breath, allowing the regret for what she had to say to seep into her voice. 'No. Raymond wasn't very understanding. I didn't like what I saw of him that day.' It was the nearest she had come to referring to her own cooling passion. She was tempted for a moment to enlarge upon the bully she had seen in Raymond that day, upon the ruthless contempt for a man who had helped to build his fortune for him. She wanted to justify herself, to show how mistaken had been Raymond's attempts to impress her with his swaggering, with his brutal treatment of his partner's attempts to secure a fair hearing.

Instead, she went on quickly, damningly, 'There were high words between the two of them. And they didn't resolve anything; Raymond was very high-handed with him. And Chris Hampson was furious. He went off in quite a huff.'

CHAPTER FOURTEEN

'There can be no doubt it's murder, John. And no doubt how he died.' Cyril Burgess, MB, ChB, spoke with considerable satisfaction.

A pathologist's job can become very humdrum. It is nowadays largely confined to the routine of postmortems on patients who have died blameless deaths in hospital, but have, for reasons of the law of the land, to have postmortem examinations conducted upon them. Burgess relished a juicy murder more than most, not just because of the break in routine, but because he was an avid reader of what Lambert saw as outdated and romantic detective fiction.

He drew the sheet back in a manner which made Lambert recoil in anticipation, but took it only as far as the upper torso. 'Our revered MP wasn't drowned at all,' he said by way of introduction. Lambert knew better than to protest that he had never thought he was. 'There has been no blood-tinged froth from the mouth or nose,' said Burgess, indicating these blameless orifices with the tip of his gold-cased ballpen. 'There is plenty of "washerwoman's skin" and gooseflesh on the belly and the legs, but they are merely the results of prolonged immersion.'

Lambert put up with the magisterial style rather than risk revelations of the ravages Burgess had wrought on the hidden body in the interests of scientific investigation. The detective constable who had attended the postmortem—one of the tasks Lambert was only too happy to delegate—was now on his way back to the station, leaving Burgess to address the superintendent. Lambert felt a rare empathy with Queen Victoria: Burgess, like Gladstone, seemed on these occasions to make an audience of one into a public meeting.

The pathologist indicated a thin purple-black line around the neck of the corpse. 'This is how Randy Ray met his death.' The mark on the throat had been apparent from the moment when the corpse had been lifted from the pond, but they needed this official confirmation for the inquest. Plus whatever else this ponderous instructor was able to give them. 'He died from strangulation with a ligature of some kind. A thin cord rather than a wire: there was the odd thread still trapped in the wound. And he died quickly, not from asphyxia, but from vagal inhibition—heart stoppage technically, from pressure on the carotid arteries in the neck. I should say he was dead within less than thirty seconds: very efficient job.' Burgess, fingering the key point on the dead white neck, spoke like one professional appreciating the craftsmanship of another.

'Was there much strength needed for this?'

'No. Force applied scientifically, that's all.' Burgess spoke with satisfaction: he knew what Lambert had been thinking.

'We can't rule out a woman, then?'

'You couldn't rule out an eight-year-old!' said Burgess happily. 'Though he might have had to stand on a chair. I'd say Keane was attacked from behind and caught unawares. Someone garrotted him with a cord. Even a slight woman could certainly have done it, especially if she had a stick to wind tight at the end of the cord. The plot thickens!' the silver-haired tormentor said delightedly, and Lambert thought he was going to rub his hands together like a stage witch.

Instead, Burgess said seriously, 'You're going to want a time of death, and I'm afraid I can't be of much help there. He's been in the water too long for me to be precise, though it's been so cold that there hasn't been much degeneration. I'd give a guess—or what you would call an expert opinion—that he's been dead for more than one week and less than two. I couldn't be much more precise than that in court.'

'That's more helpful than you think,' said Lambert. 'We know he was alive at least until Christmas Eve. You're telling us that in all probability he was dead by December the twenty-seventh.'

'In all probability,' said Burgess mournfully, articulating the phrase as though practising it for delivery in due course to a defence counsel.

'For once we can probably be more precise than you about time of death. He was under the ice during that deep frost which began on Christmas Eve; he only surfaced with the thaw. I doubt whether he would have gone through the ice later than Boxing Day: it would have been too thick. The forensic boys are working on it, but I reckon the body was dumped in that pool by the end of Boxing Day at the latest. My garden pool is smaller than the one where he was found, but it had three inches of ice on the top of it by then. I broke it for the fish.'

'The wonders of detection,' murmured Burgess in mock awe. He turned back to the row of metal dishes beside the corpse. 'Nothing interesting from stomach contents. Your man had eaten what was probably a light meal some hours before he died: the processes of digestion were quite advanced, but that and the time which has passed since death means that I can give you no account of what food was involved. There's one interesting thing, though. I showed your officer the evidence.'

'Then there's no need to show it to me, Cyril,' said Lambert firmly, as Burgess threatened to lift the sheet.

As usual, the pathologist's sense of drama had made him save his most interesting revelation until the last. 'I said this fellow wasn't drowned. More important, he probably wasn't killed at the place where he was found. The body had lain for quite some time on its back before it was moved. There is hypostasis on his shoulders, buttocks, thighs and calves, clearly visible even after those days in the water.' Lambert saw the blackening of the flesh beneath the shoulder blades, even on the limited area of the corpse visible to him. 'The blood sinks to the lowest point in the flesh in the hours after the heart stops beating: simple gravity,' said Burgess, resuming his instructional vein to a man who knew all about hypostasis.

'How long did he lie before he was moved?'

Burgess shrugged, relishing the feeling of being involved in a murder enquiry, as he always did. 'Very difficult to say at this distance. But the marks are very definite. I'd say this corpse probably lay for at least a day before it was moved, but I could only make it an opinion in court.'

'I'd like you to give that opinion in the Coroner's Court, though. There won't be any defence lawyer there to grill you.'

'No problem about that. But why should it be important there, John?'

Despite his mannerisms, Burgess was that most useful of scientific men, a man prepared to speculate, to add his own thoughts as well as his expertise to the work he did for the police. That was why Lambert was now prepared to indulge his old friend with an explanation. 'The fact that he was killed elsewhere is significant for several reasons. One of them is that that pool is quite remote. Whoever dumped Keane in it had to get him there. Almost certainly in a vehicle. Once that is accepted, I shall be able to examine the cars of all those who were close to the late Raymond Keane in the days before he died.'

*   *   *

Christine Lambert was ready some time before she saw the old Vauxhall Senator swing through the gates and ease up the gravel drive.

As she watched her husband turn in the little circle in front of the garage and leave the bonnet facing towards the gate, she put on her best burgundy winter coat. No point in saving things, now. But she mustn't make that kind of half-serious joke to John: it would only upset him. Even now, as frightened as you were, you had to think of others and how they might react. She fought down an urge to scream; it passed as abruptly as it arrived.

She watched John lever himself heavily out of the car, his movements stiffer than they used to be, the long back taking more time to straighten as he turned towards the front door of their bungalow. Through the new double glazing, she could not hear the crunch of his footsteps on the gravel as she always had heard it in the old days. That made him seem further away as he strode silently towards her. Then he looked up at the big lounge window where he knew she would be standing, and gave her a quick, anxious smile. She was suddenly very sorry for him.

'I see you're all packed,' he said when he

152

came into the lounge. He picked up the small holdall from the chair where she had set it down. She wanted to say, 'I'll carry my own bag. I'm not an invalid yet, you know. I'm still whole.' Instead, she said brightly, 'The bed's all ready for me. They rang through from the hospital to confirm it. Quite early. About nine o'clock, I suppose.'

He recognized the rapid, inconsequential phrases of someone very nervous. He had seen it often enough before. But not in this context. And not from this sensible wife and mother, whom he had seen so often comforting his children and who now needed her own comfort. Because he did not know what to say, he said, 'I'll put this in the car,' and took her bag rapidly back whence he had come, though he knew he could easily have taken it out with her: it was all the baggage they had.

She was still standing at the window, watching his movements with a pale smile, as he returned. He said from the hall, 'Shall I make you a coffee?'

'No. I had one not long ago. I'm ready to go, when you are.'

'No point in delay, I suppose.' He put his arm round her shoulders, walked clumsily with her away from the window to the door of the room, and then took her in his arms. They kissed briefly, then held each other for a long, still moment, until he fancied he could hear her heart beating, even through the thick coat.

They did not often touch each other during the day; never kissed as they parted in the mornings or met again in the evenings. 'We'll get through this, as we've got through other things,' he said to the top of her head.

I will, you mean, she thought. She wanted to be selfish, to ask how he could possibly know how it felt, to shout down his arrogance in assuming that this could ever be a joint thing. Instead, she said, 'Of course we shall. We've been very lucky with illness, over the years. Something was bound to come up, sooner or later.' And hit me, of course, not you.

The small, frightened child that was inside the middle-aged adult wanted again to scream, to indulge in girlish hysterics, to be lifted into huge, enveloping adult arms and comforted. To be told, perhaps, that this was nothing more than a bad dream and that she was now returning to the safe, normal world. Christine murmured into the warm cotton which covered John's chest, 'We'd better be going, I suppose.'

The hospital was not at all like the one where he had gone to interview Zoe Renwick. There were few carpets here, and much more noise. They had to wait behind two other people to register their presence at the desk, and there was much mysterious bustle in the corridors they walked to get to the women's surgical wards.

But the sister and the nurses were

welcoming when they got there. This was a commonplace, everyday case to them, and the fact that Christine was to be an ordinary patient in an ordinary ward had its own compensations. John Lambert found himself wishing that everyone wouldn't be so determinedly bright and cheerful, but he knew that was unfair.

The sister said, 'We shall want you to take away your wife's clothes, Mr Lambert, but you can do that this evening, if you're planning to visit then.' It was a polite dismissal, and he was cravenly glad of it.

Christine said as he hesitated in front of her, 'Get off with you! You know you're quite indispensable to the Oldford CID: I don't want a crime wave on my account!'

The sister followed him a little way beyond her office, to say to him discreetly, 'Your wife will be operated on by Mr Robertson tomorrow morning, all being well, Mr Lambert.'

That seemed like a contradiction in terms. He looked up at the windows of her ward when he reached the car park, but there was no sign of Christine's face. There were so many panes in that huge slab of wall that he was not even confident that he had selected the right ones.

As she undressed behind the screen, Christine Lambert said, 'They're nothing but big babies, these men, aren't they? We're better without them in a crisis.'

* * *

There were two police cars outside the thatched cottage of Raymond Keane. A WPC and a young constable who looked scarcely old enough to be in uniform were on their knees in the lounge. They had tweezers and small metal dishes in their hands as they covered the fitted carpet slowly and methodically, collecting hairs, threads of material, a stray paperclip, anything that might bring a suggestion from the silent room of what had gone on there. Scene-of-Crime work was ninety-five per cent unrewarding, but highly necessary for the sake of that other five per cent. A man had been found guilty of murder when a stray toenail clipping proved he had been where he denied he had ever set his guilty foot. SOC officers constantly reminded their teams of that case.

Sergeant 'Jack' Johnson had done this work for years, and he did not allow his subordinates to cut any corners. He was using different officers here from those who had combed the oozing winter ground around the pool in the woods, to ensure that concentration did not lapse through boredom or familiarity. Lambert said, without greeting him, as he came into the house, 'You've finished your work where the body was found?'

'Yes, sir. I've put a copy of the written report in your tray in the murder room at the station. We—'

'Never mind the paper. Tell me what you found. If anything.'

It was unusually abrupt. Lambert was normally brisk but polite, always appreciative of work meticulously conducted. It was one of the things which made his teams work long hours without much complaint when there was a serious crime. Today he looked white and drawn. Johnson wondered if he was suffering from the virulent flu which had caused so many absences this winter. Well, he could be rude, if he liked, without check. Superintendent's prerogative. 'We didn't turn up much, sir. The clothing has gone to forensic, but I doubt if they'll find much of interest on it. It's been in the water for days, after all, and—'

'I know that, don't I? And if anything comes, it will come from the lab, so don't waste my time with bullshit. Anything from the rest of the area? Or did you just waste a full day's time?'

'There wasn't much. The ground had been frozen, so no wheel tracks. All footprints were eliminated as being made after the body was found, when the ground was softening up. We found an old ballpen, trodden into the ground and broken in two. There was a glove by the roadside. They've been bagged and retained,

157

but in my view they predate the crime by months or even years.' Johnson spoke quickly, lest he be cut off again for stating the obvious. 'We found two things, but we've no method of knowing whether they had anything to do with the crime.'

'Well?'

'The first was a fag-end. Tipped. Sodden and flattened. Impossible to say how long it had been there.'

'Where?'

'By the pond, on the roadside. But it might have been there for months. It's difficult to tell, with a cork tip. I doubt whether there'd be any possibility of DNA testing; it looked much too far gone for that. I'm sure there'd be no saliva traces or—'

'And the second object?'

'A wooden toggle. The kind they have on duffle coats. Quite worn. It didn't come from the clothing of the old chap who found the body, nor from any of my team. But again, it might have been there for months, for all we could tell. It's bagged and at the station.'

'Right. Anything here?'

Johnson hesitated. It might not be the moment for speculation, with a chief in this mood. But the normal Lambert wanted things without delay. 'I think he was killed here, sir. I think I know where, but I've only just found the place myself.' He led the superintendent along the low hall with its irregular walls, across a modernized kitchen, into the doorway of what looked as if it had once been a large walk-in pantry, where the main fuse-box for the cottage was high on the wall. There was one of the metal dishes like the ones the officers in the lounge were using on the floor, with a pair of tweezers on its edge, which Johnson had obviously been using when he heard Lambert coming into the house.

He picked up the tray, exhibiting the few fibres upon it to the superintendent's experienced gaze. 'I found these woollen fibres on the floor. Spread over about two square feet. There are probably one or two more of them: I haven't finished yet. Forensic will test them, but I'm pretty sure they'll find a match with the sweater Keane was wearing when he was fished out of that pool. There's a heel-mark on the plaster there, too.' Johnson pointed to a dark indentation some eight inches from the floor. 'It may be quite unconnected, but I think we may be able to match it with the shoes Keane was wearing when he died.'

'You think Keane died here?' Lambert looked up at the low ceiling of a room that was little more than a large box. The floor was about six feet square. A tiny place, but big enough for a man to die in. And he saw what Johnson meant about the heel-mark; if a man had been flung down roughly with a ligature about his throat, it was just the sort of mark his foot might have made on the white emulsion paint of the wall.

Johnson said, 'Even if he didn't die in here, then the body must have been left lying flat in here. That's the only way I can see those fibres getting there.'

Lambert nodded. 'I agree. Have you found anything here yet that might have come from anyone else?'

It seemed ungrateful to Johnson, when he had just been so clever, that the man should merely ask for more. But he knew what Lambert meant. If Keane had been killed here, there would have been what the forensic people called 'an exchange' with his killer. If they could find something to link another person with this room, they might have their murderer. Johnson said, 'There's nothing yet, sir. Nothing definite. But it's early days. We're bound to find things from other people in due course. But whether—'

'Whether they'll be significant in terms of murder may be another thing. All right. Carry on.'

He went briskly out of the cottage to his car and Johnson lowered himself carefully to his knees in the doorway of the tiny room. He was excited, in spite of his years of experience, by the notion that he might find here the evidence which would solve this case. He had his tweezers inching cautiously over the surface again when he heard Lambert's feet re-enter the kitchen behind him.

'Don't get up, Jack. Carry on with the good work. And if I was a bit short with you just now, I'm sorry. I've got things on my mind at the moment.'

*   *   *

In the murder room at Oldford CID, Detective Inspector Rushton was methodically cataloguing the growing collection of items connected with the case. Most would end up as detritus, but a few as vital exhibits in court, and no one could yet distinguish between the two. The price of success in detection was eternal vigilance, in Rushton's view, and far more often than not he was proved right.

Rushton was filing reports from the house-to-house men when Lambert went into the station. There were not many residences near to Keane's thatched cottage, and what few there were strung out along several miles of lanes. But rural folk were an observant, inquisitive lot, more likely to spot strangers and strange happenings than those who lived in Britain's teeming urban streets. There had already been one quite interesting matter reported.

Lambert stood behind his DI for a moment, watching the screen on the monitor as Rushton typed in information. Often there were half-humorous exchanges between the men about the value of computers to police work, as Lambert affected a contempt he did not really feel for the new technology to tease this very serious man. Today he said nothing.

It was left to Rushton to say, 'There is one interesting report. A woman who lives a couple of miles from Keane's place goes past the cottage regularly on her way to work at a supermarket in Stroud. She's seen a vehicle parked in the trees about a quarter of a mile from Keane's house fairly often over the last couple of months. Half hidden, but she noticed it more often once she'd spotted it. Usually at weekends, she thinks. Which might mean when Keane was in residence at the cottage.'

'Any description of the vehicle?'

'No registration number. But she's pretty definite that it was an older Ford van. White, with a big brown patch on one door, where it's never been resprayed. It shouldn't be too difficult to find. Oh, and she hasn't seen it at all in the last ten days or so. Since about the time when we think he was killed, in other words.'

'Let me know when you find that van. Is there anything else?'

'Yes. Something definitely worth following up, anyway. We've been through the files from Keane's constituency office,' said Rushton. 'Not computerized, but quite efficiently kept, in an old-fashioned filing cabinet. Most of them were one-off visits from his constituents, though that doesn't mean one of them mightn't be involved, of course. If our MP rubbed someone who was unbalanced up the wrong way, they might react violently after a single meeting. But we have to start somewhere. There are five people who have been to a constituency clinic either three or four times in the last year. I've got two men going round to see them this afternoon, or this evening if they should be out. But three of them are housewives and two are unemployed. We should have reports in by tomorrow morning at the latest.'

'Good.' Lambert reacted automatically. Rushton always liked to display his efficiency, but it was so complete in these routine matters that only a defensive man would have felt the need. His superintendent registered what was said, but was too numbed to feel his usual irritation at this demonstration of industry.

Rushton half turned to look at Lambert, and found him staring at the plastic bags of clothes on the table beyond his desk. He said, 'There's one chap who saw Keane seven times in the last year, sir. I thought I might go to see him myself.'

It was a request to conduct an interview which might be important, and Rushton half expected the chief to say he would go himself with Hook. Instead, Lambert said, 'Good idea. Have you found out the background yet?'

Rushton was delighted with the question. 'I

have. There isn't much in the file, beyond repeated recordings of the name and the dates when the man attended the clinics. But I rang Keane's election agent, and he knew all about the case.' He looked at Lambert, waiting for some reaction, but the lean grey face merely showed impatience at his pause. 'Apparently the man's daughter was killed in a road accident twelve months ago. Knocked off her moped. It seems her father thinks there hasn't been strong enough action against the culprit—assuming there is one, of course; it might have been the girl's own fault. He pestered Keane to take up the cudgels for him, without much success, as far as I could gather from the agent's guarded account. The man certainly seems to have become more and more frustrated and annoyed. Whether he might have taken violent action is another matter. It's a big step from frustration to killing. I'll have a better idea when I've seen him.'

Lambert was silent, thinking of his own daughters, of his fears when they were first out alone in adolescence, of the irrational things he might have done then if one of them had died on the roads. The love of a parent for a child is one of the strongest bonds of all, thrusting down the arguments of logic in normally reasonable men, removing that balance in conduct which is one of the requirements for human beings to live with each other without violence. He said, 'Do you have a name for this unfortunate parent?'

Rushton pressed a couple of buttons on the keyboard in front of him, watched with satisfaction as the information flashed up in green letters on the screen of the monitor. 'Walsh. Joseph Walsh.' He reeled off an address on the outskirts of Gloucester, but Lambert's mind was already off in search of information stored somewhere at the back of his brain.

Joe Walsh was the name the secretary at the House of Commons had given him. The man who had pursued Keane so persistently and so ineffectively there.

CHAPTER FIFTEEN

It was very dark in the car park at Gloucester Electronics. There were only two other cars there when Lambert parked the big Vauxhall near the single light beside the windowless brick wall at the end of the building. The newer of them was a two-year-old Granada Estate, which he took to be the senior partner and managing director's car. A good vehicle, but nothing very prestigious for a company director.

Hampson was a tall man, rising from a tidy desk to greet them as he saw them through the open door of his office. The clear desk-top made Hook wonder if he really had been working, or merely getting more nervous as he waited for them.

Hampson sat them in two of the armchairs at the other side of the room from his desk, and took the third one himself. They were set very symmetrically; perhaps he had pondered hard over the careful arrangement of the furniture for this meeting.

'Sorry if we've kept you late,' said Lambert when they had introduced themselves.

'That's all right. Six thirty in the evening quite suited me. There's plenty to do. And I'm quite glad not to have senior policemen around when all the staff are here.'

'We do set tongues wagging sometimes, I'm afraid,' Lambert agreed. 'But you can't be too discreet about murder. Especially when the victim is a prominent local MP and businessman.'

'More the former than the latter of late, I'm afraid,' said Hampson. It might have been no more than a reflex action, a natural instinct to distance himself from a murder investigation, but Hook's trained ear seemed to detect a little bitterness in the words. He looked at Hampson as he opened his notebook. He was a few years older than his partner had been, probably in his mid to late forties, Hook thought. He had deep-set grey eyes and thinning silver hair.

And he was nervous, there was no doubt about it now. He had things to tell them, for sure, but he was waiting for the questions to prompt him. They took him through the details of the business: how he and Keane had started the firm twelve years ago; the excitement of the early days and new products; the elation of swift success, as the demand for computer software exploded with the spread of the new technology; the expansion of the workforce to twenty within five years, and his pride in that; how things were more difficult nowadays, for everyone in electronics, not just their firm.

'What were the functions of the partners? Or did you both have a go at everything in a small firm like this?'

A sour smile, then a quick glance up at both their faces in turn, to see if they had registered his disillusionment. 'I was the technical man, responsible for most of the new products. Ray was the salesman and PR man, in the early days. It worked, too, then. I gave him good products to sell, but Ray brought the orders flooding in. He was good, when he wanted to be.'

'But he didn't always want to be?' Lambert moved swiftly through the door Hampson had left open so obligingly.

'He didn't give the firm the time it needed, particularly in the last two or three years. Well, not since he went into parliament, really.'

'Which is now five years ago. Mr Hampson, no doubt you took this issue up with your partner.'

'Yes. Things had been coming to a head for some time. And I saw him twice in the week before he died about them.' He leaned forward on the edge of his chair, anxious to state his piece, relieved rather than apprehensive that this information was out.

'And were your differences resolved in these meetings?'

This was the moment he had known must come, and he was well aware of the implications of his reply. But there was nothing he could do about it. There was a witness to the first meeting, and there were probably people in the office who had overheard some of the second. And he hadn't troubled to disguise his own fury with his partner when Ray had left on that Friday.

Hampson ran his tongue across his lips, said abruptly, 'Do you mind if I smoke?' He did not wait for an answer, but produced a packet and a lighter from his left-hand pocket, extracted a tipped cigarette, flicked a flame at the end of it, inhaled deeply, and blew out a long column of white smoke. He got up and moved the two yards to his desk, returning with the large glass ashtray. If he was conscious of four professional eyes studying his every movement for signs of tension, he gave no sign of it. But perhaps his bloodstream's call for nicotine overrode for the moment other anxieties.

'Filthy habit,' he said, 'but I don't seem able to rid myself of it. No, I'm afraid Ray and I didn't come to any agreement. Rather the reverse, I suppose. I saw him on the last Sunday before Christmas, at his cottage. That girl was there. The new one. Ray was showing off to her, trying to impress her by the way he dealt with me, I think. Or refused to deal with me. But that wasn't her fault, of course. She didn't do anything to encourage him.'

'For what it's worth, I don't think Miss Renwick was very impressed with the way Raymond Keane behaved on that day.' It was irregular to reveal what other interviewees had said, but Lambert was throwing him a sprat in the hope of catching a fat mackerel. And that, as he recalled it, was Zoe Renwick's own phrase: she was 'not very impressed' with what she saw of Keane on that day.

The ploy worked. There was both surprise and pleasure on the grey, square face of the man in front of them, at this suggestion of support from a quarter where he might least have expected it. 'I told Ray we needed his help. That times were much harder, that the orders weren't coming in. We needed his support and his selling expertise: I told you, he was very persuasive, whenever he chose to apply himself. When he went off to Westminster, he'd promised us that he'd still make his contribution. That there'd be new

169

and useful contacts, buyers that he'd push in our direction.'

'And that hadn't happened?'

'No. He said he couldn't be seen to be abusing his parliamentary position. But he could have helped us without doing that. Just by giving us a little more of his time and energy when things got hard. That was the basis we'd agreed when he left. Otherwise he wouldn't have been getting half of all profits still: we're only a small company, and with declining sales and tighter margins, we simply can't afford to have a sleeping partner.'

Lambert did not want to get involved in questions of ethics. He said, 'And you did not resolve these questions when you saw him at the cottage?'

'No. Things went from bad to worse, in fact. I told you, I think he was showing off to the blonde lady: playing the ruthless tycoon at my expense. I could hardly believe it; we used to be very close, when we started the business and worked all hours God sends. If she wasn't impressed, I'm glad about that.'

It was a little flash of gratuitous feeling, a moment of hatred for the dead man which he had not meant to reveal. Lambert let it hang in the room for a moment before he said, 'But you saw him again, I believe. Very shortly before his death.'

Hampson looked Lambert full in the eye, feeling the threat in the phrase. He was no fool, this man, but they had never expected him to be. 'He called here two days before Christmas. On the morning of Friday the twenty-third. On his way to see his mother, he said.'

'Was this meeting at your insistence?'

'No. I'd left in rather a temper on the previous Sunday, I admit, and with nothing resolved. He rang me on the Tuesday from his Commons office and arranged to come into the works to talk. I thought at the time that he was being conciliatory, repairing a few bridges.'

'But he wasn't?'

'No. Anything but. Perhaps he intended me to think that, to put me off my guard. At any rate, he became more truculent than ever that morning. I told him we were going to have redundancies by the end of January unless there were new orders, but he just offered to come down and tell the men the bad news himself. Then we had a row over money. I told him he wouldn't be getting any money out of his partnership this year. He said the terms of the agreement entitled him to thirty thousand and he was going to take it, whatever the state of the business. We parted on very bad terms.'

Hampson's grey, exhausted face had taken on a little colour as his resentment of the dead man's conduct came bursting out. It was plainly a relief to him to express it; probably he had not been able to speak about his dispute with his partner to anyone within the troubled firm, for reasons of morale. He panted a little, expecting them to speak, becoming a little embarrassed as they waited to see if he would reveal more of himself in his anger.

Eventually, he took a long puff at his cigarette, blew smoke violently towards the ceiling, and said, 'That's it, really. I realize it doesn't sound good from my own point of view now, but that's how it was. Oh, and I didn't kill Ray. I'm sorry he's dead. We got on well, in the old days, when we were working together to build this.' He lifted his arms a little and let them drop, indicating the factory around them which had become the centre of his life. Hook, eyes cast down upon his notebook as he wrote, wondered if this place dominated his thoughts enough for him to kill for it.

Lambert said, 'Where were you from Christmas Eve to December the twenty-seventh, Mr Hampson?'

'I was at home with my family.'

'For all that time?'

'Yes. Well, we went for a walk on Boxing Day, but all together. In the woods near Westonbirt.'

'Was that the only time you left home?'

'I think so. Oh, I came in here on the Saturday, Christmas Eve. I wanted to look at the books on my own, to see if there was any chance of avoiding the redundancies.' He glanced at the top drawer of his desk, where the original partnership contract with Raymond Keane lay. There was no need to tell them that he had come in to study the detail of that: he had said quite enough already.

'Did anyone see you here?'

He paused, feigning to give thought to a reply he had already determined. 'No. There was no one around on that Saturday afternoon. There wouldn't have been on any Saturday, let alone Christmas Eve.'

'I see. Is that Granada Estate in the car park your car, Mr Hampson?'

'Yes.' His face was suddenly taut.

'Would you have any objection to our forensic team examining it?'

'Would it make any difference if I did?'

Lambert returned his mirthless smile. 'Your refusal to cooperate with the police in a murder investigation would be noted. The next step would not be up to me.'

'You can examine the car whenever you want to.' He drew on his cigarette again, tapped the ash into the ashtray, then decided that there was nothing further to be had from what remained, and stubbed the end out with elaborate care. Anything, it seemed, to avoid eye contact with his questioners.

Lambert said, 'Do you have a duffle coat, Mr Hampson?'

Hampson looked as though the question had been completely unexpected. But then it probably was. Anyone who had been aware of

173

dropping a wooden fastener near that pool would have picked it up. 'No. I had one years ago, like many people at that time. I wear an anorak now.'

'And no doubt your wife could confirm that, if we should need her to.'

'Yes, I suppose so. But I'd prefer my family to be kept out of this.'

'Of course you would. But murder investigations don't have normal rules or normal boundaries, you see.' Lambert stood up, using a favourite ploy, asking his final question at the door, when his subject might be expected to be caught relaxing, in the belief that the interview was over. He looked back at the big glass ashtray, where the cork tip of the stub still cast a tiny, residual wisp of smoke into the air. 'By the way, did the late Mr Keane smoke?'

'No. Not at all.'

They left Christopher Hampson staring white-faced from the window of his office as they drove away.

*   *   *

There were only twenty minutes to the end of visiting hours when he arrived at the hospital. Most of the other beds already had visitors sitting quietly beside them. He was glad to see the long dark hair of his daughter Jacqueline beside his wife, who sat almost upright against her piled pillows.

'I'll be off now, Dad,' Jacky said, within a minute of his arrival. 'I've a fair way to drive, and they say there's a possibility of fog later.' They had said whatever they had to say before he arrived. She kissed Christine and strode away, tall and confident on high heels, turning briefly at the door to wave and smile at her mother.

Lambert wondered if her prompt departure was intended as a rebuke to his tardiness or was merely a diplomatic ploy to leave husband and wife together. He was still not used to fencing with his daughter as an adult: it did not seem long since she had sat on his knee to watch Sunday teatime serials on television, still less to the problems of her tempestuous adolescence. He said to Christine, 'I'm sorry I'm late. I've been working until now.'

'Your murder, yes. Our late MP. I didn't expect you early. How's it going?'

He wasn't sure himself. He didn't yet feel he had what DI Rushton would have called an overview of the case. 'Early days. But there isn't an obvious candidate. No confession volunteered. No, "It's a fair cop, guv," for this one.'

It was a weak attempt to be light-hearted, and it fell appropriately flat. There was a pause before she filled in with, 'They were talking about it in the day room at teatime. Well, more about the by-election and his

175

successor, really. The waters close over even the illustrious dead alarmingly quickly, don't they?'

With her surgery on the morrow, with their fears of what might be found, the speed with which the dead were forgotten was not the happiest of topics. Lambert held Christine's hand for a little while, surprised to find how naturally the contact came to him, even in this semipublic setting. Eventually she said, 'I'm glad you're here, John. There was a time when I thought the job took precedence over any of your personal relationships, you know.'

'I know. Perhaps you were right. But it was a long time ago, and I'm glad you stayed with me.' He squeezed her hand, felt the answering pressure. 'And people can change, you know, as they get older. I think I have.'

They did not discuss the operation next day, each preferring to ignore the 'No solid food, no liquids after midnight' notice at the top of her bed. Each knew the surgery was in the other's mind, but there was nothing more to be said, now.

The bell rang to announce the end of visiting. All around them, people struggled to their feet, most of them trying not to look relieved at the end of their vigil. The Lamberts' embrace was perfunctory, embarrassed. He felt her breathing unevenly against his ear, almost overbalanced comically on to the hard bed. 'It's the first time we've had to tackle anything like this,' she muttered, holding him for a second after he had dropped his arms from her shoulders. 'I suppose it won't be the last.'

She was offering him hope, he knew, telling him that this was not going to be more than routine, everyday surgery, that the canker within her would not have progressed beyond the breast, that he was not to worry. It should have been the other way round, but he was helpless, unable to offer the comfort which should have come from the one outside this crude cutting of the body they both knew so well. She said, 'Ask for the ward sister when you ring in. You'll get the very latest news that way.'

He nodded dumbly, then picked up her bag and walked unsteadily to the door of the ward with it. He looked back from there, catching hope from her broad smile of encouragement as she watched him from her bed. It was all the wrong way round, he thought again.

He unpacked her clothes and hung them in the wardrobe. He put her underclothes in the washer as she had bidden him, ready to wash in the morning with his own. The scraps of white material looked very small, too small for a wife and grandmother.

CHAPTER SIXTEEN

Moira Yates was restless. It was only nine o'clock and the winter sun was barely creeping above the shrubs at the back of the garden, but she had washed up, opened the post, and written a longish letter to her old aunt in Ireland. Dermot Yates began to wonder quite how long his sister had been up.

She turned from the limited vista of the back garden and moved to look again through the window at the front of the house, where she could see the road outside. The children had gone now, hurried into cars by anxious parents who no longer let them walk to school, but the milk van was making its fitful way towards them. Dermot was irritated by his sister's restlessness, but cheered by what seemed an interest in the world outside his house. There had been too little of that for months now. He would ask the doctor, but he was sure he would be told this was a hopeful sign.

'I thought the CID would have contacted me about Raymond by now,' she said. 'They're sure to want to see me, you know. And perhaps you too. They'll be speaking to everyone who was close to him.'

Dermot supposed she was probably right. She had been watching television a lot during her self-imposed confinement; she must have picked up something from the many crime series, though often she seemed to him to be scarcely registering what happened on the flickering box of colour in the corner of the lounge. 'I expect you're right. You won't be able to help them, though. There must be many people they have to see more urgently.'

'Yes. But they'll have to "eliminate me from their enquiries". That's what they call it, you know.' She had two spots of colour high in the cheeks that had been so pale for so long. The prospect of contact with the enquiry into her former lover's death seemed to excite her; almost as much as the man's presence here a fortnight and more ago had excited her.

Moira was not rid of the wretched man yet, then, even with his death. Still, this would be temporary, he was sure. Dermot Yates was glad Keane was gone, after the way he had treated his sister. This death would surely mark the first stage in her recovery.

'Will you be going to the funeral?' she said.

'I hadn't planned to. Not unless you wanted me to, that is.'

'I haven't thought about that. I shan't be able to go myself, of course.'

'No.' He had not even thought of it as a possibility. For four months, he had had difficulty in getting this outdoor woman even into the garden. For a moment, he considered using the occasion of Keane's death to entice her out of the house. It would be satisfying to see the wheel come full circle, to see the man who had caused her illness with his churlish rejection of her begin her rehabilitation with the committal of his body to the earth.

But that would be too much too soon, far more than she could handle. In any case, her mental state was too brittle for her conduct to be predictable: he had a nightmare vision of her throwing herself like Laertes into the grave, or dissolving like Ophelia into a more permanent madness.

'Perhaps I should ring the CID at Oldford,' she said. 'It's being handled from there, you know, the investigation into Raymond's death.'

So she'd been reading everything in the papers. Well, he would have expected that; it was a natural enough curiosity. But she hadn't said anything about it to him, until now. There hadn't been much in the press, apart from routine stuff about pursuing enquiries on a wide front; reading between the lines, he had decided that the police weren't anywhere near an arrest yet. Dermot found their failure thus far eminently satisfactory.

He said firmly, 'I don't think you should do that, sis.' He hadn't used the diminutive to her in years; now it seemed to take them back to the more intimate days of their adolescence, when she was the younger sister he protected. 'I expect they'll be in touch soon enough if they want to speak to us.'

As if answering a cue, the phone in the hall shrilled at that moment. He hurried to answer it. Moira was still in the same spot when he came back, with both her hands gripping the rounded edge of the windowsill as she looked down the road. 'That was a Sergeant Hook,' he said. 'He and his superintendent will be here in an hour.'

Her generous mouth relaxed into the broad smile which had been so infrequent in these last fraught months. 'That's good, isn't it?' she said contentedly.

*   *   *

Alfred Arkwright, solicitor and commissioner for oaths, was preparing to enjoy himself. He had the legal arrangements of an eminent client to reveal, and the police here asking him for favours. And all this well before the morning coffee break.

'Do sit down, gentlemen.' Arkwright gestured towards the only two chairs in his office, as if indicating the correct seats from a choice of dozens. He was silver haired, erect, patrician, with just enough *embonpoint* beneath his waistcoat for his hands to fall comfortably upon it when he struck the pose of the frustrated barrister he saw in himself. He lifted his chin above them a little: the tightly stretched skin on his lower face positively shone with the closeness of his shave; a faint scent of pomade crept over the desk to their nostrils.

'The late Mr Raymond Keane chose to favour us with his legal requirements, as I indicated to Sergeant Hook when he rang yesterday. No doubt he thought a local firm would be appropriate for our MP, but I like to think he also recognized a modest reputation for competence which we have established over the years.' He fingered the old-fashioned cardboard file on his desk. 'Now, if you could begin by indicating to me just what it—'

'Don't piss me about, Alfred! I haven't time to go round the houses this morning,' Lambert interrupted harshly.

'But let me assure you, gentlemen, that—'

'But nothing. This is a murder enquiry. I haven't the time for your verbal diarrhoea. Or the inclination. We want the details of the will, and you know bloody well that in the circumstances we are entitled to have them.'

Arkwright caved in, his mind reeling. In the protected, deferential world he inhabited, he could not remember when he had last been spoken to so roughly. He gave them a truncated account of the provisions of the last will and testament of Raymond Keane, MP. It was a revision made only a month earlier, which always excited police interest. He had planned to deliver it with a proper sense of drama, building up the suspense, but that was all gone now.

182

There were minor financial bequests to the wife he had divorced five years earlier and to a nanny who must now be very aged. Items of furniture, silver and porcelain were left to his mother and his sister, presumably to keep them in the family which had held them for at least a century. The Gloucestershire cottage and the rest of his possessions were to pass to Miss Zoe Renwick.

There was no direct mention of Keane's business interests. Lambert said, 'What was to happen to Gloucester Electronics?'

Arkwright smiled, made ready to be ponderous, then caught Lambert's eye and thought better of it. He had always thought the superintendent rather a gentleman in a coarse calling; now it appeared that like most of his colleagues in the modern force he was bereft of the courtesies of decent conduct. 'I have a copy of the contract here,' he said, producing the document like a stage magician from beneath his desk. 'Mr Keane and his partner were kind enough to ask me to oversee the design of their partnership and I flatter myself that—'

'No buggering about, I said, Alfred. We've other people to see this morning. What are the terms of it? In the event of the decease of one partner, I mean.'

'The terms are that the entire business then passes to the other partner. It is unusual, but both men felt when they founded the firm that it was the best way to protect an infant business. Neither of them expected to die, of course: they were young men at the time. It may be that the time was approaching when a revision would have—'

'You're telling us that Christopher Hampson now takes over the whole of Gloucester Electronics, with no strings attached?'

'Exactly so. It's unusual, as I say, but by no means—'

'Right.' Lambert was already on his feet. 'We've got what we require, for the moment. If we need anything else we'll be in touch.' He was through the door, passing across the outer office where a secretary typed, before he called back over his shoulder, 'Thank you for your help!'

* * *

The old Vauxhall Senator moved quickly, more quickly than usual, towards the outskirts of the town. They overtook a bus as it moved away from the kerb, then had to stop with a screech of brakes as an elderly lady stepped late on to a zebra crossing.

Hook, who had not spoken in the five minutes since they had left Arkwright's office in the middle of Oldford, glanced sideways at the long, lined face beside him and said, 'There's no need for you to be working at all, John. Rushton and I could do this one, if you like. If you take us back to the station, I'll—'

'No. No, there's no need for that.' Lambert's eyes were fixed unblinkingly on the road ahead. Soon they passed from the small town into countryside. Bare hawthorn hedgerows flew past the windows, rooks rose in a noisy chorus as they passed beneath the leafless boughs of tall sycamores. Lambert relaxed the arms that were stiff upon the steering wheel with a deliberate effort and said, 'I wouldn't know what to do at home, Bert. I could only sit about, waiting for news and thinking of what she's going through.'

'Christine won't know anything about it. Not once they've given her the general anaesthetic.'

'No . . . But I'm better working. The day will pass much more quickly for me that way.' Lambert smiled, looked at the speedometer, and slowed a little. 'And I promise I won't let it affect me. I'll be thoroughly professional when it comes to questioning Miss Yates and her brother.'

'Of course you will; I didn't doubt it.' Hook sank a little lower in the passenger seat, enjoying the January sun and the patchwork of ploughed fields and green hills, clear and sharp in the pale morning light. 'We may need to go a little easy on Miss Yates, if she's as ill as we've been led to believe.' He was thinking of his chief's summary dismissal of Alfred Arkwright's pretensions.

'She may be perfectly all right physically,' said Lambert. 'The only other agoraphobic I've known got very overweight because she confined herself to the house and ate as much or more than she had done when she was taking much more exercise. The Yates woman may, of course, be unstable mentally. We'll need to play things by ear. But presumably we can eliminate her from suspicion fairly quickly, by the very nature of her complaint. If she can't leave the house, she can't go around garrotting people.'

'There should be more helpful illnesses like that!' said Hook. Then, wondering if flippant remarks about illness were in bad taste when his chief's wife was undergoing surgery for cancer, he added clumsily, 'If we have to have illnesses at all, that is.'

Lambert smiled. 'We shall need to check on her brother, though. If Moira was bitter when Keane elbowed her, her brother might easily have been enraged on her behalf. They must be very close, if she's living in his house because of her illness.'

'Old Arkwright said Zoe Renwick had only been put into a new will as the major beneficiary quite recently. Do you think Moira Yates was cut out at the same time?'

'Must have been, I expect. We should have asked the old phoney about that, I suppose; we'll check it out later. But I was thoroughly irritated with the old bugger by then. We've certainly found a strong motive for Zoe Renwick: she couldn't have expected to remain in the will for very long, once she'd told Keane it was all over between them. And the news of what happens to Gloucester Electronics bowled me over. Hampson never told us he stood to benefit by Keane's death in that way.'

Hook was delighted to hear these thoughts pouring out. Lambert was certainly better working, as he said. They ran into a village which was now also an outer suburb of Gloucester, and he used his street map to guide Lambert expertly to the little cul-de-sac of modern houses where Dermot Yates kept anxious watch over the progress of his sister.

The Irishman was waiting for them on the step of the house. 'Moira saw you coming,' he explained as he took them through the hall and into the comfortable, rather overheated lounge.

He sat down protectively beside his smiling sister on the settee, having pulled the curtain a little across the window to ensure that the sun was not in her eyes. Hook almost expected him to take her hand in his as they talked, but he did not go so far, though he looked at her anxiously each time she spoke in the exchanges which followed.

The smiling, confident woman who sat beside him seemed at first sight to need neither protection nor support from anyone. 'I gave the two of you those chairs,' she explained. 'Left us facing the light. That's how you like your suspects, isn't it, with the light full upon their faces?' She looked as though she was preparing to enjoy herself thoroughly over the next few minutes. Hook wondered what drugs they used for agoraphobia. Perhaps those who had lost the nerve to face people outside compensated by an excess of confidence in the home environment which was now their whole world.

There was coffee on the table. The CID men wondered who had made it, what contributions were made to this strange household by the smiling hostess and her nervous brother. Moira poured the coffee, added milk and sugar as they requested them, proffered the plate of thin lemon-flavoured biscuits. 'Dermot buys all these things,' she said, as if anxious not to take praise she did not deserve. 'He's an excellent housekeeper. He's had to be, these last few months.'

Dermot showed impatience at her relaxation into this domestic mode. 'What is it you wanted to know from us?' he said to Lambert.

'A little background, to start with,' said the superintendent. Hook thought he was deliberately slowing down, guarding against the impatience which had been his previous reaction to his own problems. 'Miss Yates: I believe you had a close relationship at one time with the late Raymond Keane.'

'I was his mistress, yes. For a period of almost two years. We were talking about getting married. But Raymond was busy making his way in parliament, and at the time there seemed no hurry.'

She was on the surface a model interview subject, articulate, unembarrassed about highly personal revelations, precise about times and circumstances. She wore a little discreetly applied make-up on her open, smiling face; her forehead furrowed a little in thought as she supplied them with the detail she thought appropriate; her very black hair was of medium length, tidily arranged in large waves about her very still head.

Hook wanted to ask the questions they could not ask, such as whether she normally wore make-up or had prepared specially for this occasion, what trouble she had taken over her appearance in the months of her illness, whether she was normally as voluble and as welcoming to strangers as she appeared to be to them. How much of this was a performance, a front put up for their benefit?

Lambert said, 'And when did this association come to an end?'

Dermot Yates began to reply, but she stilled him with an imperious lift of her hand. 'Four months and two weeks ago. You will want to know how it ended, no doubt. Well, it was Raymond who ended it. Rather abruptly, as a matter of fact. He rang me from Westminster.

I suppose that was to prepare me. He didn't say much on the phone, but I knew from that moment what was coming.'

Hook looked up from his notes: so far it had been almost like taking dictation. He said, 'Where were you living at this time, Miss Yates?'

She gave him a broad, friendly smile, as if to congratulate him on his percipience. 'I was living in Raymond's cottage, seven miles from here. It's a nice old place. But then you'll have seen it, I expect. I understand that he may have been killed there.'

'We think so, yes,' said Bert stiffly. He wished the press didn't reveal things so quickly; he had an old-fashioned feeling that the CID were not on top of the job if they were not running well ahead of the information which the crime reporters fed to their papers. But the modern idea was that you prevented speculation by revealing all that you could that did not help the criminal.

Lambert said, 'So you were at the cottage for most of the time, and Mr Keane only came down at weekends.'

'Yes. I have a flat of my own near Stroud, but that is let at present.' She looked gratefully at Dermot. It was the first time she had taken her attention from the police faces in their conversation, and it lasted only for a second. 'There were the parliamentary recesses as well, of course, which as you are no doubt

aware
are quite lengthy. Raymond and I were together for those, though not always in Gloucestershire.'

Lambert was irritated by her composure, when he should have been grateful to her for providing the answers they needed so readily, rather than retreating behind her invalid status. She gave the impression of conducting this interview on her own terms, when he was used to laying out the ground rules himself. Senior CID men are happier to see people a little disconcerted when they question them: it is an unfortunate effect their work has upon them. He said gruffly, 'So Mr Keane came down here and told you that he wanted to end your relationship.'

She smiled, taking her time, determined to stay calm now that the point she had known would come had arrived. 'Yes. That is a fair way to put it, I suppose.' Dermot's hand strayed towards hers again, and this time she allowed it to rest on top of her small, lightly clenched fist. 'He said that he didn't think it was working any more between us, that it would be better if we broke up quickly. So I moved out.'

'Forgive me. I know this must be painful to you, but I need to know when Miss Zoe Ren—'

'No. It's not painful! Why should it be, at this distance?' She almost shouted her interruption. The smile came back to her face

191

slowly, as if it was being applied by invisible hands. 'I found that Miss Renwick had been installed in my place within a week. There are always people who are only too anxious to tell you these things.'

Dermot said, 'Is this really necessary, Superintendent? We don't know and don't wish to know anything about this new woman who supplanted Moira in Keane's affections.'

'I appreciate that, Mr Yates. We merely wished to check Miss Renwick's version of the length of her association with the deceased, you see.' And to check the strength of feeling here about Keane and his new woman, thought Hook. Crafty old devil, John Lambert, and fully concentrated on the work in hand.

Yates appeared pacified by the hint that they were regarding Zoe Renwick with suspicion. He said grudgingly, 'We've no knowledge of how much she knew about Keane's previous life with Moira. Perhaps he didn't tell her how close he had been to my sister.' He glanced at her, then back at the policemen, getting no reaction in either quarter. He said a little desperately, 'She came here with him, you know, on that Sunday before Christmas.'

'It was the first time I'd seen her. And the last time I saw Raymond,' said Moira. 'She didn't say very much though, did she, Dermot?' Her smile seemed to have taken on genuine pleasure again now.

Dermot said, 'No one seemed to say a great deal that day, apart from you, sis!' For a revealing moment, his pride in her, in the way that despite her illness she had dominated the man who had treated her so badly, shone through. Then, as if to explain away this display of affection, he said, 'Moira's had a bad time of it, you know, since they split up.'

'Yes. I understand you've not felt able to leave the house very much in the last few months, Miss Yates.'

For the first time, she seemed prepared to let her brother answer for her, it was as if once her relationship with Keane had been dealt with, she had no energy for lesser questions. Dermot said, 'Moira came here in great distress when Keane threw her out.' He glanced at her apprehensively, expecting her to challenge the violence of the phrase, but she was looking listlessly at her spotless blue leather court shoes. 'She recovered physically within a day or two, but she's not been able to go out for months now.'

'Mr Yates, what do you do for a living?'

If Lambert had hoped to disconcert him by the suddenness of this switch, he did not succeed. Yates said, 'I'm a freelance writer, working from home. I write specialist books on horses, on the history of different breeds, on point-to-point and national hunt racing. I write articles for *Horse and Hound* and review books on horses, horseracing and tennis.' The answer tripped readily off his tongue, but no doubt he had offered it to the curious many times before.

'So you've been able to look after Miss Yates during her illness?'

'Yes. But she hasn't needed much attention.'

Moira looked up and smiled her secret smile again. 'He means you've been able to keep an eye on me, Dermot. Make sure I wasn't doing anything silly, as they say. But sure didn't y'always do that when we were kids?' She allowed the Irish brogue they had scarcely heard before to come through loud and strong in the last question, then laughed affectionately at him, as if there were no one else in the room.

Lambert said, 'Where were you on Christmas Eve, Mr Yates?'

Again there was no evidence that the man was shaken, though his questioner was sure that he appreciated the importance of this thrust. The Irishman ran a hand through his plentiful, unruly brown hair, considered the matter, then fixed his wide brown eyes upon the new page in Hook's notebook that had been made ready for this. 'Basically, I was here. I did a little shopping in the morning, then was here for the rest of the day.'

'You were out for a little while in the afternoon, though,' Moira reminded him, with a nervous little nudge of her arm.

If he was annoyed by the revelation, he gave

no sign of it. 'That's correct, yes. I went to the Humes' down the road, for a Christmas drink. They keep open house for a few hours on Christmas Eve, and people pop in as it suits them. Moira should have gone with me, but she didn't feel up to leaving the house, so I went on my own.'

'It wasn't just the house. I couldn't face all those people at once, when it came to it. But Dermot was very good, as usual. I don't suppose he was more than a couple of hours across there. And I could see the lights in the house and people going in and out for the whole time.'

'Well, I may have been a little longer. I was quite tipsy when I got back.' Dermot Yates grinned a little at his own expense.

Or you say you were tipsy, thought Hook as he wrote. Detection made a cynic of everyone. 'What time were you out of the house, sir?' he said, making it clear that the answer would be recorded.

'I couldn't be quite sure. I should think I went across there at about three thirty.'

'And you came back here when?'

'About six thirty. Maybe a little later.'

Lambert said, 'Well, we can always check your memory against other people's recollections, if that should be necessary. You say there were lots of other people there?'

'Yes. Though not all the time; they came and went. But I expect the Humes would have some idea of the time I was there.'

'Yes. No doubt they could help us, if it should be necessary.' Lambert was suddenly brisk, giving the impression that this was almost at an end, that only a few formalities needed to be completed. 'And on Christmas Day?'

'We were here all day, weren't we, Moira?' She nodded vigorously. 'And an old friend of ours, Gerald Sangster, was with us for most of the day. From about eleven in the morning until quite late at night. About eleven, I suppose. We had quite a lot to eat and drink. Gerry only lives a couple of miles away. Someone dropped him off in the morning, and he walked home at night, so that he wouldn't be worried about the breathalyzer.'

'Is Mr Sangster a relation?'

'No. I told you, an old friend.'

Moira said, 'It's all right, Dermot.' She patted his hand and turned her attention back to Lambert. 'I suppose he'd be better described as an old flame, Superintendent. He's provided a lot of moral support for me while I've been such a nuisance to Dermot.'

Yates opened his mouth to deny that she had been a nuisance, but Lambert switched the questioning again. 'You have a car, Mr Yates?'

'Yes.'

'Have you any objection to its being examined by a forensic team?'

'No. But I'd like to know—'

'We both have cars, Superintendent Lambert.' Moira Yates was on her feet. 'You may look at them now, if you like.' Lambert wanted to say that there was no point, that it needed the specialist resources and expertise of a forensic team, but it was too late; she was moving with the smooth grace of an athlete ahead of them, across the room, through the kitchen, to the door in the utility room which linked the house directly with the garage. She hesitated for the merest fraction in the threshold she had not crossed for months, then flung open the door and showed them a green Vauxhall Astra which was covered with a thick layer of dust. 'There she is, kind sirs! First time I've seen her since September.'

Lambert was at last able to deliver his thoughts about the necessity for scientific examination by a forensic team, but he was privately sure that this car as she said had not been on the road for months. Dermot Yates said, 'My car's on the drive. I use it almost every day. It's been on the road quite a lot in the days since Keane disappeared.'

'Nevertheless, I should like our forensic experts to have a look at it,' said Lambert. 'For purposes of elimination, you understand.'

'Whenever you like,' said Dermot. He followed them on to the drive as they left. 'I can't be sorry that Keane's gone,' he said in a low voice. He rubbed his broad nose, pulled for a moment at the square chin below it. 'Frankly, I'd like to shake the hand of whoever killed him. But you have to try to find the man who did it, of course, I understand that.'

He took his pale face back into the house. Lambert wondered what that close pair would say to each other when they were alone again. He looked at Yates's car as they passed it. It was a Vauxhall Cavalier hatchback, with the rear seats presently laid flat to provide extra storage space.

It would have accommodated a body quite easily when the wide rear door was raised.

CHAPTER SEVENTEEN

'She's come through the operation,' the sister said. She tried to make it sound fresh and bright, but it was difficult when you had said those words so many times.

In the bed, Christine Lambert looked small but very peaceful. She lay on her back with the sheet neatly drawn beneath her chin. Someone had arranged her hair in a dark-brown aureole around her face, so that it shut out the edges of the white oval and made the smooth, well-featured face seem tiny and vulnerable. Lambert saw too many dead bodies, he decided: this silent figure evoked for him the carefully prepared dead flesh of the funeral parlour.

He did not dare disturb the sheets to take a hold on his wife's hand, so he smoothed the marble brow gently with the backs of his fingers, and found it reassuringly warm. They had made her look like a nun, not a corpse, he decided; he preferred that image.

Words came to him now, when they were useless because she could not hear. He wanted to tell her that this thing would bring them closer, whatever happened. That they would be as close to each other as they had been twenty years ago, when they lost a child that was four days old, and for weeks it had bonded them as no pleasant experience could ever have done. Finding the words he thought his agnosticism had banished for ever, he prayed beside the silent bed that all might be well for its occupant.

The first part of what followed might almost have been scripted by Hollywood, except that there were no violins and there was a full two-minute gap before Christine's eyes opened slowly. They looked towards the ceiling and the high fluorescent light, registered puzzlement, then focused on her husband as he bent forward. A tiny smile came to her pale pink lips. John Lambert said, 'You're through it and doing fine. Don't try to talk.'

Suddenly, her throat and face were convulsed, and he thought in spite of his advice that she was trying to reply. Just in time, he snatched up the stainless-steel bowl from the top of the bedside locker and thrust it beneath the wobbling chin. Christine was sick, retchingly, erratically, surprisingly copiously. She sank back exhaustedly into a renewed unconsciousness. He drew away the bowl reluctantly and with great care, anxious not to spill even a drop of the foul-smelling contents upon the immaculate sheets.

Mercifully, a nurse appeared at his elbow, picked up the bowl, wiped the patient's mouth and chin expertly with a tissue. 'I expect it was just the aftermath of the anaesthetic,' said Lambert apologetically.

The nurse smiled briefly at his anxious face. 'Are you sure it wasn't something you said?' she teased.

*   *   *

Bert Hook had told Lambert he should take as long as he needed inside the hospital. Lambert had said he would not be more than half an hour.

The municipal golf course with its driving range abutted the hospital grounds. Hook could see club-heads rising and falling over the hedge at the edge of the car park. He had no doubt that if he lowered the window he would even be able to hear the oaths which seemed to accompany eighty per cent of amateur golf shots. He resisted temptation for almost a full minute. But he couldn't spend half an hour sitting in the car worrying about John and Christine in the hospital, could he? Morbid, that would be.

He slipped off his jacket and tie, stole to the boot, extracted Lambert's five-iron from his bag like a thief in the night, and made briskly for the professional's shop.

Just time for a basket of forty balls. And no one would know: he could have the club safely stowed away by the time the chief returned. Help him to think, the exercise would. Help him to apply himself to the analysis of that strange interview with Moira and Dermot Yates which they had just concluded. He put his coins into the machine and watched the balls tumble into the wire basket, then took them swiftly to the most private of the bays alongside him, looking over his shoulder guiltily like an unpractised shoplifter.

The first few attempts were as bad as he had feared. 'Sodding bloody game!' he said as he topped the first one miserably forward. Then, by way of emphasis after a further attempt which hit the mat well behind the ball, 'Sodding, bloody stupid, bastard game!' This, be it noted, from a bowler who had taken the blindness of umpires to plumb lbw's in his stride, who had even remained equable when edged through suddenly paralysed slips for four.

The trouble with this stupid game was that

201

there was no batsman to glare at with your hands on your hips. You could only be angry at yourself. Bert decided he was going to be good at that. Even on this crisp day in early January, his temperature was rising, despite his shirt sleeves. By the time he had dispatched forty balls, there might well be steam rising above his straining torso.

Then, on about his sixth attempt, something very strange happened. He scarcely felt the ball on the face of his club. There was merely a tiny tremor through his body, similar to that which had occurred on those very rare occasions when he had hit a six off the very meat of a cricket bat. He looked automatically at face level in front of him, expecting to see the ball careering away savagely to the right from the low, topped shot which seemed to be his normal product.

Then he spotted it. It soared gloriously against the pale blue heaven, became a speck, seemed to hang lazily for a moment, then descended lazily, until it hit the earth and bounced high and straight, coming to rest many yards beyond anything he had previously perpetrated. 'Bloody hell!' said Bert in astonishment. And then, more enthusiastically and appreciatively, 'BLOODY HELL!'

No subsequent shot matched that sublime effect. But there were several more which got into the air and travelled a reasonable distance. And Bert had quickly acquired one of the habits of the regular golfer. He now took that one perfect shot among forty as being his normal game.

He went back into the pro's shop trying not to look too pleased with himself. It was quiet in there. No one in the shop seemed to have observed that perfect stroke, which was a pity. But that also meant that there was no one to witness the move he planned now. He spoke quietly to the professional, who said he was sure he could accommodate him, looked in the large diary he kept beneath the counter, and made the entry which Bert requested there.

By the time Lambert returned, Bert Hook was sitting erect in the passenger's seat, with his jacket and tie resumed. The preoccupied superintendent seemed not to notice his detective sergeant's heightened colour and glow of rude health. Bert was pleased to be informed that Christine's progress was all that could be expected. He assured the chief that he had not been bored.

But superintendents are devious men. Bert, feeling his secret was secure as they drove away, knew nothing of the arrangement John Lambert had made a week previously with the professional.

*　　*　　*

Gerald Sangster was a surprise, even to men who had schooled themselves over the years to be surprised by nothing.

The passing references to him which had been made by others, by Moira and Dermot Yates, by Zoe Renwick, had led them to expect a worthy but rather pathetic figure. Old flames who flicker around the candle after they have been rejected compel sympathy, but they are often passive, inadequate figures, without wills of their own. Wimps, in the modern vernacular.

Gerald Sangster was clearly no wimp. They met him as he had suggested at his place of work. 'That way it won't matter what time you arrive,' he had told Hook on the phone. 'There is plenty I can be getting on with if you are delayed.'

He was over six feet, with the broad shoulders and the easy movement of an athlete as he rose to greet them. Tennis had never been Hook's sport. In the days of his boyhood, it had not been thought an appropriate activity for Barnardo's boys. It was Lambert who should have remembered Sangster's name from his Wimbledon days, but he had been too preoccupied with his wife's illness to think ahead as he normally did to the interviews he was to conduct. He made a note to delegate the next one to someone better suited to the exercise, almost as a punishment to himself for his negligence.

Sangster had been for a brief period the British number one in the rankings in the eighties. He might well have gone further than that, had it not been for a persistent knee injury which eventually forced his retirement. Since then he had built up a business in sports facilities and coaching. And obviously done it very successfully, from what they had already seen on their way to this large, thickly carpeted office, with its wide mahogany desk and elegant armchairs.

'Sergeant Hook said that you wished to see me in connection with the death of our late and unlamented MP. We shall not be disturbed,' he said, gesturing to two of the armchairs and coming from behind his desk to take a third one himself.

'Mr Keane was murdered, sir. We now know that. It is our job to find the man or woman who did it.' Lambert was stiffly formal, irritated already by the man's confidence, by Sangster's open acknowledgement that he welcomed the death of Raymond Keane.

'Woman? That's surely unlikely, isn't it?'

Lambert cudgelled his mind. Did this smiling figure with the piercing blue eyes and the blond eyebrows raised interrogatively above them know more of the detail of this death than an innocent man should? 'Why do you think it should be so unlikely, sir? What do you know about the way in which Mr Keane died?'

The broad shoulders shrugged, the close-curled yellow hair, receding a little now at each end of the broad forehead, shook a little from side to side. 'Only what I've seen in the papers. He died at his cottage, I read this morning. I think the word "brutal" was used about his killing. But I'm well aware that accuracy is not one of the virtues of the fourth estate. If you say it could have been a woman, I bow to your professional expertise.

'Keane was divorced five years or so ago, and I've never met his first wife. I think he preferred to pretend she'd never happened. But the woman whom he wronged most grievously has been confined to her brother's house for the last four months, as I'm sure you're aware by now.'

It was a challenge to comment on their interview earlier in the day with Moira Yates, but Lambert had no intention of rising to it. Privately, his present opinion was that the cool and efficient Zoe Renwick was a more likely candidate for murderer. She stood to gain a small fortune by this death and had refused to comment on the reasons for her rejection of Keane as a fiancé, but Sangster of course knew none of this. Lambert said, 'How well did you know the deceased, Mr Sangster?'

'I met him a few times. Once as an MP, when I was still a member of the Conservative Party. The other occasions I suppose you would call social; they were during the time when he conducted his—his association with Moira Yates.'

206

'And you didn't approve of him.'

It was a statement, but Sangster took it as an invitation to enlarge on his opinion of Keane. 'He was a liar and a cheat. The last person I would want to represent me in parliament or anywhere else. And he treated Moira abominably.'

He was suddenly breathing heavily, his earlier composure gone in an instant with the mention of Moira. Hatred and love are the strongest, and thus the most revealing, of all emotions, reflected Lambert. It might be worth keeping this man on a pitch where he was vulnerable. 'How long have you known Miss Yates, Mr Sangster?'

He half expected to be told this was private and irrelevant, as Moira Yates herself had indicated firmly to him when he had tried to explore the relationship earlier in the day. Instead, Sangster was only too anxious to talk. 'I've known Moira for twenty years. Since we were juniors together at Wimbledon.'

'Miss Yates played there?' He hadn't realized that she had reached such standards.

'She was the best woman player ever to come out of Ireland, in my opinion. And Moira can be very determined. She's capable of anything, if she puts her mind to it. There's no knowing what heights she might have reached, if she had chosen to push her talent as far as it would go.'

'But she didn't?'

'No. I often wonder if she regrets that, now. But whenever I try to ask her about it, she refuses to tell me. She came from an older tradition: I suppose you might call it the amateur tradition. Her family had money in Ireland, and she was good at all sports. Perhaps they came too easily to her. She qualified as a nurse in a psychiatric hospital— said she needed to do something worthwhile in life.'

'So you didn't see as much of her then as when you were both playing serious tennis?'

Sangster looked at his questioner sharply, as if he suspected some ulterior motive in this, some prying into that period of his life when he felt that he had lost Moira. 'No. She played when she could, and she was still astonishingly good. Still capable of upsetting the very best, when the mood was upon her.' His pride in that flowing, laughing girl shone in his eyes for a moment. 'But of course she couldn't play outside this country, and she had to let her ranking go. That didn't worry her. She said she played for enjoyment, and she wanted to keep all of her sports going. She's a wonderful horsewoman, you know.'

'So I believe.'

'She doesn't ride to hounds, never has done. Upsets the county set round here, that does.' But plainly not Gerald Sangster, who approved of her views on blood sports; but then he probably approved of everything the divine Moira did. Except her liaison with Raymond Keane.

'So Miss Yates didn't develop her full potential in tennis.'

'She couldn't. You have to specialize nowadays, to reach the very top levels in any sport. She chose not to, that's all.'

He was quick to defend her, even in this. Most people would have called it lack of dedication, this failure to exploit a special talent of this magnitude. Lambert said, 'Why did Mr Keane and Miss Yates decide to split up, Mr Sangster?'

It was an abrupt switch, and it caught him off guard. With a little forethought, a modicum of his normal coolness, he would have told them brusquely that it was none of their business, perhaps none of his. Instead, his desire to defend Moira overrode his judgement and he rushed to her defence. 'They didn't "decide to split up" as you describe it. Nothing so civilized. He found this new blonde woman, and promptly told Moira that her services were no longer required.'

'He was as abrupt as that?'

'He just told her to get out. Ask Moira!'

'Oh, we have, Mr Sangster.'

Sangster looked fiercely at Lambert, then snarled, 'Then why the hell are you asking me about it?'

'I'm exploring your relationship with a man who is now a murder victim. It's my job, you see.'

'You're accusing me of killing him now, are you?' Sangster laughed harshly. He seemed to get a bitter amusement from the notion. 'Well, he did enough to ruin my life whilst he was alive; why should he stop now? Shouldn't you remind me of my rights to have a lawyer present?'

'No. You are helping the police with their enquiries, in a voluntary capacity. Of course, if you think that you need to have a legal representative present, you are perfectly entitled to call for one.' Lambert held the man's gaze as the fierce blue eyes flashed angrily. He enjoyed testing wills against a strong-minded opponent.

'And if I choose to terminate this interview now? To cease helping you in this voluntary capacity?'

'You would be within your rights. We should draw our own conclusions about your refusal to help an investigation into the most serious of all crimes, of course.'

Gerald Sangster stared at him for a moment, his fine nose seeming to grow thinner for a moment with the fierceness of his breathing. Then he smiled; the broad mouth relaxed, taking defeat as sportingly as he had taken it across the net all those years ago. But this time it was a conscious effort, a policy move rather than a spontaneous reaction.

Gerald Sangster realized suddenly how few

people stood up to him nowadays; in the workings of a successful business empire, most people found it politic to pretend that the boss knew best, even when they had reservations. He said, 'You're right. You have a job to do, whatever my personal feelings might be about Keane. What do you want to know?'

Lambert looked at Hook, who said, 'Where did you spend Christmas Day, Mr Sangster?'

'With Moira and her brother. At Dermot's house. I was there from about eleven in the morning until nearly midnight, I think. But they must have told you this.'

He was accusing Lambert, and it was the superintendent who smiled grimly and gave him his answer, 'Indeed. At least, they have given us their recollections of what happened on that day. People sometimes tell us different things, and the discrepancies are always interesting to us, as I'm sure you would understand.'

They looked at each other, chins jutting a little in the air. Then Sangster said, 'It was a strange Christmas Day. With Moira being ill, I mean. I think both Dermot and I were watching her all day, trying not to make her condition worse. But she was all right, more cheerful and animated than she'd been for a while. I didn't know whether she was making a special effort for the day, or was genuinely feeling better. We all had quite a lot to eat, I think. And to drink. Well, I certainly did. I knew I was going to walk home at the end of the day, so I wasn't worried about the breathalyzer.'

It was the second time that information had been volunteered to them in three hours, thought Lambert. Was the idea to convince them that neither Dermot Yates nor Sangster was capable of driving on Christmas night? If his calculations about the ice on that pond were right, it would have been around that time that the body was committed to the water. A conspiracy between those two was quite likely; or maybe between all three, if Moira was included. He said, 'Didn't you think of getting a taxi to take you home at the end of the day?'

Sangster smiled. 'I could have afforded it, you mean? Of course I could, but I might have had to wait a long time for one, on Christmas night. And I haven't entirely lost the use of my legs, you know, as I've translated from athlete to businessman. I enjoyed the walk, as a matter of fact. It's only a couple of miles, and it was a fine frosty night, with a full moon. It helped me to sober up a little.'

'Do you live alone, Mr Sangster?'

'Yes. I have a flat in Old Park.' It was the most luxurious of the many conversions of old houses around Gloucester.

'Is there a porter there?'

'No. There are only four flats in all. It doesn't warrant a porter.' He looked Lambert evenly in the eye, and the superintendent was sure that he followed his thoughts: there was no one able to vouch for his movements, to say whether he had driven off into the night when he came home from his day with the Yateses.

'What car do you drive, Mr Sangster?'

'A Mercedes 300 SE. Dark-red metallic.'

'You drove this car on Christmas Eve?'

For a moment Sangster was shaken, as if he feared the car had been spotted in some incriminating place. Then he said levelly, 'Yes. Do you want to know my movements on that day?'

'Yes. We are asking everyone we speak to about this death to recall Christmas Eve and Christmas Day.'

'I spent most of the day here.'

'On a Saturday?'

He smiled, happy for the first time to have them a little on the back foot. 'It's our busiest day. We have four indoor tennis courts here and four squash courts. They're normally booked from eight in the morning until ten at night.'

'And you were there until then?'

'No. It was Christmas Eve, and even the fanatics among our clients weren't going to use the courts on that evening—we knew from our bookings, you see. We shut at four o'clock on that day. As a matter of fact, there was only one squash court in use in the last hour. I sent the staff away at half past three and shut the place up myself at four.'

'And where did you spend the rest of the day?'

'I spent most of the evening in my neighbour's flat. He had people in for drinks. There would be eight people who could account for my presence there, if you should find that necessary.' He smiled at Hook as he watched the sergeant write the facts busily in his notes. He was coolly controlled again, now that they had left the subject of Moira Yates.

'Times, please,' said Lambert evenly.

The wide, well-formed lips pursed a moment, affecting to give due consideration to a question Lambert was sure had already been anticipated. 'About eight to eleven p.m.'

Lambert left the obvious question to Hook, and there was a pause until the DS had completed his record of these times and looked up at Sangster's expectant face. 'We shall need an account of your movements between four and eight that evening, then, sir.'

Sangster looked from one to the other of the CID men's faces, as if he hoped to discover something there. He must have expected this obvious request, but perhaps he was wondering how precise they were now able to be about the time of this murder. Hook, like Lambert, would have been happy enough to imply that they knew the time of Keane's death to the minute. Police omniscience is a useful idea to spread among the public: it makes people nervous about what they conceal.

Eventually Sangster said, 'I ran over to look at the new centre we've just opened at Stroud. The two indoor tennis courts are already in use, but the builders are still working on the squash complex and the bar/lounge area. With the place empty, it was a good opportunity for me to check on the progress of their work. I made myself a sandwich and a coffee over there, as a matter of fact. Must have spent a good hour in the place.'

'With no observer to record your presence,' said Lambert drily.

'No. Innocent people don't consider it necessary to have their every move witnessed, you see.' Despite his smile, he was a little rattled.

'Nor do the guilty, sir. Where did you go after you'd been to Stroud?'

'Back to my own flat. I had a shower and changed before I went down for a drink with my neighbour. Without witnesses, surprisingly enough.'

'Do you smoke, Mr Sangster?'

'No, I don't. I never have done.'

No more than you drink, thought Lambert. 'Do you have a duffle coat?'

'I might have, somewhere at the back of a wardrobe. If I still have it, I haven't worn it for years.'

'We may ask you to show it to us, in due

215

course, nevertheless. Do you have a key to Mr Keane's cottage?'

'No. Why the hell should I? I've never been there.'

But he could have got hold of a key easily enough from his adored Miss Yates, thought Lambert grimly; in all probability she still had one. They checked on his movements on Boxing Day, though Lambert was increasingly convinced that the thirty-six hours from around three thirty on December 24th were the important ones. They left him with the usual injunction to let Oldford CID know if he proposed to travel outside the area.

'A cool customer,' said Hook as they drove away.

'Except where Moira Yates is concerned. He'd kill for her, if she asked him.'

Back in his office, Gerald Sangster watched the old Senator drive carefully off his premises, then dialled the number he knew so well. 'Dermot? They've just gone . . . No, I don't think so. Listen, did you tell them I drank a lot on Christmas Day? . . . Good . . . Yes, they're going to have their forensic team look at my car, too. I think they don't know anything, really. Long may it remain that way, I say!'

CHAPTER EIGHTEEN

'How is Mrs Lambert, sir?' Chris Rushton was proud that he remembered to ask this as soon as he saw the super. It might seem a small thing, but there were those in the CID division who thought of him as not just single-minded but unhealthily blinkered about his work. He'd remembered to get the right question in first today.

'She's doing as well as can be expected, I think they say, Chris. Or used to say. Nowadays they say "comfortable", when usually the patient is anything but.'

'I can bring you up to date on the various lines of enquiry fairly quickly, if you like, sir.' With his social obligations fulfilled, Rushton was positively eager to return to the job, and it showed. He was like a puppy quivering with a stick in front of its master.

'That's what we're here for,' said Lambert sardonically.

'Forensic have confirmed what you thought about the dumping of the body. There were ten degrees of frost at six a.m. on Boxing Day. They say it's "highly probable" that the pond would have been too highly frozen by Boxing Day morning for anyone to dump a body without breaking the ice. And there was no sign of that.'

'Any more sightings of Keane?'

'No. The same observant soul who told us about the van which had been parked in the woods down the road from the cottage thinks she saw Keane's Jaguar at his cottage at about seven on Christmas Eve, but of course he could have been dead or alive at that time. She can't remember whether there were any lights visible in the cottage.'

'So what time do we think Keane got there on Christmas Eve?'

'Assuming he didn't hurry after leaving his mother's house, we think probably four to four thirty. It's about forty miles, most of it on winding B roads or unclassified lanes.'

'And have forensic or the postmortem report offered any further thoughts about how long the body lay before it was moved?'

'They say that judging by the lividity on the back, buttocks and calves, it was probably at least a day. But the body had been in the water for a week: they warn that an expert witness called by the defence could soon emphasize that this was nothing more than an opinion.' Rushton as usual had the key facts in his mind. He had not so far referred to the computer, where this was but a tiny fraction of what he had stored over the last few days.

'Let's accept for the moment that the corpse lay at the cottage or somewhere else for at least a day. If we assume that it was dumped some time during the night of twenty-fifth to

218

twenty-sixth December, that means Keane was killed on the night of twenty-fourth to twenty-fifth. In all probability, within say six hours after his arrival.'

With a corpse not discovered until ten days after death, it was a more accurate pinpointing of the time of death than they could have expected. But Rushton now put it in context. 'Nothing else has turned up from the SOC team's findings around that pond. That's the other aspect of that week of hard frost: it has helped to pinpoint the time he was dumped, but it also ensured that there was no easy trace of the culprit. There isn't a tyre mark or a footprint that has any relevance; the few marks left there have been eliminated as postdating the find.'

'Nothing from the fag-end?'

'Nothing useful. No chance of DNA material from it, apparently. You can test bones after hundreds of years, but any saliva traces have disappeared from this with the damp and the frost. And they can't date the cork tip, which is really all there is left. Sometime during the last six months is all they'll say. It's a Benson and Hedges Silk Cut, which is apparently one of the most popular brands.'

Lambert nodded philosophically. In the 'golden age' detective stories which Burgess the pathologist favoured, cigarettes were usually from some exotic Turkish or French brand which immediately identified the smoker. 'Among those close to the deceased, there seems so far to be only one regular smoker. Christopher Hampson.'

Rushton made a note on his pad. He would feed that extra fact about the late Raymond Keane's partner into the appropriate computer file as soon as he was left alone. He said, 'There wasn't much at Keane's cottage. Some fibres from a woollen of some sort. Some blonde hairs, in bedroom and lounge. Both belonging to Zoe Renwick: she allowed us to check. But you'd expect to find those. She's been there regularly over the last few months. Unfortunately, Keane had a woman who went in to clean each Thursday. She went in on the Thursday between Christmas and New Year, the twenty-ninth December. As it seemed to her that Keane hadn't been there since the previous Thursday, she vacuumed the place right through.'

And possibly neatly removed vital evidence. Cleanliness was next to vandalism, not godliness, as far as Scene-of-Crime teams were concerned. Thank goodness her zeal hadn't extended to that pantry where the SOC team had found the fibres from Keane's sweater. Lambert said, 'So there was no evidence of Keane's being there on Christmas Eve? No crockery in the sink, nor unpacking in the bedroom?'

'Nothing that the cleaning lady noticed.

There was a wardrobe full of clothes that he obviously kept there. A holdall was still in his Jaguar when we checked it. Incidentally, forensic are certain that the body wasn't moved in his own car.'

So everything pointed to the fact that he hadn't been in the house very long. And Burgess's notes from the postmortem confirmed that the stomach contents showed well-digested food: probably the lunch eaten at his mother's. When Keane had been garrotted in that pantry off the kitchen, he had almost certainly not been in the house for very long. It looked more and more as if his murderer had been waiting for him to come into the cottage.

Lambert said, 'Anything interesting from forensic yet on the other cars?'

'Nothing positive.' Again DI Rushton did not need to flash up the information on his screen; he had anticipated Lambert's questions, like the experienced CID man he was. 'Christopher Hampson's Granada Estate is the ideal car for transporting corpses; perhaps Ford might think of making an advertising feature of that, in the States.'

A rare flash of humour, a glimpse of that younger and happier Rushton who was now almost lost, even to himself. He went on quickly, as if he feared being rebuked for his frivolity, 'But there was nothing to connect the car with Keane's body. Mind you, Hampson had an old blanket spread over the extensive boot area. He's a family man, of course. He says he transports a lot of kids and two dogs over short distances, and there was plenty of mud and hair on the blanket to support that story. But nothing helpful to us. Of course, he could simply have covered the floor with a different blanket, and disposed of it afterwards. The murderer had at least twenty-four hours to plan the disposal of the corpse, after he'd done the deed.

'Forensic have just phoned in some more findings. They've been over to the Yates household since you were there this morning. Moira Yates's car hasn't been moved from the garage for at least three months: they can tell that by the state of the tyres, apparently. Dermot Yates's hatchback is more interesting, but only in a negative way. He had it completely valeted between Christmas and New Year. It's spotless inside and thus completely useless to us, the scientific boys say. They're taking it in to examine it, but they don't expect to find anything significant.'

'Does Yates usually have his car cleaned so thoroughly?'

'Not known. He says it was due for its first MOT by the beginning of the year, so he put it in for a full service and thought he might as well have the car valeted at the same time. Apparently the garage offers a deal combining the two and an MOT and he thought he was behaving as a responsible citizen should.'

Yates hadn't seemed to Lambert the sort of man to have his car valeted, but these special offers could lead to out-of-character decisions, as he knew from his own disastrous impulse buying in supermarkets. 'Get a search done on all the local car-hire firms, will you? It's unlikely they'd be open for hiring on Christmas Day, but this looks like a crime planned well in advance.'

Rushton nodded, a little irritated with himself for not having offered the suggestion, or even implemented it off his own initiative. A hire vehicle was the obvious way to protect oneself against forensic investigation. He said, 'There's one extra piece of information for you on vehicles. We've identified the owner of that van with the damaged door which was seen so often near Keane's cottage in the weeks before his death. It was only a matter of time, with a vehicle as distinctive as that.'

Lambert noted that with a proper sense of drama Rushton had left the most important finding until the last, feeding in before it the evidence of his diligence in routine matters. But a man tied to a desk deserved to be indulged, at times like this. He said patiently, 'And who is it?'

'The same man who had been pestering Keane for the last year at the Commons and in his constituency surgeries. Joseph Walsh.'

*   *   *

223

The psychiatrist looked a little mad. He had hair as unruly as a clown's, hands which refused to stay still for longer than a second and eyes which grew and declined according to the angle of the thick-lensed spectacles which sat precariously on the end of his flattened nose. But he spoke with reassuring sanity about the condition which affected Moira Yates.

'Three times as common in women as men. The essential problem is a fear of something awful happening. Panic attacks occur when sufferers feel that something awful is about to happen to them—usually asphyxia, heart attack or some other means of dying. They may be aware, especially if they're long-term sufferers, that these disasters aren't likely to happen. But whilst they accept that intellectually, fear will override logic—hence the condition.'

'Could it be brought on by some disastrous occurrence in the life of the patient?'

'Yes. In practice, it usually is. A death of someone close, a serious accident at work or on the road, a broken love affair. These things make people subject to irrational fears. They feel that there is now no reason why one unpredictable disaster should not be followed by another one. The mind may react to such fears in a variety of ways. In the case of agoraphobics, it is a retreat into environments

224

which are familiar. Sometimes they are all right in their own cars, as if they are travelling in a capsule which is part of their homes. In extreme cases, they feel unable to leave their houses; occasionally they even confine themselves to one or two rooms in their homes.'

'Is it treatable with drugs?'

The specialist's uncoordinated hands fluttered in front of him like escaping pigeons. 'Drugs are certainly resorted to. Self-prescribed alcohol is one of the things doctors need to watch out for: people confining themselves to their homes have their own hideaways for bottles, and can become dependent without anyone realizing it until it's too late. The most commonly prescribed drugs would be benzodiazepines, like diazepam— our old friend valium.'

'And could an effect of such drugs be a kind of heightened awareness, a sort of unnatural confidence in social exchanges?' Lambert was thinking of the strangely brilliant Moira Yates and the way she had seemed to be positively enjoying their exchanges. Zoe Renwick had described what seemed to be a similar effect when she had spoken of her visit to the house with Keane on December 18th.

'Certainly. Indeed, the condition itself can sometimes lead to short-term effects like that. When panic threatens, it brings an excess of adrenaline surging into the system. That can bang about and have all kinds of effects; the commonest are dizziness and physical sickness, but a surface confidence couldn't be ruled out as an effect. But valium could certainly lead to a brilliant but artificial performance: artificial in the sense that it is drug related. Was the subject warned in advance of these meetings?'

'Yes. In both cases, I think.'

'Then if she was anxious, she probably took medication immediately before these meetings. Even overdosed mildly, perhaps, if she perceived them as important or threatening. These things are not always predictable, of course. But what you have postulated to me so far is a classic case of agoraphobia.'

'One more query, then you're rid of me. Would someone suffering from agoraphobia be able to use drugs to build up to a supreme effort to overcome the condition? For a special occasion. Let's say to go into the town on her own after not leaving the house for months.'

'No. Almost certainly not, in my experience. If the drug was as effective as that, there would hardly be a problem in the first place, would there?' The psychiatrist, who had been addressing the ceiling as an aid to thought, switched his wild eyes back to Lambert's face disconcertingly. 'If the agoraphobia was as intense as you describe, she wouldn't get further than the garden gate. She'd be looking for support, for a start. And even then she

226

wouldn't be able to do it, unless she was so drugged as to be almost insensible.'

In which condition, thought Lambert, Moira Yates would certainly not have been capable of the violent physical action involved in the murder of Raymond Keane.

CHAPTER NINETEEN

Joe Walsh was talking to his daughter. An observer would have seen only a man in scruffy garb muttering over a headstone, but Joe knew what he was about.

'The police haven't been to see me yet, but they will, Debbie. But don't worry, they won't be able to do anything to me. Lack of evidence, they call it. You remember that, don't you? Lack of evidence. That's what Keane said. Well, he's dead now. And they won't get me for it, because of lack of evidence.'

He laughed a little, listened for a while to her reply, looked round the deserted cemetery, thrust his cold hands deep into the thick woollen pockets of his duffle coat. 'I went to the inquest, you know. But don't worry, I sat at the back. No one saw me. Murder by person or persons unknown, they said. Well, we could have told them that, couldn't we? Raymond High-and-Mighty Keane's going to have a burial, not a cremation. Over at the family vault, near Chipping Sodbury. Next Tuesday, it is. I might go and see him put into the earth. Finish the thing off.'

He stood up, looked round again at the rows of stones, the mostly neglected graves. 'Bit warmer today. No frost now. I might be able to bring you a little plant tomorrow. Brighten the place up a bit. 'Bye, Debs.' He walked briskly away from the grave, with its fading flowers beneath the glass dome, waved cheerfully from the gate, and got into the van with the big patch of brown on the door.

He felt better than he had for months. Hungry, even. He pulled into the car park at Sainsbury's and walked into the brightly lit interior, cringing a little at the prospect of moving among people, though to most eyes the store was quiet with an early-afternoon hiatus. In another hour, the place would be crowded with young mothers and their clamorous children, newly released from school. But to Joe Walsh, unused for so long to any form of contact, this seemed a very public place.

He filled his basket quickly, impulsively, snatching at whatever caught his eye on the brightly lit shelves. Cereals, tins, eggs, milk, bread, potatoes. He had no list and there was nothing systematic about his selection. He was a curious, scarecrow figure, even to the checkout girl, who had trained herself to look at purchases rather than purchasers. But he produced two new ten-pound notes to pay, which was all that really concerned her. She plucked the notes fastidiously from his dirty fingers, provided him with plastic bags as his goods accumulated beyond the till, and turned a professionally blank face to the next customer.

Joe Walsh found he was beginning to notice things again. True, he hardly registered the streets of terraced houses and allotments between the store and his council house. But when he turned the van between the drunken gates of his council house, he saw the uneven row of sprouts in the garden at the side, the grey-green tufts of January grass on the lawn that should have been mown in the summer and autumn, the peeling light-blue paint on the front door as he inserted his key. Things to do. He had not thought of things to do for a long time now.

As he turned his key and pushed the door open, the thought that he was going to be able to get on with his life again entered his mind for the first time. Well, soon, anyway. Once Raymond Keane, MP, had been safely committed to the ground.

*　　　*　　　*

Lambert felt very tired when he got into the house. It felt strangely empty without

Christine there. He often popped in during the day, when his wife was out at the secondary school where she taught, but the place had never then seemed as deserted as it did now.

He rang the hospital, got the news that Christine was resting comfortably, sent the message that he would be in that night. Then he checked his answerphone. There were three messages from friends of Christine, showing their concern, hoping things had gone well, promising visits when the time was appropriate. He would have to ring them back in due course. Or perhaps he would give that job to Jacqueline, when she called that evening as she had promised. Nothing more important than effective delegation, they told you at all the police management courses.

Then came a call which cheered him up, even in his fatigue. It was the pro at the municipal golf course, grassing on Bert Hook, as he had agreed to do. 'Your sergeant popped in here whilst you were in the hospital. Hit a basket of balls.'

'I thought he might. I'd let him know my clubs were in the back. He didn't say anything when I came back, though, crafty old bugger.'

'And there's more. He's booked a lesson with me.'

If the professional had had any scruples about informing on a detective sergeant, his reservations were surely removed by the delighted superintendent's laughter with which this revelation was greeted.

*   *   *

DI Rushton parked the police car immediately behind the battered van in the drive of Walsh's council house. Off the road was best, in an area like this. Though the street looked respectable enough at the moment in the twilight, there was plenty of unemployment on the estate, and the devil found work for idle young hands.

The inspector took in the stuccoed walls with their small cracks, the rotting windows with their grubby curtains, the neglected garden, the blue front door badly in need of a coat of paint. He had visited hundreds of houses like this in his thirteen years in the police force. Too many for the dinginess of this one to depress him now; coming armed with what he knew, he scented a result here. He was surprised the super had let him do this one. But Detective Superintendent Lambert, whatever else he might be, was never predictable, as far as Chris Rushton was concerned.

He paused for a moment by the van, looking with satisfaction at the big brown patch on the driver's door, testing the lock on the back doors. He would like to have examined the vehicle more closely, but you never knew what eyes were watching from within houses like this. He might bring Walsh out to open it for him, in due course.

He rapped hard on the door. It opened within two seconds. 'Mr Joseph Walsh?'

The narrowed brown eyes took in the tall figure in the grey suit, the old-young, arrogant face, the police car in the drive, blocking in his van, as though to imprison him. 'Come inside.'

Rushton followed him. He had been prepared for more resistance, had been ready to thrust his way in, to begin with a burst of aggression. It was almost a disappointment when these things were unnecessary.

There was a scratched oak table, upright chairs covered with vinyl, a threadbare Indian carpet from which the design had all but gone, a three-piece suite whose draylon had long succumbed to grease and dirt. The television set had a film of dust over its face. The tiled fireplace within a wooden fender was occupied by a two-bar electric fire which glowed dully; the only object in the room which seemed to be polished and shining was the crucifix on the wall above it. After the cold in the hall, the room was unpleasantly hot.

'Sit down, won't you?' said Walsh, and Rushton had again the feeling that his visit was almost welcome. Perhaps the man was at the end of his tether, was waiting to confess. Confession always brought a kind of relief. That was why it was such a pillar of the faith in which Christopher Rushton had been brought up; to which it appeared that Joseph Walsh might still be committed.

Rushton sat in one of the armchairs. He had been in much worse places than this. His experienced eye told him this was neglect, not real squalor. Not yet, anyway. There was no smell, no expensive damage to the property. Nothing malicious. The place had just been let go. Like its occupant. 'You live here alone, Mr Walsh?'

'Yes. Now I do. For the last year.'

'Since your daughter died.' Rushton had done his homework, as always.

'Since she was killed by a drunken soldier, yes. Killed by a man who got away with murder.'

'Not murder, Joe. It would have been manslaughter, even if we'd been able to make it stick.'

'He hit her with a car when she was riding home. Debbie never had a chance. Killed her in the gutter. Never even stopped. I call that murder.'

She had died on the way to hospital, in fact. And it seemed likely that the vehicle had stopped briefly, a hundred yards beyond the point of the impact. But there was no way Rushton was going to get involved in the detail of an old tragedy which had not even been his concern. He said, 'I might well feel the same, in your place. Nevertheless—'

'Have you a daughter?' The eyes blazed at

him from beneath the lank hair; the listless figure was almost on its feet, transformed by the passion which had driven out all else for a year.

'I have as a matter of fact, yes, Joe.' Rushton was relieved to be able to deflate the man. No need to tell him that she was only four, that he scarcely saw her now, since the divorce, that her absence gnawed at him as harshly as this man's tragedy affected him, even if the loss was different.

'You'll know what it feels like, if you ever lose her.' Walsh sank sullenly back into his chair, and Rushton knew suddenly that he was right: his own loss was as nothing compared with the devastating, final severance of death.

He said, 'You've no wife, Joe?'

'Not for twenty years and more. She walked out with her fancy man. Left Debs and me on our own. I brought her up myself, you know.' His pride was as manifest as if the smiling girl in the photograph above the television was standing beside him.

As Rushton felt the bond strengthening between hunter and hunted, he reminded himself that he might well be talking to a murderer. 'It wasn't CID that investigated the case. It was traffic division that was involved, Joe. And they did all they could. It was CPS who wouldn't bring a case.'

'CPS?'

'The Crown Prosecution Service. It's they

who make the ultimate decision about whether these things come to court, you know. The lawyers.'

Often you could get sympathy by reviling the lawyers, building up a momentary alliance between questioner and questioned in a mutual frustration against the stupidity of the law and the pusillanimity of lawyers. But Walsh waved the idea angrily aside. 'It wasn't you lot. It wasn't even the bloody lawyers. The army posted the bastard to Northern Ireland, so that we couldn't get at him.'

Rushton shrugged. 'Perhaps. Insufficient evidence, they said. That's what the CPS always come up with when they won't bring a case.' He picked up the newspaper from the edge of the table, looked at the rectangle of print which was heavily outlined in blue ballpen. It gave the details of the forthcoming funeral service for the Right Honourable Raymond Arthur Keane, MP for Gloucestershire West.

Walsh was regarding him steadily when he looked back at him. Rushton noticed for the first time the green of a nearly healed bruise on the right of his forehead. He folded his arms across his chest, oblivious or uncaring about the holes he revealed in the sleeves of his grubby sweater. 'That bastard stopped me getting justice,' he said, 'and now he's got justice himself!'

'How so, Mr Walsh?' Rushton was

deliberately cool, ready to provoke the anger which might be revealing.

'You know that! Or you should do. He could have got that corporal returned from Ireland for more questioning, got him to face charges. I've found a lad who was drinking with him that night, who was a passenger in the car behind him. We'd have had him, if only you could have questioned him again. But my MP wouldn't help. My representative in parliament didn't give a damn for justice for my Debbie. We were only little people, you see. Raymond bloody Keane had nothing to gain from helping the likes of us!'

Walsh was almost in tears with the pity and the fury of it. He had lived this many times in the last year, but over the last few months, as people had got bored with his anger, he had not had many chances to voice his fury. Now it was pouring out, whatever the danger it might bring to the speaker.

Rushton wasn't going to get involved in the rights and wrongs of these wild claims. The important thing was that Walsh felt like this, that his emotions were strong enough to drive him beyond the counsels of reason. Rushton said quietly, 'So you killed him, Joe. Brought your own brand of justice to him.'

For a moment, he thought Walsh was going to claim the murder, to glory in his guilt and his revenge. It flashed through his mind that he might go back to the station with a murderer under arrest, a prize to display to a superintendent who had floundered uselessly among the other people who had surrounded the dead man. Then Joe Walsh said, 'No. At first I wished I had. But I'd have been locked up then, wouldn't I? It's much better this way, for Debs and me.'

For a moment, Rushton felt again a strange kinship with the tattered, defiant figure who sat so close to him. This man was a loner too, as he had been himself for nearly two years now. This was a warning of what loners might be reduced to, when obsession preyed on solitude. It didn't need much, to tip a man over the edge, when he lived alone.

Then the work Rushton did, the work he was good at, reasserted itself. He said, 'You were seen there, Joe. At his house, I mean. In your van. It's quite distinctive, you see.'

' 'Course I was. I was watching our Mr Keane, wasn't I? I might well have had a go at him. In time. When I could choose the moment. But some other bloke saved me the trouble, didn't he? Well, good for him, I say!'

'Come off it, Joe! Your van was seen near the house several times, including probably the day of the murder itself. And you want us to believe you had nothing to do with it?'

He had chanced his arm, hoping for a slip which would be revealing while Walsh was still excited. He had made no revelation yet of the police thinking on the time when Keane had been killed. If Walsh denied his presence at the scene on Christmas Eve, it would show that he knew that time. For a moment, Rushton thought the ploy was going to be successful, for Walsh almost rushed into a denial.

Then he shut his mouth firmly, as though trapping within it the spider which had almost spun his downfall. 'I don't deny I was watching the house in the weeks before this happened. I don't deny that I wanted him dead. But you can't prove I killed him. Lack of evidence, you see! Just like it was with my Debs!'

He clasped his thin arms across his wiry body, allowing his grimy fingers to creep round his shoulders, and Rushton thought for a moment that he was going to laugh in his face. The DI said stiffly, 'It's our job to get evidence, Mr Walsh, and we shall do that. We shall arrest the man or woman who killed your MP in due course. You said a moment ago that it was a man. Had you any reason for that view?'

Walsh looked puzzled. Then he gave a small, crooked smile and turned his palms marginally upwards. Perhaps he thought he was off the hook, that his assurances were being accepted. Well, he'd find out differently in a few minutes, thought Rushton grimly: you didn't escape investigation as easily as that. Walsh said, 'I just thought it had to be a man, that's all, a crime like that. He was strangled with a cord or a wire, wasn't he? Don't see a woman doing that.'

Privately, Rushton didn't see it either. But neither he nor Walsh should be generalizing about what they still thought of as the weaker sex: hadn't they both failed to keep their wives? Hadn't those wives both shown a ruthlessness in leaving that had been wholly unexpected? He growled, 'You'd be surprised, Joe, what we see women getting up to, these days. So why were you watching Mr Keane?'

If he thought the sudden switch would catch his man out, he was disappointed. Walsh looked with narrowed eyes at the dull red element of the electric fire, scratched his stubbled chin, and said, 'We're off the record now, aren't we? I'm not going to put this in a statement. But I was going to kill him, when I got the opportunity. I owed it to Debbie, you see. But I don't think I'd ever have got round to doing it. I can see that, now that it's happened.'

'Very convenient, I'm sure. Where were you on Christmas Eve, Joe?'

Caution dropped like a curtain over Walsh's face. He had known this would come, had rehearsed it often in the last two days. 'Here, most of the time. I did have a run out in the van.'

'Which took you to Mr Keane's cottage, no doubt.'

'I did have a look round there, yes. I was

239

expecting him down for Christmas, you see. With that blonde he'd been brandishing for the last four months. I'd watched him say goodbye to her on the previous Sunday night. I was close enough to hear what they were saying, you know.'

There was something chilling about his pride in his cleverness, even to a policeman. And something quite sinister about the image of this ragged, unbalanced figure, motionless beneath the firs opposite Keane's cottage, watching his every move, listening to his cheerful goodbyes and his plans for the following week. Rushton said, 'What you heard enabled you to be waiting for him on Christmas Eve, didn't it, Joe? It'll be easier in the long run for you to tell me everything now, you know.'

'You won't get me for it, Mr Rushton. Lack of evidence, you know. Can't proceed any further for lack of evidence.' He rocked to and fro on his chair, repeating the phrases which had given him such pain over the last four years, finding them now exquisitely comforting.

'We shall need to examine your vehicle. In detail!' snapped Rushton. He delivered the last phrase waspishly, but was aware of his peevish futility as he did so.

Walsh seemed aware of that also. 'Come and look now, then!' he said, and he was on his feet and through the door, before the DI could stop him, could tell him that this was a job for the forensic team. Rushton followed him through the open front door. Perhaps even now he could pick up something from the van which would clinch the guilt of this manic little figure and give him his capture.

Rushton looked as he was bidden at the driver's and passenger's seats. He didn't expect to see anything there, and his inspection was cursory; he did not even put his head inside the vehicle. 'Open the back doors, please,' he ordered.

Walsh had a crooked, knowing smile, but he said nothing as he flung open the twin doors at the rear of the battered vehicle, like a stage magician revealing an empty cabinet.

Rushton was prepared for a slightly musty smell of damp winter van; it would have been too much to expect any vestiges of the sweet-sour smell of death from the day-old body that might have lain here. What he was not prepared for from this man and his vehicle was the overwhelming smell of cleanliness. The odour of bleach and disinfectant was so strong that he recoiled from it physically, as if he had been struck in the face by some invisible adversary.

When he turned round, he found Walsh grinning at him, so widely that he could see for the first time how uneven and yellow his teeth were. 'Cleaned it out on Monday, didn't I? Cleaned it out good and proper.' He seemed to think this was a tremendous joke.

'Why, Joe?'

The skinny shoulders shrugged elaborately. 'Ponged a bit. Carried some boxes of hen manure, hadn't I? Strong stuff, that is. And blimey, does it pong!'

Rushton looked at the bleak, windswept garden. No one had worked in it for a long time. 'Used enough disinfectant, didn't you?'

'Disinfectant and bleach. Too strong to put your hands into. Show you, if you like.' He gestured with his head towards the house behind them.

Rushton bent his head cautiously and looked inside the little van. There was no carpet, no mat, nothing but the steel of the floor and the sides. He could see the brush marks where the energetic scrubbing had taken place. Even the inside of the roof had been brushed. He couldn't see that there would be much left in the way of evidence, but at least the vigour of this cleaning suggested that the man thought he had something to hide. Making it sound as menacing as he could, he said, 'The forensic boys will need to look at this van. Surprising what they can come up with, you know.'

'Sure. Send 'em round whenever you like.'

'What did you scrub it with?'

'A stiff brush. Yard brushes, my old mother used to call them. Put the stuff in a bucket.'

'I'll take the brush away then, for

examination.' Rushton was trying not to lose face, but the man in the torn jeans and ragged sweater seemed to realize it. Walsh grinned at him, then went and pulled open the garage door and handed him a long stiff brush. The DI took it gingerly by the handle, affected to examine its formidable bristles, which smelled still of the disinfectant, then put it carefully in the boot of the police Sierra. 'I'll pick up my notes from inside, then be away,' he said. 'And I'd better take the container that the disinfectant came in.'

It was his last throw, but it was successful. Whilst Walsh went uncomplainingly into the kitchen and burrowed beneath the sink, Rushton pulled open the door of the shallow cloaks cupboard in the dingy hall. There was a woman's red winter coat hung carefully upon a hanger on the left. Debbie's, presumably. No doubt her bedroom was still neatly preserved as she had left it upstairs.

But it was the other garment that interested Rushton. This had no hanger, but was flung carelessly upon a hook. It was a thick, well-worn, navy duffle coat. With the bottom toggle fastener missing.

CHAPTER TWENTY

They let him into the ward for a few minutes, even though visiting time was over. The night sister, one of the old school with a will to rule and forearms to match, said disapprovingly, 'We relaxed the old visiting times some years ago, you know. There were at least ten hours during the day when you could have come.'

But murder carries its own mystique, even in this violent age, and it gave the superintendent conducting the investigation into the killing of the local MP the status of a VIP. A penitent Lambert was conducted to his wife's bedside; his daffodils were put in water, waved briefly in front of the patient, and taken away for the night.

Now he sat awkwardly at the bedside, a big man upon a small chair, conscious of his health among the sick, conscious of his maleness as the preparations began in an all-female ward for the early hospital night. 'You vomited when I saw you after the operation,' he said.

'Did I? I don't remember that.'

'I expect it was the anaesthetic.' He felt like a distant relative upon a duty visit. That earlier intimacy, the closeness he had felt when she lay helpless and unconscious at his side, was seeping mysteriously away. He had no idea how he might hold on to it. 'How are you feeling now?'

'Oh, much better. I think I might have some breakfast, in the morning.'

'They say the operation is successful. As far as they can tell at this stage.'

'Yes. So far so good. They have to do a biopsy on the tissues they took away for analysis. We should know the results of that in a day or so.'

'Yes. I'm sure it will be all right.' The naivety, the effrontery, of the phrase hit him even as he said it, and he went on in confusion, plunging deeper into dangerous areas. 'Did they—did they take much away?'

'Most of the breast, I'm afraid. I haven't dared to look myself yet. They give you a false tit, you know, to fit into a special bra compartment. Indistinguishable from the real thing, they say, under clothing. But not to the human hand, I'm sure! Inevitably an expert on these things like John Lambert will know the difference.'

She smiled bravely through the joke, like a woman in a black-and-white English film of thirty years earlier. He thought she was going to burst into tears, almost willed her to do so, since he knew that would restore the closeness he felt unable to bring himself.

Instead, she said, 'You look tired. You've had a long day, haven't you? Are you making progress on the case?'

'Some. But I can't prove anything. And I can't see how it all fits together.'

She didn't press him further. It was unusual for him to say even as much as this, and she was content that it should be so. She had not wanted the harsh world of serious crime in her home, had demanded that he switch off from work when he came into the house, and for years he had found that very difficult. She was not going to break the pattern she had striven so hard to establish, even in these extreme circumstances.

And so for another five minutes they talked of trivia and reminisced sporadically about the days when their daughters were small, whilst the staff bustled about the ward with the trolley of evening drinks.

She was glad he had made the effort to come, and he was glad to see her with more colour in her face. But in the end, they were both relieved when it was time for him to go.

*   *   *

It was an awful morning, with a north-east wind blowing sleet almost horizontally from a pewter sky. Lambert and Hook were glad of the efficient heating system in the old Vauxhall as they drove through the undulations of Cotswold hills that were now invisible. Dermot and Moira Yates might not see the car visiting that other house in their cul-de-sac in this weather, thought Lambert. But it wouldn't matter if they did; he often preferred to let suspects see the police screw turning tighter.

'Mrs Doris Hume? Detective Superintendent Lambert and Detective Sergeant Hook.'

'Come in, please.' The elderly woman with the still bright green eyes and fading red hair was plainly one of those who delighted to be involved in a murder enquiry, to have a place on the fringe of it, whence she might glimpse the workings of the police machine without feeling personally threatened. She led them into a tidy lounge, where there was already a tray with crockery and biscuits on a coffee table, and bustled away into the kitchen.

When she came back with the coffee pot, she had discarded her apron and looked remarkably trim in her dark-green woollen dress. Plainly this was to be the highlight of her week, an experience to be retailed and perhaps enlarged when she spoke to her friends. Lambert certainly wasn't going to complain about her attitude: her eagerness was a relief after the caution and the concealments he had met among the principal figures in this drama.

She probed them a little about the case, but they parried her thrusts with an expert, experienced politeness as they consumed her coffee and biscuits. 'We'd just like to check a few things about the drinks party you held on Christmas Eve. To help us eliminate people from the enquiry, you see,' said Lambert, noting Hook attacking the biscuits with gusto.

'Yes. Mr Yates said you might want to ask me about it. I've made a list of the people who called in on that night. I can give you their addresses too, if you think it would be useful.' She handed him a carefully written list on her best notepaper.

'That shouldn't be necessary. Did Mr Yates give you any indication of the kind of thing we wanted?' What he was really interested to know was whether the Irishman had asked her to cover up for him in any way: that was the only reason why he had not let a DC conduct what should be no more than a routine fragment of a major enquiry.

'No. He just said you might want to confirm that he was here that night. Which I can do, of course.'

Yates hadn't been unwise enough to try to adjust her account of those fateful hours, then. A pity. 'If you can just give Sergeant Hook here a few details for his records, we needn't take up much more of your time, Mrs Hume.'

She looked quite disappointed that her contact with great happenings was to be so brief. 'Well, we always hold an informal little party for neighbours and a few friends on Christmas Eve. Gets the celebrations off to a bright start after everyone's finally finished work for the holiday, I always think. We hold open house from about half past three until about ten or eleven, depending on when the last ones go. No formal meal, but I do plenty of sausage rolls and cheesy—'

'But Mr Yates wasn't here for the whole of that time, was he, Mrs Hume?'

'Oh, no. People pop in when they can, and leave when they feel like it. It's very informal, and a lot of people have other commitments, on that day. People with families and—'

'Yes, of course. And as hostess, it must be difficult for you to keep track of the comings and goings. So perhaps you won't be able—'

'Oh, I remember Dermot Yates coming, quite clearly. He was one of the first, you see.' Lambert had put her on her mettle, by suggesting she might be too vague to be of help. She felt her hold on dramatic events slipping away from her, and was determined to hang on as long as possible.

Hook said, 'So he arrived here at what time, Mrs Hume?'

'Soon after half past three. He was one of the first. I think there was only my friend Alice, who'd been helping me with the food, here when he arrived. I remember him explaining about poor Moira not being able to come after all. It cast a bit of a dampener on things for a while, because she's been in other years, and she's such a lively girl normally.'

'And he was here until what time?'

She paused, pursed the lips she had made up so carefully for this occasion, wrinkled her brow, allowed them to see a little grey at the roots of her red hair as she bent her face to the carpet in concentration. Lambert had the impression, despite all these trappings of thought, that she had decided on the time she was about to deliver to them before they had ever come into the house. 'It would be about seven. I know because the Petersons arrived just as he was leaving. I'm sure they could confirm the time for you, if it should be necessary.'

'Thank you. And as far as you know, Mr Yates was here for the whole of that time?'

The pensioner's face narrowed in conspiratorial mischief, so that the CID men glimpsed the impish schoolgirl she must once have been. She hadn't thought this was going to be important, but now she suddenly divined that it was. Or at least it might be. She could see herself in court in her best hat and coat, answering the questions of a grateful counsel with precision and dignity. 'Dermot popped out, didn't he? Popped out and came back again.'

They couldn't conceal the rise in their interest, and she smiled her delight. Then, a little guiltily, she said, 'I expect he was just checking that Moira was all right, wasn't he? He worries about her, even though you can't see anything wrong, you see.'

'Yes. He's very fond of his sister, we could see that for ourselves. Can you give us any idea of how long he was gone?'

250

She hesitated before she reluctantly shook her head.

'Not really, no. Well, it wouldn't be fair, would it, if I'm not sure? There were lots of people coming into the house at the time when he slipped out, you see. It was quite noisy and confused.' She smiled a little at the recollection of herself as a busy, capable hostess, on the one day of the year on which she now entertained.

'You probably have some idea when he left, though? It might just be important, you see.'

'Well, I am sure that he hadn't been here very long when I saw him going up the road towards his own house. Some time around four, I should think.'

'And can you give us any idea how long he was away?'

'No, not really. I was too busy, you see. And my husband wasn't here until about half past five. Dermot was here then, because I remember him greeting George when he went into the lounge. But he might have been back here well before then. I really couldn't be sure.'

So Yates might have been gone for a few minutes or an hour and a half. They could check with other, less busy people who had been here on that night, if it should be necessary. And it might well be: Yates had certainly chosen to give them the impression that he had been in this house through all those vital hours.

The two big men stood up together. Lambert said, 'Thank you, Mrs Hume. You've been most helpful. I'm sure I hardly need to mention that you should keep the nature of our enquiries confidential.' He hadn't much confidence that her discretion would hold for very long, but he thought she would hardly talk to Dermot Yates, at least.

As they reached the door, he said, 'Do you know a Mr Gerald Sangster?'

'Oh yes. Been very good to our over-fifties tennis club, Mr Sangster has. Let us use an indoor court at half the usual rate. And he's been a friend of the Yateses for years, I think. Very keen on Moira, if you ask me! And who can blame—'

'Mr Sangster wasn't here on Christmas Eve, was he?'

'Oh, no. He has been once before, and I did invite him. I think he might have come, if Moira had. But it's not his scene really, as they say nowadays. With him not drinking at all, you see. You don't need to, of course, but you can feel a bit out of place if everyone else is—'

'Mr Sangster doesn't drink?'

'No. Not at all. Makes quite a thing of it. Jokingly, you know, but he says fit sportsmen can't afford to drink. Is it important?'

'Oh, probably not. We must have picked up the wrong impression somehow. Our fault, I should think.'

She waved them off from the top one of the three steps below her front door, an animated, erect figure. She could not possibly know how unexpectedly interesting she had been to them.

*   *   *

Joe Walsh insisted on watering the bright little polyanthus he had bought before the two uniformed constables took him to the station. 'It's for Debbie, you see,' he said to the two unimaginative young men who had never heard of his daughter, as if that immediately made everything clear.

At Oldford Police Station, he looked round the bare little interview room, which seemed impossibly crowded, with Lambert, Rushton and Hook all crammed together on the other side of the square table. 'Top brass out for me this morning,' he said. His smile was nervous, but not fearful, as they might perhaps have hoped.

Walsh wore the same clothes that Rushton had seen yesterday, the same soiled jeans and ragged cardigan. The frayed collar of his blue shirt, half inside and half outside the pullover beneath the cardigan, was noticeably grubby. In the tiny, overheated room, they caught the stale odour of his neglected body. His lank grey hair did not look as if it had seen a comb this morning. He looked from one to the other of the impassive, watchful faces which confronted him. 'Are you going to charge me?' he said.

Rushton said, 'No, Joe. Not yet. You're just helping the police with their enquiries. What happens after that depends on you.'

The thin head nodded. 'That's all right, then. I told Debs you might want to talk some more with me. She'll understand if I'm not back for a while.' None of the three men confronting him knew whether he meant back at the house or the cemetery.

Lambert said, 'You've been concealing things from us, you see, Joe. We don't like that. But we're giving you the chance to put things right now.'

Walsh digested this for a moment, looking again round the little semicircle of three faces which were so close to him. Then he said, 'I'm glad that bastard's dead. I'm not going to help you catch the person who killed him.' The pinched features set in a determined line: he hugged his skinny body with that folded-arms gesture which was familiar to Rushton from the previous day.

Rushton said, 'Oh, but you are, you know. Even if you killed him yourself.' He glared at the dishevelled figure, willing him to look into his eyes, to realize his danger.

'Did you kill him yourself, Joe?' Hook, speaking for the first time, was very quiet, speaking in the way he spoke to his sons when he caught them out in their childhood sins, as if he might agree to forget the crime once it was admitted.

'No. I thought I was going to, but I didn't. I don't think I could have done it really. Not even for Debs.' He said it reluctantly, as if it was a failing in him, turning the normal moral canons on their heads.

Rushton was watching him intensely. He said, 'That's what you said yesterday, Joe. It won't wash, you know.'

Walsh shook his head, his regret now manifest. 'I didn't kill him,' he said again.

At a nod from Lambert, Rushton put the polythene bag with the wooden toggle from the duffle coat on the table between them. Walsh stared at it for a moment, then looked up at the expectant faces opposite him. For the first time there was fear in the brown eyes. Rushton said, 'Don't touch it, Joe. It is yours, Joe, isn't it? The one that's missing from your coat.'

'It could be. How did—?' Suddenly he was aware of what Rushton had done on the previous evening, of the look the DI had snatched at the coat in the hall whilst he had been getting the disinfectant from the kitchen. His voice was harsh as he said, 'Where did you get that?'

'Wondered where you'd lost it, did you, Joe?' Rushton could not keep the excitement out of his voice as he scented a triumph. 'And

255

well you might. This fastener was found by the pool where we recovered the body of Raymond Keane.'

Walsh looked desperately into Rushton's hungry, triumphant face; looked from there to the other faces alongside him, searching for a denial that this was so, for some phrase of consolation. 'It might not be mine. How do you know it's mine? Mine's been missing for a long time!' His voice rose in panic on each phrase, until it came near to hysteria. His breath stank now as it came at them in gusts.

It was Lambert who said quietly, 'But it is yours, Joe. Don't be under any illusions: the men in our forensic laboratories will have it all matched up with the other toggles on your coat by the time the case comes to court.'

'Court? But I didn't do it. I keep telling you. Honest, I didn't do it!' For the first time, it seemed important to him that he should convince them of that.

Lambert leaned back, relaxing the pressure a fraction, anxious to keep the pathetic figure talking when it seemed he might degenerate into sobbing at any moment. 'You know more than you've told us, Mr Walsh. If you want us to believe you, it's time to be more honest.'

The trembling figure had been almost on his feet, his frame rising with his panic. Now he sank back again on to the hard upright chair, his small chin nodding a little, as if to convince himself, as he stared at the table. 'I was there on Christmas Eve. You said my van had been seen.'

'Why, Joe?'

'I—I don't know. I think I felt that as long as I was watching him, as long as I knew what he was doing, and he couldn't see me, I had him in my power.'

'All right.' Lambert had heard psychopaths talk like that in prison cells. This man had not their air of excitement at the mention of violence, but there were many gradations of madness. And something within him said that there was madness in this crime somewhere. 'Did you see Mr Keane arrive, Joe?'

'No. He was there when I drove past, though. I saw his Jaguar.'

'And you parked in your usual place?'

'Yes. Under the trees, a hundred yards on. I could see the cottage from there.'

'And what did you see?'

'Nothing. I was expecting the blonde woman to arrive, but she didn't. She might have already been there, though. There's parking round the back. There were no lights in the cottage, not that I could see. I decided eventually that they must have gone out. It was bloody cold that night. I went home as soon as I decided that he wasn't there.'

There was silence in the room. Lambert looked at the sweating, exhausted figure who held the key to this case and said, 'See if you can rustle us up some tea, Bert, will you?'

It was a relief to have the door open for a moment, for all of them. Rushton announced the suspension of the interview, then leaned over and stopped the tape recorder turning. The slight figure watched the silent machine balefully, as if it were a living thing, as if it and not the human tormentors opposite him were the source of his danger. All that he said while Hook was away was, 'I didn't kill him!' muttering the words in a low voice, as if it were necessary to convince himself of it.

Hook was back surprisingly quickly with four steaming mugs. He pushed the largest across the table to Walsh. 'Hot and sweet, lad. Standard police issue,' he said, not unkindly.

Walsh nodded absently, folded his fingers around the beaker, lifted it with two unsteady hands, took a cautious sip. He watched Rushton's hand move to set the tape in motion again, then, without waiting to be prompted, said, 'I was there on the Sunday as well, you know. Christmas Day. In the morning.'

They didn't know. No one had seen him. A bonus for them, at last. Lambert said, like a man floating a fly past a nervous trout, 'And what did you see, Joe?'

'I saw the blonde woman come, didn't I? Come and go, as a matter of fact.'

'Miss Renwick, Joe. That's her name. Do you know what car she drives?'

'Yes. A Fiesta Sport. A black one. That's how I knew it was her, when she came. But I

258

saw her get out and go into the house, as well.'

'What time was this, Joe?'

'Quite early. There was no traffic about, on Christmas morning, when I drove there. She must have arrived at about half past nine, I think.'

'And how long was she in there, Joe?'

'I don't know. Not very long, though. Perhaps ten minutes or quarter of an hour. She came out in a hell of a hurry, I can tell you!' He took a long, reminiscent pull at his tea, seeing that moment with the distraught woman fleeing from the cottage, thinking she was unobserved.

'You thought she was upset, did you, Joe?'

'She came out of there like a bat out of hell.' For once, the cliché seemed an appropriate one, considering what Zoe Renwick must have left behind her in the cottage.

CHAPTER TWENTY-ONE

Zoe Renwick's Cheltenham flat was within four hundred yards of the hospital where she was a sister. When Hook rang her on the ward, she showed no surprise that the CID should want to see her again. She said, 'I shall be off duty at two. I think it better that we meet away from here this time. I'll see you at home.'

She had sounded composed and in control

on the phone, as she had meant to do. As she walked through the tree-lined streets to her flat, huddled in her thick coat against the rawness of the January day, she felt much less assured. How much did these quiet, relentless men know now? How long could one woman stand up against the massive, impersonal police machine that was operating in pursuit of Raymond's killer?

Zoe felt very much alone. She was used to that, but she felt her isolation more keenly than she ever had before. Despite the cold, she walked slowly, trying unsuccessfully to prepare her thoughts and her tactics for the meeting ahead. How could you prepare for a battle when you had no idea of the enemy's strength?

From behind the double glazing of her first-floor apartment, she watched the blue Senator turn silently into the car park and come to rest beside her own Fiesta Sport. The superintendent, whose name she could not remember, levered himself a little stiffly from the driver's seat. Sergeant Hook checked the numberplate of her car, then studied the interior curiously for an instant before he turned towards the communal entrance doors of the flats. In that moment, she realized somehow that they knew she had lied to them.

She had hoped that things might be more relaxed if they saw her at home. And if it came to an arrest, at least she wouldn't be ushered past the curious eyes of the hospital's corridors and reception areas. An arrest? Was she being melodramatic? But didn't deceiving the police in an enquiry make you something called an accessory after the fact? She realized how ignorant she was of the law and of her rights.

Lambert was brisk, even abrupt. This woman had now forsaken her right to the courtesy he had afforded her in his previous interview at the hospital. He said, 'We have heard statements from others involved which conflict with your earlier account of events, Miss Renwick. We are here to establish the truth in these matters. I should warn you that any further attempts to deceive us would be very ill advised.'

She had been intending to offer them tea or coffee. Now she knew that it would be refused; they barely accepted her invitation to sit down in the elegant lounge. With its Georgian silver tea service on top of the china cabinet, its gold-framed etchings of Bath and old Bristol on the high walls, its period armchairs upon the Persian carpet, this room seemed to her as well as to them a curious setting for what must now transpire.

She said, more calmly than she felt, 'I told you. I had nothing to do with the murder of Raymond Keane.'

It was the first time she had produced the full name of the man she had once intended to marry, as if she sought by the use to distance herself from the events of his death. With her blonde hair dropping almost to her shoulders, her bright blue eyes trained observantly upon their faces, her slim form perched gracefully on the edge of her tapestried armchair, she presented a much changed appearance from the efficient professional they had seen in her sister's uniform at the hospital.

Yet she was just as careful, just as intelligent, thought Lambert. Only her clothes were different. He stared back at her for a moment before he said, 'You had more to do with it than you pretended when we saw you two days ago, Miss Renwick.'

'In what way?'

He was suddenly impatient with her prevarications. 'I could take you through your statement line by line and expose its falsehoods. But we haven't time for that. You told us earlier that you hadn't been near the cottage since a week before Christmas, that you did not go to meet Mr Keane as you had arranged to do. But we know now that your car has been there, on one or more occasions.'

'On one. Only on one!' There was fear in the way she spat the words from between her pale lips. In that one moment of vehemence, she had admitted her earlier lies. Lambert, who had backed the tale of the dishevelled, half-crazy Joe Walsh against the account of this cool-looking woman, breathed a huge but entirely inward sigh of relief.

They glared at each other for a moment,

realizing the implications of her words, each of them measuring the strength of the adversary. Then Lambert said, 'If you expect us to believe you this time, you had better not try to hold anything back.'

She nodded. It was almost a relief to have it out, without further attempts to disguise it. She had known from the moment she received Hook's phone call that it must come to this, she told herself, so she had lost nothing so far. She said carefully, 'I didn't go there on Christmas Eve. What I told you was correct, apart from one omission.'

'A very important omission.'

She frowned impatiently at him. The comment was a distraction, a mere underlining of what she had already admitted. If the wretched man would only shut up, she would tell him. 'I rang on Christmas Eve, to tell Raymond I wasn't going to arrive as he expected. I put off the call until about eight o'clock, because I wasn't looking forward to it. I thought he'd have rung me by then, but he hadn't, so I had to take the initiative. When I'd screwed myself up to tell him we were finished, there was no reply.'

She paused, allowing them to picture the scene she was now putting to them, with the phone ringing in the silent cottage and the man it was intended for lying dead a few yards away. They said nothing, and she found their silence chilling: even a question would have been somehow a comfort, an assurance that at least they were taking her latest story seriously. She said, 'I was deflated. I'd expected to have to give an account of myself, to confess that I wasn't going to marry him any more. I expected an argument; I was going to suggest that he came over to discuss things with me on the next day. Instead, there was nothing. I couldn't even leave a message on his answerphone, telling him to ring me; it wasn't switched on. I didn't go there.'

'But you went on the next day. Christmas Day.'

'Yes. I drove over there in the morning.'

'Why?'

'Because Raymond hadn't rung back. Because I thought there might be something wrong with his phone. The answerphone still wasn't on, so I presumed he must be there. And I wanted to have it out with him. To get that over with.'

'So you drove over there. At what time?'

'Quite early. By other people's standards, not the hospital's.' She smiled nervously at that thought. 'It must have been about half past nine when I got there, I suppose.'

Some time in the last few seconds, she had ceased to look at them. They could see the tension in the drawn muscles of her long neck; a tress of the blonde hair had fallen unchecked over the top of her right cheekbone. Lambert, speaking more gently now, said, 'Tell us what

264

you found at the cottage that morning, please.'

'Raymond's Jaguar was parked round the back: I could just see the end of the boot. I went inside—I have a key, you see. I called his name two or three times. There was no sign of him, and no heating on. If it hadn't been for the car, I'd have thought he'd never arrived. I went to the answerphone to play the messages back. I thought there might have been some family emergency, you see, or some political thing needing attention. I couldn't see why his car would still be there if he'd gone off somewhere, but he might have gone with someone else.'

'And did you find anything among the messages that might have explained things?'

'No. The answerphone tape had been cleared. I thought at the time that Raymond must have done that.'

'But now you're not so sure.'

She shook her head silently. They knew why she was so tense with that thought. If Keane had not cleared the tape, it had almost certainly been the murderer who had erased it. The two men watching her so closely knew that the tape had indeed been clear when the Scene-of-Crime team tried it. Sooner or later, they would have to know whether this latest story was the real one, or whether it was the cool Nordic figure before them who had cleared that tape and any evidence it held, after killing the owner of the cottage. She was staring now at the carpet between them as if hypnotized, as the key point of her story was at hand. Lambert, as if offering a stage cue to move forward the action, said, 'Go on, please.'

Zoe Renwick spoke slowly now, reluctantly almost, though she knew there was no turning away from the course she had decided upon. 'I looked upstairs. The bed hadn't been slept in. I went into the kitchen, to see if he had cooked anything. I found him there. In the old pantry. Underneath the fuse-box. He had already been dead for some time.' Even with the last words, she did not look up. It was as if, in recounting an ill dream, it was important to her to get every detail correct.

It was Hook who broke the spell as, looking up from his written record of this, he said, 'You're certain of that?'

She looked at him with widening eyes, as if she had forgotten for a moment that he was there. 'I am a hospital sister, Sergeant. We are not unfamiliar with death and its trappings.'

Lambert said, 'Quite. And your opinion is that Mr Keane had been dead for some hours at least?'

'My immediate thought was that he'd been killed on the previous night. He was cold, you see, when I felt for a pulse. But I'm afraid I didn't think in professional terms for very long. I just wanted to get out of the place. And I did. I drove away as fast as I could.'

Like a bat out of hell, Walsh had said. Their

stories tallied in that, at any rate. 'Did you lock the door behind you?'

'I can't remember. I was in a panic. I'm sure I pulled the door to behind me: I was terrified that whoever killed Raymond might still be around somewhere, anxious to put any barrier between me and him. But I went out of the back door. It doesn't have a Yale lock like the front one. So it may be that I left it open. Does it matter?'

'It may do. If you are telling us the full story this time.' Lambert looked at her for a moment, assessing her credibility, without attempting to disguise the fact. Then he said quietly, 'So you knew Mr Keane was dead for a week and more before his body was found. You realize this makes you an accessory to murder.'

There it was, almost the phrase she had thought of for herself. But she didn't care now. She was drained with the effort of what she had told them. She said dully, 'I suppose it does. I hadn't thought of it like that, until today. All I wanted to do at first was to get away from the place. And when I had done, I thought, "If I say anything, they'll think it was me." That seemed more likely the longer I left it, until after a day or so it became impossible. I was waiting all that week for someone to find him. I couldn't understand why no one did.'

She brushed the hair back from the pale flesh of her face now and looked straight into

Lambert's cool grey eyes as she said, 'I hated Raymond by this time. I know that sounds a stupid reversal, within a week. But I hated what I'd seen of him with his business partner, and with his former mistress. So when I found him dead like that, I felt guilty anyway, even though I hadn't done it. Because I wanted him out of my life, and I suppose there was a part of me which was glad to have him dead.'

Lambert returned her gaze silently for a moment, then gave a curt nod. 'And when did you go back to move him, Miss Renwick?' he said.

'I didn't. I haven't been near the cottage from that day to this.' She was alarmed now, earnest in her attempt to convince them.

'You realize that your earlier concealments have made it more difficult for us to believe you, of course. All right, if you didn't move the corpse, who did?'

'I've no idea. I've thought about it, but I haven't got any nearer. Do you—do you think the murderer was at the cottage when I went there?'

Lambert ignored the question. To answer it would be tantamount to admitting he believed her story. Instead, he said, 'Most innocent people who come upon a body think at first that there has been an accident of some kind. You immediately assumed murder. Can you explain that to us?'

'Yes. I felt for the pulse in the throat

immediately to check that he was dead. The mark of the ligature was quite plain upon the throat. I touched it as I felt him.'

She shuddered a little at the recollection, but she was happy with her answer, a professional woman giving a professional account of herself.

*   *   *

Moira Yates had worked for almost an hour in the garden of her brother's house. It was the first time in four months that she had declared herself happy to move even this far from the security of the interior. Dermot had worked with her in the raw north-east wind, keeping a discreet but watchful eye upon her, trying to ensure that she became absorbed in the work, ready to desist as soon as she suggested it.

They had cleared the dead tops of perennials that had been waiting since the autumn, collected the myriad small branches blown from the oak and the beech at the end of the plot by the winter gales, assembled the debris into a conical heap which they would fire on the following day. Dermot would have liked to light the fire immediately, moving close to its crackling flames on the raw afternoon, but he thought that Moira had been outside the house for long enough.

She declared that she had enjoyed the unaccustomed physical work, and her cheeks were indeed warm from the exertion and the fresh air. Dermot sent her for a shower to warm herself up after the unaccustomed cold. When he stood in the hall and heard the water running above him, he made his phone call, his hand sheltering the mouthpiece, his eyes cast apprehensively up the flight of stairs, his voice low and terse with the trepidation he felt.

When she came down, relaxed and smiling in dark-green cashmere, he said, 'I have to go out, sis.'

She looked the question he had expected about his destination, but he did not volunteer an answer. He had a story ready about meeting a writing friend in a pub, which did not sound very convincing, even to him as he rehearsed it. But she did not press him, so he did not offer it. When he reached the end of their cul-de-sac, he set off in the opposite direction from the one which would take him directly to his goal, in case Moira was watching, as she often did, from the lounge window.

He drove the Cavalier swiftly through the familiar lanes, beneath scudding clouds which ranged from the near white to the almost black. He watched his rear mirror more closely than usual. It was only after three miles that he realized that he had been checking for police pursuit. Had it come to this then, now? Had he been expecting his own house to be watched, his vehicle to be followed?

Perhaps he was too imaginative. Certainly

there was no sign of police surveillance. As he took the circular route to his goal, he had the roads almost to himself, on one of those January days which seem to be little more than breaks between nights. He saw seagulls, wheeling in wide, swift arcs on the wild wind above the Cotswold rises, but no cars until he was near his destination.

The courtyard where Dermot Yates parked was deserted. He went swiftly through the empty communal hall and up to the heavy mahogany door. It opened as he prepared to ring: this man at any rate had noted his expected arrival. He went swiftly into the elegant apartment and turned to face its owner.

'We need to talk,' was all he said to Gerald Sangster.

CHAPTER TWENTY-TWO

'Do you think she did it?' said Chris Rushton, He was feeding the timing of Zoe Renwick's amended story into his computer, pondering the best way to cross-reference it with the other information he had collected from so many sources.

Lambert watched him with interest as the green print flashed on and off the monitor and the earnest DI operator switched to different computer files. 'That machine doesn't reveal who is telling the truth and who is lying,' the superintendent said. 'Still less does it show what is true and what is false within a single statement.'

'If it could do that, we wouldn't need superintendents,' said Rushton daringly. 'And you still haven't answered my question.'

'Zoe Renwick? She could have done it. I'm keeping an open mind. She's well organized, and in the right circumstances, she could be ruthless. She changed from being prepared to marry Keane to hating him within a week. Women who have their eyes opened like that tend to be bitter, even unbalanced.'

'Only women?' said Bert Hook with a smile.

'These liberal attitudes will get you into trouble, Bert. Unbecoming in the police force in any rank below Assistant Chief Constable, they are. Sexist and homophobic, we're supposed to be, certainly up to the rank of detective sergeant. All right, let's say, as a generalization, no more, that women, being finer creatures, tend to feel these things more deeply than men. Therefore their reactions may be more extreme. Will that do?'

'Could Zoe Renwick have moved the body?'

'Yes. With difficulty. Nurses are trained in lifting techniques, for the sake of patients. Keane wasn't a big man: a hundred and fifty-six pounds, the PM says. She's strong enough, even though we all know that dead weight is a bugger to move. It seems that there was no heating on in the cottage in that bitterly cold weather, so rigor mortis would be delayed. Keane's corpse probably hadn't stiffened up by the time he was collected for disposal.'

Experience of death and its consequences made them as dispassionate as surgeons about human remains. Rushton said, 'The computer hasn't thrown up any new leads. Nor has it ruled out any of our leading suspects yet. Have you?'

Lambert grinned, glad to be absorbed in the intellectual puzzle, despite its grim theme. 'I should be surprised if it was Chris Hampson. Because this death will probably save the business which is at the centre of his life, he has gained more than anyone from it, but nothing anyone else has said has suggested him. Unless of course someone is deliberately protecting him—but none of the others seems close enough to him to take the risk of shielding him like that.'

Hook said, almost reluctantly, 'Zoe Renwick had plenty to gain. She inherits almost everything from Keane except that business and some family heirlooms. Once he'd found out everything was over between them, he'd have been down to old Alfred Arkwright to change that will pretty smartly.'

Lambert nodded. 'But don't rule out the three musketeers over at the Yates household. I include Gerald Sangster with the other two, because in the matter of Raymond Keane at least they become a trio. Moira Yates is seen as a woman scorned and the other two are close enough to her to want revenge on her behalf. They've scarcely troubled to disguise it.'

Rushton said, 'Well, we know Moira Yates couldn't have done it, because she's been confined to the house with agoraphobia for months. She could have alibied one of the other two, I suppose.'

Hook said, 'You haven't seen her, Chris. There's something very odd about her. She seems to be in control of herself and what's happening, and yet at the same time in a world of her own.'

Lambert nodded. 'That could be an effect of the medication she's on, don't forget. One of the effects of the diazepam she's been prescribed can be an excess of short-term confidence—especially if she takes a double dose before facing what she sees as stress situations, like interviews with us. Or the one Zoe Renwick attended with Keane a week before he died, for that matter. Moira Yates seems to have surprised everyone by taking control on that occasion.'

Hook said, 'Have we ruled out a conspiracy? It seems to me the kind of killing and disposal that is easier to accomplish if two, or even three people were involved. Actively involved, perhaps, as well as covering each other's traces. The disposal of the body, for instance, would be easier if more than one person was involved in it.'

'That's why I called Sangster and the Yateses the three musketeers,' said Lambert. 'The two men are both devoted to Moira in their different ways, both resentful of her illness and the man they see as causing it. We've caught them out in at least one lie, the one about Sangster's drinking. Maybe that's only the tip of the iceberg, but we need proof. They've already shown they'll stick together if one of them is threatened. Neither Yates nor his sister mentioned that he'd left that party on Christmas Eve.'

'You seem to be discounting Joe Walsh,' said Rushton. 'He strikes me as the most unbalanced of all of them, and we've thought from the outset that we should be looking for a nutter. Or a nutter at least in respect of Raymond Keane, MP. Walsh certainly has tunnel vision about him. I found I was very sorry for him. But he wouldn't be the first murderer I've felt sorry for. He's channelled all his grief and resentment about his daughter on to one man. He certainly seems more contented now that Keane has gone. He has the air of a man with a job well done.'

Lambert was pleased to see his DI confessing a sympathy for a man who might be a murderer. A year ago, he would have thought it unprofessional for a detective to declare such feelings; he was more confident and flexible now. Lambert said gently, 'He seems to have put himself increasingly out of touch with other people since his daughter died. People who do that lose touch with reality, until their obsessions seem quite natural to them. In this case, a man channelled all his grief for his daughter into an obsession against the man who would not help him to get justice for her. But did Joe Walsh do the job himself, Chris?'

'He's changed his story. I think he might still not have told us everything he knows.'

'You could be right. When he told us about Zoe Renwick's visit to Keane's place on Christmas Day, we went haring off to see her, because hers was the first major lie we'd unearthed, and she seemed likely to be our killer. She still may be. But Joe Walsh was visiting that cottage every day: I don't believe he ceased to go there at that point.'

Lambert looked at the two faces waiting for a lead from him. 'Pull Walsh in again, Chris.'

*　　　*　　　*

There were flowers on the table in the middle of the ward, sunlight streaming through the high windows. The place was more cheerful and animated this afternoon than he had previously known it, with patients moving about and talking to each other. Christine's bed was empty when he got there.

'She's in the day room, love,' said the young nurse, spotting the forlorn visitor with an expert eye as she hurried past with hypodermic and drugs.

Lambert found his wife sitting at one end of the high, glass-roofed room with a book, not watching the afternoon television soap with the others. 'I'm bored,' she said, stretching her slippered feet cautiously, setting the paperback crime novel face down upon her lap. 'That's supposed to be a good sign, you know. Shows you're getting better.'

Lambert said, 'You look better, too. Much better.' She did. There was colour back in her cheeks, and the dark-brown hair was neatly combed and brushed. He fancied he saw more life in her eyes, but that was probably just his imagination. He sat down awkwardly beside her, setting aside the thick woollen shawl which someone had left on the chair. He was uncomfortably hot in his suit. Hospitals had to be heated for the sick, he knew, but they were always much too hot for him. He said awkwardly, 'Did they tell you anything today? Anything about . . . ?'

It was absurd that someone who spent so much of his time framing questions for people should be unable to complete this one, but he could not.

Christine grinned at his discomfiture, the same mischievous grin he remembered in her thirty years and more ago, when he had first known her as a twenty-year-old. 'The tests? Yes, they did, John. There's nothing further showing up. The biopsy was all clear.'

He felt an immense relief, a relief he could not show. He wanted to take her in his arms and hug her, as if he and not the doctors had brought her this cheer; he wanted to show her how important her health was to him. He was not sure he could have done it in private; in public, he had no chance.

Whilst he resented the innocent backs of those women who watched the television, he knew that he would have struggled for the words, even if the two of them had been alone together. And now Christine reached out cool fingers and set them warningly on the back of his hand. 'No demonstrations,' she whispered. Then with an explanatory gesture of her head towards the line of unconscious backs he had found so inhibiting, 'Not everyone has been as lucky as me with the results of the tests, you see.'

They chatted quietly for a few minutes. He tried not to look at Christine's breast where it curved softly beneath her dusky-pink dressing gown, to wonder which of the laughing women on the row of chairs a few yards from them had had the evil, perhaps fatal news. Death was very different in places like this, more inevitable and straightforward. The puzzle here was not who or how but why.

He was getting awkwardly to his feet, dismissed after his audience, when he remembered to ask, 'Have they said anything about when you can come home?'

'Just saved your bacon there, didn't you, John?' Again there was that old, familiar grin, and he realized for the first time quite how relieved she was. 'As a matter of fact, the consultant said that if I have a good night I might be able to come home tomorrow.'

* * *

Joe Walsh used his trowel carefully, resting on one knee on the turf, disturbing as little of the soil as was necessary to bury the small pot almost to its rim.

He talked all the time in a low, confidential voice. 'I can get the trowel in now, Debs. Much better than when we were in all that frost.' He levered himself upright, stood back for a pace to admire the effect of the bright-blue petals and yellow stamens of the polyanthus, then put the wide glass dome carefully back in place over it to protect its fragile winter beauty. The colours were more brilliant now, in the early January twilight. 'Should last you a few days in flower, that should.'

He clasped his hands under his armpits, trying to ease warmth back into his fingers after their contact with the cold soil. The wind was raw, but he was reluctant as always to leave this place. 'That Keane's to be buried on Tuesday. I still think I might go to the funeral. But as you said, that isn't really important. I told the police about that blonde woman, the way you told me to, Debs. And I'm sleeping better, now. Perhaps I might do a bit of decorating, in a week or two. Just the lounge, you know, not your room. I shan't touch that, don't you worry. Your posters look quite good, now I've got used to them.'

He backed away from the grave for a few yards, like a courtier leaving the presence of a Tudor monarch. It meant he did not see the man behind him until he almost trod on his toes. Joe started violently as he felt the presence at his shoulder.

Like a guilty thing, thought DI Rushton. 'No need to worry, Joe,' he said. 'Time to come in and have another little talk with us, that's all.' He led the shabby figure away very gently.

*   *   *

Joe was given a cup of tea and a sandwich. He sat alone in the small square interview room for a few minutes, looking at its blank walls without resentment. He thought this was the room where they had talked to him last time, but he could not be quite sure of it. He was neither bored nor fearful; he had lived with much worse than this in the last twelve months.

And now it was almost over.

The same three men who had talked to him before came presently into the room, scraping the plastic chairs into the limited space available to confront him. He nodded to them, a little nervously but quite affably. They were the only people with whom he had exchanged more than a few words in months now: the nearest thing he had to friends.

It was the tallest one, the one who seemed to be in charge, who said to him, 'We need to know more about what happened on Christmas Day, Joe. And we think you're the man to help us. Very important to us, you are.'

Joe nodded, a little smile playing about his emaciated lips. Very important, eh? It was a long time since anyone had considered him important. It gave him a little feeling of power; he was surprised how pleasant that felt. People said you had to be careful with the police, but these blokes seemed all right to him. He finished the last of his tea, careful not to slurp as he sometimes did when he was alone.

Lambert said, 'You told us last time that you saw Miss Renwick drive away from Keane's cottage in a hurry. "Like a bat out of hell," you said.'

'Yes. If that's the name of the blonde woman he'd been knocking off.' He felt quite daring, throwing in the slang like that. He was getting back into the real world. Debs would like that. But he wouldn't have used that coarse expression in front of her; he mustn't let his standards slip.

'And what happened after Miss Renwick had gone, Joe?'

He was immediately guarded, though he was unaware of how his face shut as suddenly as a book in front of them. 'I went back to my van, didn't I? Drove away, but not as quickly as she did.'

'I don't think you did, Joe. I think you were curious, when you saw her come out in such a panic. You thought you'd go and see what she'd been doing, what had upset her, didn't you, Joe?'

It was touch and go. For a moment he was sullen, and, had he chosen to deny them, they would have got no further, even though they would have known he was lying. Then he looked at the scarred square table, as he had done when he made his previous revelations, and said, 'I'd never been inside Keane's place before. Wouldn't have got in that time, if she hadn't left the back door open.' For a moment, he was resentful of the woman's omission, blaming her as a child might have for his own actions.

'Tell us what you found inside the cottage, Joe.' Lambert's voice was a monotone in his ears, low and hypnotic.

'I found Keane, didn't I? Lying cold and dead.' A smile spread slowly across his face at the recollection. Then he looked up into the three attentive faces and said fearfully, 'I didn't kill him, though.'

Rushton realized suddenly that this was progress in the man's rehabilitation. The Joe Walsh he had seen when he first went to that shabby council house might well have been proud to claim the murder. The DI found himself hoping, quite unprofessionally, that the man he had spotted for their murderer had not in fact committed it. Lambert said, 'So tell us what you did, Joe. You know that you can't hold back anything now, if you want us to believe you.'

And Rushton knew somehow in that moment that Lambert had decided that the ragged figure in front of them had not killed Keane.

Walsh said, 'I didn't know what to do. I remember feeling glad that he was gone. I thought at first that the blonde woman had killed him. She might have done, mightn't she, even though he was cold? She might have done it the night before. Anyway, I think I was a bit confused. I stood there for a moment, with my head reeling. I nearly got myself a drink of water, but I didn't want anything from that house. You'd have had my fingerprints, if I'd had a drink, wouldn't you?'

'Yes, Joe, we would. But you've told us now that you were there. That's good. What happened next?'

'I drove away. Not as fast as the blonde woman, though. I wasn't scared. I drove to the cemetery. Told my Debbie about it. Told her we needn't chase him any longer over the accident. I don't know how long I was at the grave. There wasn't anyone else around on Christmas morning. I remember I passed one old woman coming in, as I left. Crying, she was. I went home then. Had something to eat. Beans on toast, I think.' He looked as if the most elaborate Christmas dinner could not have been more of a celebration.

Lambert's voice, gentle, insistent, irresistible, said, 'But that wasn't the end of it, was it, Joe?'

Joe, staring at the table, wondered vaguely how they knew about these things. The tall man seemed almost clearer than he was himself, as though he was merely helping him to remember. He was surprised what a relief it was to talk, after keeping it between Debs and himself for all these long days. 'I watched some television in the afternoon and the evening. Can't tell you what was on, though. Can't remember it myself, you see. I was thinking about Keane lying there. Wondering when he'd be found. Wanting to help whoever had done it.'

They were the words Lambert had wanted to hear, but his tone never wavered with his excitement as he said, 'You went back there, didn't you, Joe? Back to the cottage.'

'Yes.' Walsh's voice was scarcely audible now, even in that small room where the three men listened so tensely. 'I thought, "If I move his body, nobody need ever know what happened. He might not be found for years."'

And if you'd thought to weight him down, you'd have been right, thought Lambert. The body might have been at the bottom of that pond for years. He said gently, 'What time did you go back there, Joe?'

'Late. Very late. The television had finished. I knew it would be quiet then, you see. It must have been about two in the morning, I think.'

'So you put your duffle coat on and went out to your van.'

'Yes. I had to scrape the frost off the windscreen and the wing mirrors. It was cold. Bloody cold!' Debbie wouldn't mind him saying that, he was sure; bloody wasn't very strong, not nowadays.

'But you got the van started and drove over to Keane's cottage. Did anyone see you?'

'No. There was no one about. It was a clear night, but very frosty. But it was two o'clock on Boxing Day morning. There was scarcely a light on in the houses I passed. Those who were still up weren't going to be driving, I reckoned.'

'So no one saw what you did at the cottage?'

'No. There wasn't a soul about. If there had been, I'd just have driven past without stopping.' He grinned slyly; for just an instant, he was proud of his cleverness.

'All right, Joe. What did you do?'

He looked up at Lambert, for the first time in minutes. For a moment, it looked as if at this key point he was going to deny that he had entered that sinister, silent house. Then he said, 'I parked round the back. Keane's Jaguar was still there, with frost all over it, like a dusting of snow. I tried the back door of the cottage. It was still open.'

'And was anything different from the way you had left it in the morning, Joe? Had anything been moved?'

He looked startled by these questions, which he had not expected. 'I don't think so. I only had a torch, because I didn't want to put on any lights in the place. I didn't go into the lounge, but everything in the kitchen looked just as I'd seen it in the morning.'

'And the body hadn't been moved?'

'No. I'm certain of that, because his head was twisted a little to one side, resting on the skirting board. His—his eyes were open, you know.' He was stilled for a moment by the memory of the staring eyes of the man he had hated, glinting wide and unseeing in the spotlight of his torch beam.

'So what did you do with him, Joe?' It was curious that a voice as quiet as Lambert's could seem quite so relentless.

'I thought for a minute that I might just leave him there, after all. Then I remembered

286

how he had treated me and Debbie, how he had refused even to see me, even to consider the new evidence I was bringing him. So I pulled his legs into the kitchen, to give myself more room to pick him up. I got him over my shoulder and took him out in a fireman's lift. He was heavy, but I knew I could do it.' He looked as though he expected to be praised for the huge effort he had made.

'Was he easy to move, Joe? He hadn't stiffened up in the time he had been lying there?'

'No. I didn't notice anything. His face might have been a bit set, but I got him over my shoulder without too much difficulty. And he straightened out again when I threw him into the back of the van.' Like fresh dead meat, they thought. Which was how Walsh had been treating him.

'And then you drove to the place where you dumped the body.'

'Yes. I drove very carefully. It was frosty, and there were patches of ice where the road was damp under the trees. But there was no one about, and I made myself take my time.'

Despite your grim cargo, they thought. It took nerve, even in a man as unbalanced as Walsh was, to drive carefully, with those staring eyes waiting to be discovered behind your shoulders. Lambert's voice, prompting like the psychiatrist who would surely be assessing this man's state of mind in the next

287

few days, said, 'And you knew just where you were taking the body.'

'Yes. I'd walked past the pool with Debbie, in the old days, when we used to take picnics out. It seemed, well—appropriate. I'd driven out to check the place exactly during the day. The ground between the pond and the lane was more overgrown than I remembered it. But that seemed a good thing. I found it easily enough that night. There was almost a full moon, you know.'

'Yes.' Lambert remembered Gerald Sangster telling them the same thing about his walk home from the Yates house. 'Did you leave your van on the road, Joe?'

'No. I drove it under the trees, through what had once been a gateway to a track. I didn't think I could drag him all the way from the lane to the pond. And it meant that if any cars came past, they wouldn't see my van, under the trees and thirty yards from the road. But nothing did come past while I was there.'

'Did it take you long, Joe?'

'No. I reversed almost to the edge of the pool, so that the water was below me. Then I pulled him out by his shoulders. I dragged him to the edge of the pond by his feet and flung him as far as I could over the ice.'

Walsh, who had been all intensity as he lived again through that macabre journey, was now suddenly shaken by silent laughter, until they thought he would dissolve into hysterics. But the internal, silent giggling passed as abruptly as it had arrived. A small smile remained on the pinched face, as it stared at the cassette turning silently in the machine at the side of the square table.

'What is it, Joe?' said Lambert.

'He nearly didn't go into that pond at all, you know. It was frozen and he slid across the surface a little, then stopped there. I thought it was frozen too thick for him to sink. But then it cracked. Like pistol shots, it was, in the quiet of those woods. I watched him disappear. Then I stood for a few minutes, until the patches of ice stopped rocking and came together again, and everything was still.'

They didn't remind him about the toggle from his duffle coat. There was no need now. There was a pause before Lambert said, 'Did you drive straight home from there, Joe?'

He looked up at them, reluctant for a few seconds to leave that scene he had recreated so vividly in his own mind. 'Yes. I didn't see a single vehicle on the way. I remember thinking, "Well, they won't find Mr Bloody Keane in a hurry now, will they? You've done your bit, Joe Walsh."'

CHAPTER TWENTY-THREE

At nine o'clock the next morning, the forensic laboratory rang through with unexpected news. The bristles on the stiff brushes used by Joe Walsh to clean the inside of his van had retained minute fibres. These appeared to be from the sweater taken from Raymond Keane's body. Chris Rushton received the news philosophically. Ironically, this unexpected bonus finding scarcely mattered, now that that tatterdemalion figure had confirmed the details of Keane's last journey in his van.

It was while Lambert was driving the old Vauxhall through the intermittent mists of a still, cold morning that he told Hook who had killed Keane.

The DS said nothing for a full minute, an interval that was enlivened by his chief's narrow failure to hit an unkempt sheep, which had heard about the free grazing afforded by the common land in these parts but not about motor cars. 'Sheep were here before cars were!' said Bert smugly in response to Lambert's relieved expletive. Then, as another sheep appeared through the mist on top of a stone wall like the monarch of the glen, he said, 'Can you prove it?'

Lambert mused on this, visualizing the

actions and reactions of that old CID bugbear, the wily counsel for the defence in a British law court. 'No, not yet. But I don't think proof will be necessary, after this morning. I rang from home: they're expecting us. I shall need your judicious help, as usual, of course.'

The chief was hoping for a confession, then, thought Hook. Well, they certainly wouldn't have needed proof with Joe Walsh, if he had done it: he had spilled the beans about his role as accessory quite completely, in the end. But he was a special case, an obsessive excited by the death he had yearned for months to encompass. Hardly your typical murderer.

They were losing height now, as they passed Robinswood Hill and the road wound along gentle Cotswold slopes. Then the sun burst suddenly upon them, illuminating a huge patch of blue sky which seemed the more brilliant after the previous grey gloom. As the car turned a bend, they caught a glimpse of one of the Severn's wide, still curves, motionless as blue glass and brilliantly clear. Hook could see the markings on the herd of Herefords that were unexpectedly present on the field which rose steeply to the farm on the far bank.

Unusual for cattle to be out this early in the year. The farmer must be expecting a mild spell; Bert retained from boyhood a faith in the absolute reliability of farmers where weather was concerned. His mind was reeling from what Lambert had said; as always, he tried to steady it by a contemplation of the natural world, which had so often represented a working release for him during his teenage days in the home, when puberty had added its insistent distractions to the problems of finding out who he was.

There were few obvious signs of activity in this village which had become a distant suburb of Gloucester: it was that hiatus time when people had gone to work and the children had been safely delivered to school, and the rows of respectable, gardened houses paused to catch their breaths before getting on with the rest of the day's business. There was no human presence visible as they turned into the cul-de-sac and drove carefully to the house which still had its secrets to reveal.

There was, however, a large red Mercedes parked in the drive behind the blue Vauxhall Cavalier, Lambert noted with satisfaction. The news of their coming had brought out the third musketeer.

Standing slightly above them on the stone step of his house, his right hand still on the catch of the door he held half open before them, Dermot Yates affected to be pleased to see them. Bert Hook did not think the pleasure extended to the wide brown eyes, which were within two feet of him; perhaps eyes were, as the romantics said, the windows of the soul.

'You'd better come in,' Yates said. He led

them reluctantly through the neat modern hall and into the long lounge, with its three-piece suite and extra armchairs. Gerald Sangster was here, as they had expected when they saw his car, sitting well back in one of the wide, heavy chairs of the suite, smiling a welcome he did not feel, trying to look at ease and unworried by this visit.

Dermot went to the foot of the stairs and called up to his sister, 'The policemen are here again, Moira,' though all of them felt that the invisible woman was well aware that they had arrived. Dermot followed them into the room and sat down, opposite the two supplementary armchairs which were already occupied by the CID. There was an awkward silence. No one wanted to begin without Moira present.

Within a few seconds, that lady was with them, moving gracefully and unhesitatingly down the length of the room, settling herself elegantly on one side of the settee, composing her long legs and shapely arms without haste, turning her brilliant dark eyes fully towards them only when she was ready. In every sense, she had made an entry.

Her brother made an attempt to take back the initiative she had seized from him without speaking a word. 'What can we do for you, Superintendent?' he said quickly.

'I think you can help us to complete our enquiries into the murder of Raymond Arthur Keane,' said Lambert calmly. 'If, that is, you are all prepared to be more frank with us than you have been previously. I advise you to be honest this time; we shall arrive at the truth, you see, with or without your assistance. If you do not cooperate, it will merely take a little longer.'

Gerald Sangster said smoothly, 'I'm sure no one here has deceived you, Mr Lambert. Not willingly, certainly. It may be that in having to recall events from—'

'No!' Lambert's monosyllable came like a pistol shot. 'All three of you have lied, in a deliberate attempt to frustrate the course of justice. If you now plan to continue that policy, you can do it at the station, with your lawyers present if necessary.'

Moira smiled brilliantly at them from the settee. 'I'm sure this can all be resolved quite easily. What is it we have said that is troubling you, Superintendent?'

Dermot Yates flicked up a nervous hand as he attempted to stop her. 'You can have no quarrel with my sister, surely, gentlemen. And I must remind you that she is still a sick woman, in no condition to be upset by needless arguments.'

Lambert had not taken his gaze from Moira's face; their eyes held each other's steadily, as if connected by some invisible beam. He did not look at Dermot even as he said, 'Then I suggest you begin by telling us about why you lied to us about your movements on Christmas Eve, Mr Yates.'

'Christmas Eve? My movements?' It was always a sign of guilt when they repeated the question, thought Hook: it meant they were playing for time, that they had no answer ready. Dermot Yates's broad, open face looked suddenly shifty as he said, 'I told you. I went to the Humes' house, just down the road. I was there for three or four hours. From about half past three until about seven, I think. I'm pretty sure George Hume could confirm that I—'

'Mr Hume wasn't home until half past five, was he? And his wife tells us that you were missing from the house for a considerable period immediately before that: possibly as much as one and a half hours.'

Yates must have been expecting this, but nevertheless it hit him hard. He raised a hand pointlessly to his mouth, then let it drop limply back to the arm of his chair. 'I—I'm sure it wasn't quite as long as that, Mr Lambert. And I don't quite see how—'

It was Gerald Sangster who cut in smoothly with an attempt at rescue. 'I hardly think Doris Hume can be completely reliable, Superintendent. She's a nice woman, but you must have noticed that she's getting on in years. And she must have been busy with other guests at the time you mention.'

'Mrs Hume is entirely reliable, Mr Sangster. We've checked her recollections with some of those other guests, you see. Incidentally, she also told us that you don't drink at all. Whereas you went out of your way to tell us that you had been drinking heavily here on Christmas Day, before you walked home late in the evening. A clumsy lie, that. And a pointless one, in the event.'

Sangster looked at them, his hands still steady on the arms of his chair. Whereas Yates had been immediately ruffled, he seemed to be calmer, to be gathering strength in the crisis. 'All right. I admit I was stone-cold sober on Christmas night. I walked home, exactly as I said. I could have driven over to Keane's place—I was perfectly fit to drive and do anything else I thought fit. But you may have difficulty in proving that I did that.'

'We should find it impossible. As you anticipated. You knew that we'd find out from someone that you didn't drink; you could even have let it slip yourself, if necessary. But you didn't go over to Keane's cottage that night, or at any other time in that period. You were simply setting up a false trail for us. That is a serious offence, and you may find yourself charged with it in due course. What concerns me at this moment is why you attempted to divert us.'

Moira Yates, her nyloned legs still elegantly crossed as she sat slightly side-on to them on the sofa, smiled a wide smile, perfectly motionless, still perfectly assembled in the

296

pose she had chosen for herself when she came into the room. Then she delivered the words she had also prepared for the occasion. 'This insight into police procedure is all quite fascinating, Superintendent Lambert, particularly so for innocent people like us. But you have already told us that you believe Mr Sangster had nothing to do with this crime. May we ask what is the point of your detailed investigation into Mrs Hume's Christmas Eve celebrations?'

Lambert regarded her steadily for a moment, willing her to more speech. She seemed again keyed up for this meeting, though whether the adrenaline was natural or drug-assisted he had no idea. To his disappointment, she said no more. He turned abruptly back to the unhappy Dermot Yates. 'You left the Humes' house within half an hour of your arrival. You were away for the best part of an hour and a half. What did you do in that time?'

Yates ran a hand through hair that was now tousled, then looked at his palm as if it enjoyed a facility to move on its own, without his approval or control. 'I didn't think I was away that long. I came back to check on Moira. I knew she'd been excited and upset before I went, you see, and I wasn't happy about leaving her.' He looked desperately at Moira for support, for some confirmation of the fact that she had been in this room and in need of his help, that he had come back to give it on that fateful afternoon.

She spoke, but what she said filled her brother with horror. 'Dermot didn't commit your murder, Superintendent Lambert. And neither did Gerry. But I expect you know that. You seem to have worked most things out.'

Sangster had started forward at last to the edge of his armchair with her words, and Dermot shouted, 'Moira, don't! You mustn't—'

'Oh, but I must, Dermot!' She turned her dazzling, unreal smile from Lambert to her brother, and it softened into a genuine affection. 'You've done everything you can for me. Both you and Gerry. But it's time to stop the protection now. I'm not having the two of you getting yourselves into more trouble on my behalf.' She was as masterful as a mother taking charge of troublesome children.

And she had the same effect as a mother upon her charges. The two resourceful, intelligent men to whom she spoke were cast into immediate defeat and dejection by her words. Their shoulders slumped, their heads dropped, they stared in dull defeat at the carpet by their feet. Their controller turned her attention back to the two CID men opposite her. 'Dermot left that drinks party on Christmas Eve because he saw his car drive past the Humes' window. When he came home, he found that I had been at the wheel of it.'

Dermot made another feeble effort to check her, raising both arms, then dropping them hopelessly as she stilled him with a slight, imperious gesture of her slender hand. Lambert said quietly, playing to the central figure in this drama, 'Tell us where you went in your brother's car, please, Miss Yates.'

'I think you know that. I went to Raymond Keane's cottage. Though why you should suspect an agoraphobic of going out, I still don't know.'

'Because we have trained ourselves to be suspicious. Because you were described to me as "a classic case" when I outlined your symptoms to a medical man. Too classic, perhaps, especially when I discovered you had trained as a psychiatric nurse. Perhaps you simulated the symptoms almost too well.'

She pursed her lips, smiled a small, regretful smile. 'It was genuine enough at first, you know. When Raymond ditched me so suddenly, I just didn't want to leave the house. Couldn't leave it, for a week or two. Then I thought to myself, "You can use this, girl. He's brought you to this state, and now you can use it to get back at the bastard." '

She turned to her brother, who was still staring at her aghast, fearing what was to come, yet powerless to stop her. 'I'm sorry, Dermot. I didn't want to deceive you, but I had to, if you weren't to be involved. And you too, Gerry. You were both so concerned about the agoraphobia that there were times when I longed to tell you what I was about, but I knew I mustn't.'

Lambert, pointing her back the way he wanted her to go, said, 'None of the doors were damaged at Keane's cottage. That pointed to someone who had a key to the place.'

'Which I had, of course. I returned all his presents in high dudgeon at the time when we split up, but I found the key two months later, when I was well into my plan. It seemed like a sign to me.' She nodded to herself at the recollection, seemingly contented.

Hook recalled how they had talked of Joe Walsh shutting himself away in his own private world, losing touch with reality, creating the personality which might do abnormal things. This woman had shut herself away from reality just as firmly, with a more awful result.

Lambert said, 'Was the cottage empty when you got there?'

'Yes. Rather to my surprise, it was. I hadn't expected the opportunity to fall into my hands as easily as it did. I took my car down the road and parked it under some trees, where it was invisible from the house. There had been vehicles there before; you could see the tyre marks.'

Not vehicles, thought Hook, but a vehicle. Joe Walsh's van. Strange how these two people who had never met each other had made up a combination of which neither of them had been aware. Speaking for the first time, he said, as if merely checking the details of a minor burglary, 'What time would this be, Miss Yates?'

'About quarter past four, I should think. It was a bright frosty day, but already going dark. I let myself in with the key I'd taken with me. It was curious being back in there. Nothing much seemed to have changed. I looked into the lounge and the dining room. Listened to the messages on his answerphone, as a matter of fact, then wiped it. The kitchen was neat and tidy—I expect Mrs Brownlow, the cleaning lady, had been in on the Thursday, just as she used to do in the old days.'

For a moment, she seemed to have been stopped by the memory of those old, contented days, when she had thought that Raymond Keane and she were going to live happily ever after. Then she said harshly, 'I didn't go upstairs, though. I expect the new woman's night things might have been in the bedroom we used to use. If she wore any.'

Lambert said, 'Did you take the cord with you?'

'Yes. I'd made it up weeks earlier, with the wooden bits at the end to tighten it. I kept it in the underwear drawer in my bedroom upstairs. I used to practise with it in front of the mirror up there sometimes, when Dermot was out.' She turned to the armchair beside her, saw her brother weeping silently in the face of this awful image, reached out her hand to touch his temple as gently as if to a baby, and said, 'Sorry. Don't cry, brother.'

'And you decided to wait for him in the pantry,' Lambert prodded her forward relentlessly.

'Not really. I mean, it wasn't as planned as that. I heard his car coming. That big Jaguar. For a moment I lost my nerve—I thought I'd just scream abuse at him, tell him just what I thought of him, and run away. Like a hysterical female. Then I could hear him using that very phrase, and I hid. I found myself in the old pantry, looking up at the fuse-box. And it seemed like a sign again, as if events were conspiring with me, you see.'

'You just stood in there and waited?'

'Waited until it went dark, yes. It was already almost dark in the pantry. As it was designed to preserve food in the days before fridges, it's on a north wall, and there's only one tiny high window. I just shut the pantry door and waited behind it. I heard him come into the kitchen and put on the central-heating boiler. I watched the circle on the meter begin to revolve as the pump started. Then I heard him walk down the hall and into the lounge and switch on the big standard lamp. It was just like the old days. I could almost see him reading his paper in his big armchair by the fireplace, as he used to do.'

302

But this cosy domestic scene had induced no mercy in the woman who pictured it, thought Hook. Lambert said, 'How long was it before you made your move, Moira?' It was the first time he had ever used her first name: they were united now by this oldest, most primitive of crimes.

'I don't know. It seemed a long time to me as I waited, but it probably wasn't more than ten minutes. I watched the little window at the top of the wall beside me until it seemed quite dark outside. Then I reached up and put off the main electricity switch. I heard Raymond curse, then come stumbling down the hall and into the kitchen. I could hear his breathing as he fumbled for the handle of the pantry door. My eyes were quite accustomed to the darkness, and his weren't. I stayed behind the door as he opened it, then slipped the cord round his neck, as he reached up to the fuse-box.'

She paused, looked at them as if to see whether they had any questions, then went calmly on. 'I was surprised how easy it was to kill someone like that, how quickly he died as I twisted the wooden handles at the end of the cord. I had my gloves on, of course, and it didn't even seem to need as much pressure as I'd expected. I don't think he ever knew who it was who was killing him.'

It was not clear from her even, matter-of-fact tone whether or not she would have

303

preferred Keane to know who it was who was twisting away his life. Moira Yates stared straight ahead of her, recreating in her mind's eye the last moments of the man she had once loved. When they thought she had ceased to speak, she said reflectively, 'It's strange how easily and how completely love can turn to hate.'

It was as though she was commenting on someone else's story, drawing generalizations from particular events from which she was now detached. Lambert drew her quietly back to the tale she had almost concluded, the tale which would see her locked away for years. 'What did you do next, Moira?'

'I checked he was dead, that there was no pulse in the carotid artery. I put the power back on. Then I went and switched off the central heating boiler and the lights he'd switched on in the lounge. I had a last look at him before I left the house, but I didn't touch him again. I went out of the front door and pulled it to behind me. There was still no one around. I drove home as quickly as I could in Dermot's Cavalier. I thought with a bit of luck he'd still be at the Humes' and no one would have known that I'd even been out, but that wasn't to be.'

She seemed entirely philosophical about that now. And had her luck held and her absence from Dermot Yates's house not been spotted, she would probably have got away with it. It was Dermot Yates's discovery of her absence, his subsequent realization of what she might have done, which had set him and Gerald Sangster off on their series of deceits and diversions. As they had sought to deflect suspicion away from Moira and on to themselves, they had created tracks which in the end would always have led nowhere for the CID.

Lambert recalled Gerald Sangster's pride in the woman he had loved for so long as he described her to them two days earlier: 'Moira can be very determined: she's capable of anything, if she puts her mind to it.' All strong emotions are dangerous, and love perhaps more so than any; it can often be more revealing than any malice. He wondered if it was these words, from someone so anxious to protect Moira, which had first set his mind thinking on the possibilities of her involvement.

Now, with her tale almost complete, it was Moira Yates who asked a question. 'Why wasn't he found more quickly? I locked the place up and left it, hoping that he wouldn't be found immediately, but I couldn't think it would be longer than a day or so. Then we heard that Raymond had become a "missing person". I couldn't understand why no one had discovered his body at the cottage. Then I read that he wasn't found there at all.'

He owed her an explanation at least, after

the way she had condemned herself. 'Someone else had the same idea as you. That the body shouldn't be discovered easily, I mean. Someone you've never even met, I think. He took the corpse away in his van, more than a day after you'd killed Mr Keane. Dumped it in a pool in the woods, as you probably heard.'

He had thought there might be some reaction now, some tears, some sense of the awfulness of what she had done. Instead, she said, 'You might not have found him yet, if he had weighted the limbs.' Her hatred of Keane had apparently not been mitigated a jot by his death.

And she was right; Keane could well not have been found for months, if the careful, unbalanced Joe Walsh had thought of this one more detail. And if that had happened, this woman would almost certainly have got away with her crime. He stepped forward and arrested her. With the formal warning that she was not obliged to say anything but that it might prejudice her defence if she kept silent about issues she intended to raise in court, she nodded gravely and stood up. 'I've packed a small bag,' she said. 'I left it in the hall.'

It was as clear-sighted as she had been throughout. She had expected this, then, from the moment when she heard this morning that they were coming again to the house. When she got to the door of the lounge, she looked with a smile at the two ashen-faced men who had wanted so desperately to save her from this. 'I want you to know, Superintendent, that neither Dermot nor Gerry knew what I had done. They knew that I had taken Dermot's car and been out for a while, but nothing more. They may have suspected all kinds of things, but I never told them what I had done: they have heard the story for the first time just now, with you.'

Her coolness even now, as they led her to the car, was striking, even shocking. She rode beside Hook in the back with her handsome dark head held high, a slight smile still on her wide lips. She was as serene as any bride.

*   *   *

An hour later, Lambert, easing himself stiffly from the same driver's seat, tried to dismiss the disturbing image of that calmness and give the whole of his attention to his wife.

He took Christine's case and led the way into the house. She followed him, walking a little gingerly, as if she scarcely trusted her legs. The raw air felt bitterly cold to her; it was the first time she had been outside since her operation. Less than a week, but it felt much longer.

'Daffodils!' she said delightedly when she got into the lounge and saw the splash of gold in the fireplace.

'There wasn't much else available, in

January,' said Lambert awkwardly. 'I'll go and make us some tea.'

'Come here a minute, John,' she said. She put her arms round him and he held her, feeling the warmth of her body through her clothes, stroking the shoulders which had never before seemed so fragile, banishing the image of that other woman he had just seen locked away.

'Welcome home, love,' he said at length.

Then, when they sat with their cups steaming and she was telling him about the others at the hospital, he looked at his watch. 'I'll have to be off in a minute. Just for a while.'

Christine sighed. 'The demands of crime are incessant,' she said without rancour.

Lambert shook his head. 'It's Bert Hook. He's having his first golf lesson, with the pro at the municipal course. He thinks I don't know. If I'm quick, I'll catch him in the act.'